MANTIS FORCE

MARIUM KAHNET

REBIRTH

A novel by

R. J. Amezcua

ISBN: 978-0-9980748-6-3 (Pbk.)
ISBN: 978-0-9980748-7-0 (Ebk.)

WWW.MARIUMKAHNET.COM
WWW.MANTISFORCE.NET

To

MY WIFE

SHERYL

who blessed me with her editing skills

for my first book trilogy

and to whom

this book

is

Lovingly Dedicated

CONTENTS

Chapter One

REDIQUIN

A bevy of audible alerts jarred Rediquin out of her meditative state. Her eyes darted over the control panel to find out what could possibly be happening now. "Cloaking systems are fine," she noted with a frown. Then she figured it out. Her loud gusty sigh of relief made her laugh. "Oh…that's why…resetting it now." After the system re-calibrated, she deactivated the automated audible warning systems, irritated by the constant adrenaline rush of emergencies. She was glad she had finally arrived at Ausertane One. It was time to retrieve the rogue sisters before they went so deep that no one would be able to find them.

The mountainside reminded her of the massive Mogwatto creature back in Tomongusta. The memory sent a shiver down her spine. *At least retrieving Fay will be much easier than facing those beasts.* For a fleeting moment, her thoughts dwelt on Zeta Three's amorous gaze.

But only for a moment, because the silhouette of a group of ships in the distance caught her attention. They were traveling in tight formation on the same flight path. *A Necropis military convoy. Why are they coming into Maluminian territory?* Her prickly first-hand experience with the xenophobic reptilian Maluminian race had proven how fiercely independent they were. She had gained great respect for their innate intelligence and strength. They had helped hone her negotiating skills in a moment of great personal danger that she would never forget. *They must know this type of incursion will not be tolerated and will certainly be met with force. Why would the Necropis government take military action against them?*

Then it hit her. *They're searching for the Stadageo saboteurs.* A deep sense of certainty that she was correct settled in her spirit. She confidently maneuvered her cloaked ship closer to see what would happen.

"Wow!" she exclaimed as a volley of energized weapon fire, shot from dozens of tall stone towers, struck the armada of Necropis military ships. Surprisingly, it did very little damage. *They must have Class II shield plating.* The miniscule trails of smoke from the defensive response of the Maluminians quickly dissipated from the vessels. One by one the unrelenting attacks of the armada silenced each defensive tower. It was shocking how quickly they were leveled to mere crumbling rubble as if they had not just been jutting imposingly into the sky. *How pride quickly comes to a fall.* Her lips pressed together at the sight of the armada relentlessly pressing forward toward the cliff city of Nassau.

"Looks more like an all-out war than a skirmish," she murmured. She was surprised at the scale of engagement. *Should I go now or wait a little longer to see if there is more action?* Before she could decide, hundreds of Marauder Class single-seat fighters streamed out of the mountainside like packs of metal birds-of-prey screaming in challenge toward the armada. Moments later, several of them were engulfed in flames and violently exploded, sending colorful hot metallic shards shooting in every direction. Many others crashed into the steep mountainside.

She swallowed hard, seeing how many were lost. *Maluminian pilots are brave, but they are no match against the superior firepower of Targa class warships.* She was relieved to see the remaining defenders break off and scatter into a labyrinth of chasms. "The Magiathep Council is risking civil war searching for the sisters," she murmured. "I'd better reach them before they are captured and executed."

Overcome with urgency, she re-engaged the previous flight plan and sped off. She had no doubt the military would use ground troops to search every one of their structures. *I wonder how many radicals will die protecting their homes.* A red blinking light on the communications screen broke her muse. "A network message... Now what?" Grudgingly, she activated the visor on her helmet.

"Warning: Air regenerator power cell at extremely low levels," she read.

Somewhat perturbed, she dismissed the warning and activated the network security mechanism in her helmet. A beam of blue light from the visor scanned for specific DNA markers. Text flashed on her visor:

```
Identity: Rediquin
```

"Receive message," she commanded, curious now.

```
Sender: Zeta Three
```

Message: I terminated my mission. It's most urgent that we meet. I am heading to Ausertane One. I will arrive shortly. End of message.

"Zeta Three?" Perplexed by the request, she uncharacteristically hesitated to respond. "Send reply." His behavior lately was unusual, to say the least.

I will honor your request. End of message.

She retracted her visor. "What's so urgent that he canceled a very lucrative mission to speak to me? Is this mere coincidence that we're meeting in a safe house? No, that can't be it; he knows where Fay is." Her voice trailed off. She took a measured breath, taking control of her racing thoughts. In a semi-meditative state, she reached outward with her spirit, searching for the threat of a double-cross from her mercenary ally. *I don't sense any danger.*

Feeling somewhat more relaxed, she replaced the empty power cells for fully charged ones and let her mind wander back to how admiringly he'd looked at her the last time they were together.

The *Furies Scepter* flew through a narrow chasm. "Beautiful… but way too humid for my liking," Rediquin marveled aloud. The lower plains of the Ausertane continent were visually stunning, brimming with life and vegetation, so unlike the frigid arctic climate of Tomongusta, where she had just been. A hundred meters below, a stampeding herd of red-striped Gallapelle streamed between vivid turquoise pools of water. She entered the precise landing coordinates, all the while keeping at bay a dreadful foreboding. *If the Necropis government fails to contain the spreading radiation, things could get out of control very quickly. So many will be lost...* Her thoughts sent alarm thrumming through her veins.

With determination, she set them aside to deal with a more immediate problem: the Kritokhaan and their barbaric customs. "They're almost as bad as the Maluminians. They don't trust anybody." She sighed a bit impatiently at yet another obstacle to be overcome, getting past these brutal beings.

She skimmed her ship closely above the low-lying mountain range, occasionally glancing at the high humidity atmospheric readings. The air was going to make her feel like she was in an outdoor shower. *Yuck. Oh, well. I've been in a lot worse.* She reached over and grabbed a metallic flask, popped open the top, and drank the rest of the Kravajava and flung it under her seat. It clanked loudly against other objects under there. She absently wiped her mouth with her gloved hand. *I'm certain the Grand Dukar will release Mirinda and Orisa into my custody with a large payment of Cymbratar. It will be amusing to see the expression on Fay's face when she sees me and not her cadre of wayward sisters.* She laughed at the thought, knowing that her reputation would precede her when she introduced herself. She hoped Fay wouldn't do something foolish like try to escape. But then again, it might get Fay to be more cooperative.

As she reached her destination, a vexing memory flitted through her mind and her wide grin faded. During a previous mission, she had unwittingly become a victim of the luminescence of velvety blue flower petals that hid a toxic pollen. She had leaned down, plucked a flower, raised it to her nose, and smelled deeply of what she was sure was going to be as lovely a smell as the beauty of the blossom. Instantly, her body had been seized with a wave of noxiousness. With her eyes watering and her breathing shallow, she had staggered back to the ship and collapsed in a heap, just barely conscious. As she lay writhing on the deck in her ship, excruciating pain had racked her body. It had taken her many long moments to crawl to the med-kit to get some relief. The image of her innocence in smelling the vibrant, but deadly blossom sent a wave of chastisement running through her mind. *That was not smart…you knew better yet look at what you did.*

Rediquin swallowed hard and cleared her throat that even now seemed to be swelling at the memory. "That won't happen again." Her determined tone was reassuring, and she followed the words with action, activating her helmet visor before even leaving the bridge, just in case. "Good, the air recirculation system is working just fine." Her voice held a note of relief. "That looks like a good spot." She landed on a lower ledge that extended out of the cliff's face.

Peering out the side viewport, she spotted a path down to the pristine primordial jungle floor. *That should be easy enough.* Her lips pressed together decisively. She strode to the cargo hold and armed herself. Then she swiftly secured a small box containing half a dozen Cymbratar units to her utility belt. But her hand hesitated on the box. "This is not good. After I bestow these and then pay a large homage to the Grand Dukar, I'll only have a small supply left." She pursed her lips, contemplating her options. *I will have to make a trip deep into the Rakia Expanse to retrieve my stash. That will not be a pleasant or safe trip.* At the time she had thought it was a brilliant idea to hide her horde of the valuable substance in one of the most inhospitable regions of space, where ships vanished without a trace. "I definitely need to upgrade my ship's weapons and shielding before I go. That will be a costly endeavor. I believe the bounty on the sisters' heads will suffice…" She smiled, anticipating a great outcome. *Systems all green, time to go.*

Standing at the cargo door, she pulled out her weapon, reached over her left shoulder with her left hand, and grabbed a booster barrel. With well-practiced dexterity, she attached it to the pistol. "Open cargo bay door." Her visor instantly adjusted to the brightness of the cloudless sky. With her weapon at the ready, she leaped off the ship, and landed firmly on solid ground. "Activate cloaking." After the door slid silently shut, the *Furies Scepter* vanished.

Data displayed on her visor indicated that there were various small and large life forms just inside the dense jungle. Her only concern was some of the more dangerous predators, whose scales and hides gave them the ability to go undetected by conventional sensors. She decided to hold off using her body armor's environmental blending technology for now. She renewed her grip on the weapon, then moved down the hoof-beaten small path with her senses on high alert.

A few moments later, Rediquin reached a cluster of the toxic flowers that had almost killed her before. "Not you again." She curbed an urge to blast them into oblivion. She gave them a wide berth, releasing the breath she had unconsciously been holding. Just ahead was an open field. She broke into a trot to get there a bit faster.

"There it is." She halted and stood there, looking at the distinct outline of the camouflaged dwellings of the Kritokhaan on the edge of the small valley. Her lip curled with disgust, thinking about how they'd built some of their shelters using secretions from their bodies. *Thank Abba El they don't do that all the time. Not what I want my home built of. Stinky too…*

She switched on the EBT, then turned up the external sensors to maximum at the bottom of the slope and hid behind a large boulder. "Only a few hundred meters to reach the other side." She looked around to find the best angle of approach, then froze as her sensors alerted her to a single bio-mass just a dozen or so meters away.

She silently spun to see emerging from a cluster of rocks a red and black striped beast. Its narrow, angular head rose high, sniffing at the air. *It smells something…must be me.* Her teeth clamped down tightly in frustration as she weighed her options. *I could kill it, but that would alert more dangerous predators.*

But it appeared that had already happened, because just then her visor lit up with a second bio-mass, slightly larger than the first. The brush moved subtly on the other side of the field of rocks. Then the movement stopped. Whatever it was, it had vanished just as quickly as it appeared. *Must have been a Kritokhaan lookout. Thanks for all the help.* Her sarcastic muse did little to alleviate the danger of her current predicament.

Rediquin braced herself, then darted out and swiftly knelt, bracing her forearm on her left knee. She was not surprised to see the beast already in a deadly charge coming straight at her. "One shot." The sound of her voice uttering the words she had spoken so often in practice and in other life-threatening encounters helped steady her aim. She calmly pulled the trigger.

A muffled roar of pain emanated from the large cloud of dust that marked where the heavy animal had fallen, but the roar quickly sank to silence. She shot to her feet, placed her weapon in the holster across her back, and began running through the rock field. Already she could see two other beasts fast-approaching on her visor screen. Adrenaline flooded her body, adding a burst of speed to her already fast pace.

"Damn your crazy Kritokhaan traditions!" She knew it was a deadly test of her honor and trustworthiness before they would conduct business with her. *Just a little farther.* The words repeated helplessly in her mind to the beat of her racing heart. The beasts were in sight now, advancing very rapidly with large ground-eating strides. Her spirit quailed, knowing she was about to meet her end.

Seemingly out of nowhere, a very large group of her hosts appeared in an arc formation. "Yes, finally some help." Her panted words huffed out between her deep gasping breaths, courtesy of the full run she was in. They were brandishing sharp-tipped spears pointed in her direction, but not at her. The spears were laced with the same toxins and the secretions as the poisonous mucus on their exposed upper torsos that glistened in the sunlight. *I made it.* Her spirit soared as she ran past the first line of warriors. Once safely behind the venomous barrier, she abruptly stopped, though her forward motion had her hydroplaning a few meters on the slick grass. She spun around to see the beasts that had been pursuing her. *Not exactly a Mogwatto, but dangerous all the same.* The scaly bipedal predators roared angrily in challenge before backing down, then retreating.

The leader of the formidable warriors of the more than sixty-strong force was impressive in height and he exuded the power of authority befitting his position. Rediquin bowed her head to him respectfully. "Thank you." The genuine gratefulness in her tone was not lost through her visor.

He nodded in acknowledgement. "Come." He lifted his spear into the air then strode past her, uttering a guttural word that she assumed was a command of some kind. The others waited for her to move. She groped at her utility belt, instantly relieved to find the precious box still attached after the desperate run for her life. Turning, she followed the leader down a clearly marked path. *There they go.* She watched the warriors melt into the jungle as if becoming a part of it. This was familiar to her, as they had done the same on previous visits. *I can't decide which is worse—being chased by predators or the deadly flora and fauna.* She deactivated the visor and immediately felt the humidity that drenched her exposed face.

There was a rustle in the vegetation nearby, and she turned to see the tribal sovereign King Tegga Kutar emerge from behind a curtain of vines. His steady consumption of Cymbratar had made him larger in both height and mass and his skin was a deep blue. Rediquin removed her helmet, greeting him with a warm smile. She had grown quite fond of him over the course of fifteen years. She returned his deep bow with one of her own.

"Welcome back, Hiagawa." His deep voice was warm and rather loud. The "wiry red-haired one." was the only nickname she had ever been dubbed with by anyone.

She laughed lightly and said jovially, "Thank you. It's an honor, King Kutar, to return to your kingdom once again." Although completely focused on him, her eyes tracked groups of warriors dispersing in every direction. *This is certainly new. I wonder what all the commotion is about.* Half a dozen warriors remained standing by the king with their energy weapons drawn. Even from two meters away, the acidic odor from the king's toxic skin caused her eyes to water.

"I believe you have something for me." He bared his sharp teeth in joyful anticipation.

"Yes, of course." She removed the metal box and opened it, revealing six sparkling tabs. "Here is your tribute and thanks for the use of the safe house." She placed it gently in his outstretched hand, then took several steps back.

The king's expression turned somber. "If you are not aware, our sources tell us that chaos has swept across Necropis and in some regions civil war has broken out." His voice was filled with deep concern. He turned to a Kritokhaan who'd just arrived in the clearing and motioned for him to come forward. "Speak," he commanded.

Rediquin watched the exchange in their guttural clicking native language. *Doesn't seem to be good news.* The king's face went rigid and his tone was rock hard. She had never seen the king so angry before. He dismissed his subject with a curt wave of his hand and took a moment to regain his composure. "I hope you will leave as quickly as possible," he said with a slight urgency and warning in his voice. He cleared his throat then continued, "We are going to have guests that you don't want to meet."

"Yes, I understand, your majesty," she said. "I will do as you ask."

He motioned for her to enter the outskirts of the settlement. She bowed her head slightly and left. She could feel his gaze remaining on her for quite some time as she headed for the safe house.

Rediquin knocked hard on the rough-planked door, then stepped back and waited. She knew her aggressive stance and the darkened visor that masked her features would make a big statement to Fay.

The door flung open. "It's about time you got here!" The small, dark-skinned woman's mouth dropped open wide, then snapped shut immediately, realizing her mistake. "Who are you?" Her brow furrowed in consternation and she quickly moved to try to close the door.

"Stop! We don't have time for this," said Rediquin, stepping forward to block her. "My name is Rediquin. I know who you are and how much trouble you are in." She quickly peered into the room to make sure they were alone. "Fay, let me in. I need to discuss an urgent matter with you."

"Very well, come in." Fay stayed at the door after she shut it behind them, looking her up and down. "Why are you here?" She crossed her arms and waited with one eyebrow cocked suspiciously.

Rediquin moved to the nearest window. "Wait a moment. I need to make sure we don't get any surprises. The situation out there is getting worse." She removed a recon sphere from her utility belt and placed it on the windowsill. "That should suffice." She moved to stand by a small table. Her right hand rested on the pistol she had just holstered. "First…I am not here to harm you. Second, I know that you, Mirinda, and Orisa were directly involved in the destruction of the Stadageo." She watched Fay swallow hard and saw the look of shock on her face that she could not hide.

"You have no proof." Fay's voice was thin with fear.

"Listen to me," Rediquin drawled in a knowing tone. "I am trying to save your life and that of your…sisters. I also know you are from Ramah and you were all at one time members of the Marium Kahnet." She felt a swell of pride at this revelation. "I am doing this partly because of a reward to bring you back to Ramah, and for other reasons that are for me alone to know." She drew her weapon and waited threateningly for the rogue sister to comprehend that she was now a captive.

"So, you are here to take me prisoner," said Fay, her mouth forming a tight line. "For who? And what about Mirinda and Orisa? Are you going capture them or, as you say, help them?" Her somewhat sarcastic reply somehow ended in a plea.

Rediquin was unmoved. "I'm waiting for an associate before we can leave." She noticed a large bowl of fresh Ausami berries on the table. They looked quite appealing, she had to admit. "Do you mind if I help myself to some?" Not waiting for a reply, she scooped up a handful and began eating them, all the while staring piercingly at the sister.

Fay nonchalantly walked over to the wall and leaned against it. "How long have you been a mercenary?"

"Long enough," Rediquin said around a mouthful of the berries. She holstered her weapon and, without asking permission, went over to the basin of water and used a neatly folded cloth to wipe her purple-stained lips clean.

"How badly did we damage the Stadageo?" Fay's curiosity was piqued.

"Damaged…?" Rediquin cocked her head to the side then continued callously, "It was completely destroyed, releasing massive amounts of Cremindraux and other deadly radiation. Countless millions have died as the result… Matter of fact, chaos has spread across Necropis because of it. Now, I've heard exploits of other saboteurs, but they pale in comparison to what you've done." She mockingly clapped her hands and bowed slightly. "I am very impressed that you were able to accomplish such a feat. I can't imagine how you pulled it off."

Fay burst into tears and dropped to her knees, then folded forward, pressing her forehead onto the floor. "It seemed so simple to just put the Overseers and the Stadageo out of commission. How come I could not see what would really happen?" Her words were muffled, but Rediquin could still make out what she was gasping between sobs. After a moment, Fay lifted herself back up, scraping the wetness off of her cheeks, then continued in a harsh dead tone, "I'm a heartless murderer—my hands are stained with blood. Look at what I have done… My soul is damned forever." The condemning words hung in the air. Her heartfelt plea for mercy on her soul touched Rediquin's ice-cold heart.

"In war, casualties are a surety. More often than not, the innocent are caught in between the weapons of destruction." Rediquin made a move as if to console her but stopped. "According to the Kodashah, you can be forgiven. But that is something I can't do for you." She leaned over and gently touched Fay's heaving shoulder. The reference to the sacred tome appeared to cut through her grief and brought back a semblance of composure. Her breathing calmed, and she nodded, accepting the truth that Rediquin had given her.

"Who are you?" she asked again. "How do you know about the Kodashah?" Fay's tone was bewildered. She took a breath as if to continue, but then seeing Rediquin was not going to answer, she stopped.

"Tell me, how did you make it safely across the rock fields?" asked Rediquin, abruptly changing the subject. "Your clothing offers you no protection whatsoever."

Fay sniffled. "Years ago, a tribal leader named Vtak sought me out. When we met, he told me about a dream he had in which a divine being of light instructed him to provide sanctuary to a human female. Of course, I…" Her voice trailed off when Rediquin's left hand shot out, gesturing for silence.

"Quiet, someone is coming." Rediquin moved to one side of the door. "You stand over there." Looking frightened, Fay obediently moved to the other side of the door.

Chapter Two

ROGUE

Rediquin's eyes were riveted on two red dots on her visor that were heading their way. *I recognize those weapon power cells' signatures—it has to be Zeta Three. Careless assumptions will lead to your death.* Heeding the internal counsel, she had gained from a countless number of dangerous missions, she palmed her weapon. She gave Fay a hard stare, testing her grit. "On my signal, open the door." Her tone made it clear there would be dire consequences if she did not obey. She waited for Fay to nod her acceptance, then stood ready to engage any threat.

A momentary silence ensued after a series of hard knocks on the door. "Reach out and pull the door open. Stay behind it until I know it is safe," she whispered. Rediquin braced the butt of her weapon with her other hand. The door swung wide open.

"Well, I guess you are glad to see me," Zeta Three said smugly and laughed as he removed his helmet.

"Come in, why don't you," said Rediquin. She cocked an eyebrow and jutted the weapon at him in a mock threat. This banter felt a lot more familiar. She holstered her weapon with a grin. "Go ahead and close the door."

Zeta Three glanced at the rogue sister as he did so. His unkempt hair and the dark stubble of facial hair indicated that he had been very busy. *He's a little too scruffy for my liking, but he has potential.* The passing thoughts surprised Rediquin. For decades her only pursuit had been for riches and influence while simultaneously orchestrating the deaths of those responsible for the massacre of her family on Ramah. She determined that she would not let his charming good looks get to her.

She steeled her gaze and placed her hand on her hips. "So, what's so urgent that you canceled your mission to meet me here?" She noticed his eyes were riveted to her lips. She wondered if they were still stained from the berries she had just eaten. Her full lips were a feature she'd always been proud of.

"I received a transmission from my associate on Letalis. He has the bodies of Nia and Taona. They died from radiation poisoning." His eyes were locked on Fay's face over Rediquin's shoulder. She heard a harsh gasp escape Fay and turned to see her run over to a small couch and sit down heavily, placing her hands over her face. Fay would just have to cope with the news the best she knew how. Rediquin turned back to find Zeta Three just a half an arm's length away from her.

"I canceled my mission for reasons I can't divulge." His voice was soft, with a sense of intimacy that she was not used to. "But I can tell you that I am going to meet my associate on one of the Letalis moons. Here is what I propose." She pursed her lips, not sure how to respond. He appeared to assume it was something else altogether.

"Wait, let me guess, you want me to hand over Fay, so you can collect the bounty and impress your old mentor and cut me out of my share?" she said with narrowed eyes. Her scowl did nothing to diminish what was clearly an amorous look on his face. He leaned a little closer.

He laughed lightly as she drew back a little, then continued, "Look, my associates most likely have secured Nia and Taona by now. So, tell me what you think about this. I will take Fay to Letalis where they will be safely taken to Ramah, while you find the others." He crossed his arms and the room fell silent. Rediquin was aware that Fay was listening closely to the exchange now.

"Taken safely back to Ramah?" She huffed with a contrived indignation. "You have a strange concept of what is safe. Let's see…was mining in a Mogwatto breeding ground safe? We almost got eaten!" She shook her head in disbelief but could find no true anger at him in her heart.

"True enough, but you wouldn't have died alone." His unbroken gaze cracked the barrier over her heart. *What is this? Am I beginning to be attracted to this miscreant?*

"I'm not amused, but you have a point." Rediquin cocked her head to the side and raised an eyebrow at him in light challenge. "Shall we split the percentage for bounty cooperation?" She waited for his nod of acceptance, then turned to face Fay. "You are going with Zeta Three. I'm going after Mirinda and Orisa. Don't worry, appearances can be deceiving." She looked laughingly at him, then said, "He's actually quite trustworthy."

He had moved over to peer out of the window at the increasingly loud commotion outside. "I have a bad feeling about this," he said. "Take a look." He stepped away from the window.

She activated her EBT to camouflage herself and moved to the middle of the window, noting more than a dozen weapon signatures. "There are Necropis military personnel entering the market. They are wearing Class I body armor. They seem to know outsiders are hiding here." She reappeared next to him. "Obviously a Xenophobe must have reported us. Not good." She set her mind to finding a way out of this alive.

"Excuse me. Although I detest being a prisoner of lawless mercenaries, it's a far better prospect than being publicly executed." Fay's dry tone broke into her feverishly racing thoughts.

"Are you saying there's another way out of here?" Rediquin couldn't help the impatience in her voice.

Fay pointed to the back of the dwelling. "There is a hatch under the bathtub that leads to an underground tunnel system. One of those passageways will take us just outside of the encampment." It was clear Fay knew her way around.

"It's worth a shot," said Rediquin. "What do you think?" She turned and caught the doting look in Zeta Three's eyes.

"Sounds good to me." His tone sounded a bit playful and somewhat out of place in light of the danger waiting outside.

"Would you just stop already? I'm not going to fall for your charms like your other women," she snapped in an undertone.

"There are no others here, pretty lady, to ensure you get your share of the bounty." He lifted her hand and placed a red marker in it. The atmosphere shimmered with the attraction growing between them.

Rediquin stepped back. "We better get moving."

"Well then. After you, Fay." He gestured with an expansive wave of his arm and followed her to the back room.

"Together on one…one!" Rediquin said. With a little effort she and Zeta Three slid the bathtub across the floor enough to expose the hidden escape passage. "Easy enough, looks like we'll be able to fit through," she said.

"Since I know the way I'll go first," said Fay, before quickly lowering her body into the opening, vanishing into the darkness below. Zeta Three followed. Rediquin removed a micro recon drone from her utility belt and dropped it into the opening, then fluidly lowered herself in. Then, with every bit of strength she had, she heaved the bathtub back into place.

In the stygian darkness, the recon drone relayed a series of tunnels with Fay and Zeta Three just ahead. Carefully, she waded through ankle-deep sludge. *I'm sure the Grand Dukar Namtar received my request for an audience. I just hope reaching Musterion won't be a problem with all the civil unrest.* In a few short moments they reached a dim oval cave with half a dozen tunnels branching off it. Zeta Three and Fay stood just inside to her right.

Fay pointed across the small cave. "That one will lead you to the other side of the rock fields, out of danger. I assume that's where your ship is."

Rediquin nodded, then looked at Zeta Three, unsure of what to say.

"I will see you very soon…" he said warmly. It made her feel like she had someone who cared about her for the first time in a very long while.

"Very soon," she repeated with a grin, then spun around and broke into a trot, willing herself not to turn to see if he was still looking.

Her flashlight beam powered up to its full strength as Rediquin walked into a large cave. In the distance, she could see the light of day and swung the flashlight rapidly around the cave as she headed in that direction. The repetitive dripping of water echoed loudly in the deep silence.

A sudden, large shuffling sound from somewhere behind her compelled her to move faster toward the opening with her weapon palmed. *Please… I don't want to fight anything else right now.* Gratefully, she reached the opening and peered out, checking for danger. *All clear. This ledge is definitely large enough for my ship to land.* She entered a series of commands into her wristband, summoning her ship. She moved to the side of the mouth of the cave and waited. Her visor lit up with data, indicating ships with weapons charged were approaching from a kilometer away. "What's going on over there?" she muttered, frowning. It looked like a full on Necropis military invasion. *Why are they doing this? They know that the Kritokhaan, just like the Malumine, retaliate with force.* Her muse was interrupted as a volley of missiles was launched from the nearby hillside. One hit its mark, resulting in a spectacular explosion. "Good for you! I don't care for the Varkrato League of Worlds anyhow." She felt a sort of dark joy watching the ship streaking downward in a smoking ball of fire. Just over the ridge, a menacing, much larger cadre of military ships came into focus. She hoped Musterion, the Choshek headquarters, would be free of this chaos. "I need to meet the Grand Dukar and make a deal to secure Mirinda and Orinda quickly." Her visor indicated her ship was descending to land, and she moved back near the rock face. *I sense something strange about those ships.* Her narrowed gaze remained fixed on the newly arrived reinforcements. The rocks crunched loudly with the weight of her ship landing. "Open cargo bay door." Rediquin took long strides up the ramp and into her safe haven.

"Systems check." Moments later, she sighed in relief. "Everything is looking good. Thanks, Zeta Three, for those parts." She removed her helmet and tossed it onto the seat next to her. "Finally, no issues. Well, we'll see how long this lasts." She paused, noting the pessimism in her tone. It was time to get out here.

As she was lifting off she noticed the Necropis military ships were now firing upon each other. "What in the world—?" She was puzzled momentarily at this brother against brother battle, but then the realization donned on her. The separatists' movement to break the Necropis government from the Varkrato League of Worlds must have begun in earnest. *I'm sure the same is happening at Letalis.*

Their leadership must have decided to strike now in the midst of the global chaos caused by the destruction of the Stadageo. "I suppose I would have done the same," she said dryly.

The fray began to move in her direction and she entered an alternate flight path over the Sabsha Ocean. *Now reaching Musterion will be that much more difficult.* Frustrated, she slammed her clenched fist against the armrest.

Skimming a hundred meters over the choppy foam of waves cresting out at sea that were kicked up by the high winds, Rediquin adjusted her speed to maximize the ship's power. The display screen identified a wide swathe of radiation encompassing hundreds of square kilometers of ocean. It almost seemed as if the whipping wind was in response to this unwelcome wave of destruction. "I'm thankful I don't have to go through that." Her stomached grumbled with hunger. She engaged the autopilot, then stood up and stretched backwards before heading for the food storage locker.

"Let's see. What do I have left that tastes good?" She rummaged through the food storage shelves. "Nothing looks good…" Her lip twisted wryly. Shaking off the disappointment, she grabbed a precooked meal package. "This will have to do for now." She closed the cabinet with a quick flick of her hand.

Unceremoniously, she plopped herself on the square metal storage box she usually sat on to eat. "Sometimes I wish I could trade all of my Cymbratar for a place I could call home. For a normal family life…get married and maybe even children." She let out a laugh at the thought. "Me married… to who, Zeta Three? Ha, I can imagine them asking me questions about my past. 'Mom, what did you do before you met Dad?' 'Oh, I was an elite mercenary, traveling throughout the galaxy eliminating those responsible for the murder of your grandfather, aunts, and uncles.'" The reality of that statement wiped the grin off her face. She peeled off her gloves and opened the meal pack. "That's not likely to happen."

Her stomach growled loudly, so she took a big bite of protein bread. "This tastes delicious, I must be hungrier than I thought." Her words were muffled by her full mouth. She blissfully slurped down a large container of her own unique blend of Kravajava. Her hunger satiated, she rubbed her hands clean, then placed the crumb-laden tray into the recycle bin.

Still sitting in the cramped galley, she stared at a Cymbratar tab in her hand for what seemed an eternity. *There is most likely trouble ahead. I have to be as strong and sharp as possible.* She took it and immediately felt the rush of renewed strength course through her body. "Exactly what I needed to top off my meal." Rejuvenated, she stood and tucked her gloves in her utility belt, then looked directly into a polished metal panel that she occasionally used as a mirror. *If I am successful at securing Mirinda and Orisa, I will have to bring them to…Ramah.*

Her mind and heart wrestled with uncertainty, realizing she was returning home. "Mother." Her voice held a longing she didn't realize was there. Sometimes she wondered if she resembled her more now than when she was a child. *"You're beautiful like your mother."* The voice of her father echoed in her memory. He had said it many times to her and to others. The memories brought a warm smile to her jaded and guarded heart. She had found out many long years ago that her mother had not died but had ascended as the spiritual leader of the Marium Kahnet. She had decided not to make contact with her mother, making it that much easier to avenge the slaughtered, no matter the cost. "She is holy, and I am not. She will reject me." She stared at her watery-eyed reflection. "Look what I have become. A killer for hire…an assassin." Tears streamed down her cheeks. She looked at her hands, which seemed to be blood-stained somehow.

"You will never love me, Mother. But I will not be twice dead to you." In her mind, Rediquin wrapped her arms around the image of her mother. "It does not matter what you think of me. I love you, Mom." She took in a measured breath and released it. Taking every emotional thought captive, she locked them away in the recesses of her subconscious.

Yaqal 322

My hope is held captive in the dark towers of misery. They give me bitterness to drink and fear is my portion to eat. My heart is held in ice. Beauty has been removed from my eyes. The howling wind of anguish buffets me. Sorrow comes to mock my wounds. Who will rescue the orphaned?

The malevolent essence within the Cymbratar quickly repaired the breaches in her heart against remorse and abandonment. "I am what I am now." She sniffed loudly and straightened her shoulders. "My actions are justified. They murdered my father, sisters, and brothers and with incomprehensible fierceness consumed infants, children, and the unborn, laying waste to untold millions of lives. No, Mother, I have been transformed into the instrument of righteousness and the weapon of justice and retribution."

Her teeth clenched with indomitable resolution to bring the blade of destruction and agony deep into the heart of her enemies the

Krauvanok, and those allied with them. "This is just another bounty mission. Once completed, my next objective will be to replenish my supply of Cymbratar."

She placed her hands on her hips, then broke away from her reflection and surveyed the ship. *I've never had to do so many repairs to the* Furies Scepter *in such a short time.* "Maybe I should pay the price and completely upgrade the entire ship."

The proximity alert alarm jolted her into action and she headed back to the bridge. *Eighty-five kilometers to Vonku.* Her gaze flew from one panel to the next. The display panel was lit up with multitudes of weapon discharges on the ground, and above the city a large-scale aerial combat lit the sky with fire and fury. The familiar rush of adrenaline flooded through her veins and her body tensed as she flew directly into the midst of the fray. "Disengage autopilot." She slowed the ship and swung wide around the larger pockets of the unceasing volleys of weapon fire.

The city was dotted with plumes of smoke spiraling into the cloudy sky. Musterion was still a few kilometers away. "I need to get closer." Her mind weighed the pros and cons of each option like a machine. "No, I have to land now." To avoid detection from cloaking scanners, she maneuvered the *Furies Scepter* toward a row of a smoldering cluster of buildings. *If I can land here, I won't have too far to go to reach Musterion.* She landed in a clearing where no one in their right mind would traverse because of the raging battle.

"Maintain cloaking. Code Alta-Teph." Rediquin rose out of her seat and swiftly moved to the weapons cache near the cargo area. Her previous experience in a battle zone had been years ago, but it was not forgotten. In that instance she'd been exiting the theatre of war, not entering it. *I will definitely need these.* She holstered two AR72 pistols, then grabbed an extra EBT power cell and placed it securely on the back of her utility belt. "Oh, and I'll need some of these." She carefully checked to make sure the firing pins were secure on three metal explosive disks, then placed them on either side of the utility belt. Her gaze hit the heavy assault weapon. "Next time…" She switched her favorite black bio-flex cape to a Class IV camouflage cape capable of withstanding small weapons fire. *I will never be more ready to go.*

Rediquin touched the side of her helmet and switched the mode to battle. The red visor slid shut. "Open cargo bay doors." She quickly jumped out before she could change her mind. The doors closed even before she landed. From a protective crouch in the shadow of the ship, she watched three single-seat strike fighters strafe a building opposite the one she was about to enter. One of the fighters was struck by a missile and enveloped in a ball of fire. Despite the piles of rubble and the dense smoke all around her, she could see a small crevasse on the side of the partially collapsed building. *Okay, it's only a few dozen meters. Time to move.* With that encouragement, she moved forward in a fluid crouch, staying low to the ground. She swept her AR72 in every direction, looking for ground troops.

As she slid stealthily forward, the ground shook with the ferocity of the back and forth fire, causing her to nearly lose her footing. The noise was deafening, and she was grateful her helmet filtered the air. As best she could, she avoided contact with the bodies of dead soldiers strewn everywhere. She noticed some of them had a large red mark on their helmet and a red metal utility belt. *Looks like some hand-to-hand combat took place.* She visualized the movements of the combatants as they'd fought to the death, judging by their final resting positions. *Enough of that. This is bad!*

Navigating around the last large pile of rubble, she halted and sank to a crouch when an intense firefight erupted just over two hundred meters away. Quickly changing route, she began to move, then transitioned to a full sprint as pieces of debris rained down on her. *Oh no!* Her visor tracked a stray missile that exploded above her point of entry. Chunks of the wall were toppling toward her.

With little choice, she hurled herself toward the entrance. "This could be it." Her voice was loud with the finality of the statement. She closed her eyes and prayed for her life as she rolled, coming to rest just inside.

A loud crack sounded, and the wall partially collapsed around her, seemingly entombing her. But the horrible pain of death she'd been expecting did not come.

Moments later she opened her eyes in relief and took stock of her situation. "I'm alive. Now let's check for injuries." Using discernment techniques, she'd learned in the Monastarium, she searched for any damage to her vital organs. "Good, no broken bones either. Seems I am buried under sections of wall." Rediquin inspected her sarcophagus and saw a crack of light a meter away. "How am I going to fit through that?" she muttered.

Always alone. Always in peril, a taunting voice whispered in her mind.

"Shut up already!" She grimaced at her predicament but refused to give in to despair. She rolled to her stomach and, using her elbows, began crawling through the opening that was now less than half its former size.

Chapter Three

MUSTERION

Ever cautious, Rediquin slid a reconnaissance drone from the left side of her utility belt and released it just a scant meter in front of her face. It skimmed over the debris and secured itself to a stack of metal pipes. She waited with bated breath for the stream of information that should have been coming immediately. *Maybe there is an active communication disruptor…Come on, come on…I need that data.* "Good," she murmured when it appeared. The relief helped her relax momentarily. A bead of sweat rolled down her temple as she read the data on her visor.

```
Tactical Data:

Life forms: 0

Weapons detected: 93
```

"This must have been quite the battle. I'm glad I missed it." The silence, with death looming all around her, magnified how dangerous this mission was. Rediquin chose her next position, attached the long-range barrel to her AR72, and then cautiously emerged from the crevasse. She made her way to a wrecked battle drone and slid behind it for protection. She looked up at a network of mangled gantries. The twisted scaffolding looked like it was about to fall as well. *Must be some kind of maintenance facility.* Her head jerked to the left where a piece of the ceiling hit the ground with a dull thud, sending a cloud of dust into the air.

Using that as a cue, she darted to the other side of a damaged pillar, and in one fluid motion removed the micro drone, then flung it over a collapsed wall. *Come on, find me a way through!* She gritted her teeth in frustration. A sense of urgency pooled in her belly. *Move… too much debris.*

The helmet dampened her grunt as she looked at the data feed, which showed her escape route was blocked by a labyrinth of collapsed storage containers and loose sparking power lines. *I have no choice; I have to go up and over.* As she scanned the area again, she noticed a ladder that connected to the catwalk above and confidently strode straight for it. "Yes, finally a break!" She called the trusty drone back to her, then read the feed on her visor.

```
Caution: EBT power cell at 50% capacity

Warning: High levels of toxic gases detected
```

She was sure glad she'd brought that extra power cell. Her chances of survival without the EBT would've been greatly diminished. Rediquin swept the area with the tip of her weapon, while deciding if she would be able to traverse the missing sections of ladder. Reluctantly, she secured her AR72 weapon on her back and began to nimbly climb with intermittent leaping spurts, pulling her body with only the grip of her gloved hands to bridge the gaps in the ladder.

That was easier than I thought it would be. She reached the catwalk and took one step, then stopped as she watched a battle drone skim over the carnage below. It exited through a gaping hole in the wall. *Must have energy masking technology. I hope I don't run into one of those outside.*

She continued stealthily onward for several hundred meters and came upon a broken window. The boom of small arms' fire echoed through a narrow open space separating the sections of industrial buildings from a residential district. *No easy way down. Hmmm, that dead tree looks solid enough.* "I haven't done this in a while." She removed a spool of high-tension line and a dart from her utility belt and attached it to her long-barreled weapon. *That's about fifty meters, no problem.* Aiming at a thick branch close to the ground, she held her breath, and squeezed the trigger.

The sound of the squealing line shooting out seemed louder than it actually was. Rediquin hit the target dead center. She wedged her weapon behind the exposed metal bars above the window and tightened the line. "I better not slip." She looked momentarily at the fast-flowing water of the canal below, not wanting to fall into it. *Here goes nothing!*

The hum of her exhilarating, controlled descent vibrated up into her neck. The second she hit the ground, she removed the second holstered weapon and sprinted through one of the many large holes in the single-story complex. She counted five bodies lying in the main hallway. The skirmishes had spread into the residential district. *I can't seem to catch a break.*

```
Caution: EBT power cell at 20% capacity
```

I wish these blasted power cells lasted longer. I better swap them out now while

I have a chance to do so. That looks promising. She entered a large room and stood behind a stack of chairs and, seeing no immediate danger, deactivated her EBT system.

A scuffling sound and whimpering cries of terror sent her scrambling to draw her weapon again, and she whipped around ready to shoot. But there was no one at eye level. She realized that it was children—they were under a table. With a sigh, she stuck the weapon back in her belt and retracted her visor. She motioned with a finger to her lips to quiet them and kneeled near them.

"Come here," she whispered in a reassuring tone, motioning to a humanoid boy who seemed to be older than the others. They were all huddled tightly together. He looked to be about eight or so. Their cries quieted, but the silent tears streaming down the cheeks of the little ones who peeked out at her shot an arrow into her heart. She kept her expression empty of anything but concern.

"Is anyone hurt?" she asked and waited for a reply. "Where are your parents?" She was drawn into the helpless look in the boy's deep blue eyes. "What is your name?"

"My name is Peter… They're in the main hallway. They told us to hide in here… Is it safe now?" His voice was soft but held a note of bewilderment because of circumstances that he could not begin to understand. His eyes looked hollow with the knowledge his parents were gone, like his aloneness was just then dawning on him.

She patted him on the shoulder, leaning closer. "Not yet." A couple of the other little ones wiggled around each other, trying to come to her. "Children, I have to leave you. You can't come with me. It's very dangerous out there right now." A small plump girl looked as if she was about to cry; Rediquin drew her to her side, patting her little back. "You must trust me. It's safer right where you are. But I know that all the fighting has moved to another housing complex." The sounds of explosions in the distance emphasized her point. She removed a small sphere from her utility belt. "Take this and activate it by squeezing these points together. It will call for help. But I need you to wait until morning."

Rediquin handed it to the boy. "My mother has one just like this," he said, more confidently this time. He turned toward the others and showed them the beacon sphere.

"Do you have food and water?" Rediquin asked, turning to the other children, waiting for them to meet her gaze one by one. She was pleased to see they had no visible injuries.

"Yes, behind the table inside the wall," the boy replied, obviously reassured at her presence.

"Good, take the others and hide now. Peter, you can do this. You are strong and smart." He nodded and wiped his nose with his sleeve.

Rediquin remained kneeling, watching him herd the others behind a pile of rubble that looked like a fort as she switched out her EBT power cell. She then stood up, checking on them one more time. "Stay quiet, little ones. Turn it on in the morning." Her whispered words were met with silence.

I hope they will be safe. Abba El be with them. A memory surfaced of her mother just then. *"You can do this, Minna Lavine Vallo. You are strong and smart."* Her heart squeezed with emotion. She swallowed hard and set it aside and moved swiftly out of the building.

"One more block to Musterion." Rediquin crouched behind a crumpled and smoking military vehicle. She scanned the local market bazaar. *Dead bodies everywhere…can't go through there.* She felt the cold presence of death hovering over her as if mocking her. Sweat broke out on her forehead as she watched dozens of weapon signatures on either side of the market square. Sporadic fire between the opposing forces kept her senses on high alert. On her last visit to this bustling market, she had purchased delicious Swetilli fruit. Now the place lay in ruins.

Feeling trapped by the continued exchange of fire, she was pressed to decide from which merchant shops to approach Musterion. *You are strong and smart; you can do this.* The words echoed again in her spirit. *Should I go to the left, or right? If I approach from the left I will have to go through the Pools of Serenity. But that's a bad idea. The area is most likely littered with any number of death traps. They might as well be called pools of death…On the other hand, going to the Shentar gardens is not much safer.* Between the two, she had to choose the lesser risk.

A whistling sound from above drew her attention to a military ship hovering over the marketplace. A second volley of missiles with streaks of smoke trailing behind them landed in several shops to her left. They erupted in balls of fire that engulfed the buildings; debris flew everywhere. Immediately, the ship was hit by a missile and listed sharply to the side. Direct hit. She watched the vessel spiral out of control and fall like a dead weight to the ground.

What is going on here? Is it a rival faction trying to overthrow the Choshek from power? Who is powerful enough to make this move? I don't know of any that have the influence or numbers, for that matter. I'll give them this—they are all in. That military shuttle attacked those on the left. Only the Choshek have sufficient connections and influence in the Necropis military to request assistance like that. Well, at least this made her decision easier. *I'm going to the right.*

"I've never been in combat before, what was I thinking?" she muttered. "I am the blade of vengeance. I do not fear death, for I am dead already." The well-rehearsed mantra placed an impenetrable wall around her heart. Fearless now, she entered the fray.

Just to the side of a string of overturned merchant tables lay the still body of a Drevka woman. Rediquin paused to examine the gaping wound between her shoulder blades. Judging by the dried blood, she'd died quite some time ago. These people were obviously caught in the middle without warning. Just beyond were other civilian casualties strewn across the bloodstained cobblestones.

The ebb in the fight was broken by a large exchange of fire. Blue and red bolts of energy laced the grey skies. Using the melee as cover, Rediquin bolted to a side entrance at the edge of the row of shops.

Without any hesitation, she deftly navigated the rows of collapsed partition walls and stepped over a dead soldier slumped against the pockmarked retaining wall. *I just need to stay against this wall.* Pieces of rock bounced off her helmet from the battle occurring just on the other side. She looked around the large, decimated shop. She was surprised by the presence of so many soldiers; there were over thirty dead, she estimated. *Those are Class II mobile shield generators*, she noted, impressed. *The Choshek have more influence and connections than I thought.*

"Almost out of here." Her lips barely moved with the words. She fought off a sense of revulsion at being surrounded by so many violently dead. Then, the floor shook as a blinding explosion decimated the retaining wall at her back. Large chunks of brick smashed against her, throwing her violently across the rubble-strewn floor. She opened her eyes and remained still, taking stock.

```
Warning: Body armor shield offline.

Warning: EBT systems require repair.

Caution: EBT power cell at 10% capacity.
```

At least her EBT was still operational, for the time being. Reaching into her utility belt, she removed her last mini recon drone. *Time to move, quickly. I need to know what's in the last shop.* She rose to her knees and flung the recon drone along the wall. The readings came back swiftly. No survivors. That last hit had taken them out. *I'd better get going. I'm sure the Necropis military will come to shore up this position.*

She stood up and peered outside toward an area of grass littered with dead soldiers. Her visor lit up with warnings of a minefield just outside. Carefully, she made her way across the expanse, expecting a shot between her shoulder blades at every step. She breathed a sigh of relief as she passed through the still intact metal gates leading to the Shentar Gardens. *Thank you, Abba El, for your mercy in helping me this far.* She could hear weapon fire on the other side of the thick hedge. *Strange, no bodies, and I don't see any indications of any traps being set off. Is that good or bad?* she wondered, frowning. She slowly pushed through the thinnest section of the yellow and orange shrub wall and stopped when her helmet cleared the other side.

Just inside, twenty meters away and tucked into a carved-out section of the hedge wall, manning a sniper weapon, was a familiar individual. Magula, second in charge of Musterion security. Rediquin was just about to announce her presence to help him repel the attack when a check rose up in her spirit. *Wait.* Something didn't add up here. The attackers were to his left. His weapon was pointed in the opposite direction.

Any doubt she had was erased when Magula fired two shots in quick succession. Her eyes narrowed angrily. "Traitor!" she said through gritted teeth. *If it's one thing I hate, it's someone who betrays their own for self-gain. I will enforce the Dukar rule and like all traitors, Magula will die.* Rediquin pointed her pistol at her target and gently squeezed. Perfect kill shot to the back of the head.

She stood there frozen for a moment as his body slumped to the ground. Her first kill by her own hands. *What am I doing?* Her mind and body recoiled with horror as the murderous realization struck her. Her breathing began to quicken, then she immediately shut her racing thoughts down. *Keep on task or you will die.* The echo of the words gave her the will to go on.

```
Warning: EBT power cell depleted.

Warning: EBT system offline in 5,4,3,2,1.
```

Rediquin pushed through the shrubs, then ran to Magula's still body. She grabbed his wrists and dragged him out of the pathway.

Fully exposed now, she quickly shoved his body partly into the shrubbery. As she turned back around, a mercenary emerged from around the corner of the maze. With her enhanced speed, strength, and agility, she moved just enough to the side to escape being impaled by his energized spear and easily disarmed him. With all her might, Rediquin smashed the attacker's exposed forehead with the butt of her weapon, sending him back into the shrubs, out cold or dead. She did not care which. She pivoted back to face two large mercenaries who simultaneously pointed their assault weapons at her and shot green bolts of energy that whizzed by her body in a dance of death.

In the lethal manner of a master of death, her mind, body, and weapons merged into one. Her environment seemed to slow to a crawl as she reached back into the bushes with her left hand and grabbed the long spear. She spun around and thrust it with all her might between the protective upper body plating of the closest man, impaling him. He lurched backwards and fell heavily to the ground with blood spurting out of his chest. Using her forward motion, she whipped up her pistol and calmly, with deadly accuracy, shot the narrow visor of the second man. He fell forward, and his head bounced off the dirt path. He lay still. Adrenaline pumped in her veins as she scanned the area, prepared to eliminate any new threats that might come her way.

"Let's hope I don't get any more surprises." She moved inside the carved-out hedge and retracted her visor. The municipal building, known as Musterion, was clearly under siege. *I thought so. Those upstarts joined forces to take out Choshek leadership.* She estimated the assault force to be over a hundred strong. *I know Musterion is sufficiently fortified against a small contingent of attackers, but not against this number of well-equipped men,* she thought, shaking her head. *I can't take out that many. I will die for sure. There must be another way.* She noticed that there were no heavy energy cannons used in the attack. "They need Musterion in one piece. Most likely to make a statement to everyone that a new authority has replaced the Choshek." She pursed her lips tightly, knowing that her mission had not changed. She had to keep going.

To her right, just out of sight, was an auxiliary access way. It was most likely guarded. She weighed her options as she peered below. She counted four guards manning two large energy cannons pointed at the access. *It's no wonder no one has tried to use that exit. So, how am I going to do this? Take out all four guards? I only have one explosive device left. Here goes nothing.* She removed it from her utility belt. *On 3…1,2,3.* She activated the explosive and flung it at the nearest energy cannon at the same time she jumped.

The guards turned to shoot, but the blast knocked the two farthest guards off balance while killing the other two. Rediquin landed hard on the concrete slab and allowed her body to dip, absorbing the force of her controlled fall, and fired her weapon at the two remaining guards. On her feet again, she sprinted to the undamaged energy cannon and fired multiple shots at the still closed door. *Now the Choshek can mount a counterattack,* she thought. Through the smoke, she could see that it had been partly ripped inward. Immediately, she moved the energy cannon in the other direction and placed it atop the ramp just in time to fire at the approaching assault forces.

The cannon quickly did its deadly work, holding back the wave of attackers. Bolts of energy shot past her from behind. Moments later, scores of Choshek soldiers streamed past her toward the enemy.

"Reinforcements, finally!" She stopped firing and stayed quiet on one knee with her weapon loosely gripped. Soon, the sounds of weapon fire slowed then stopped. *Looks like a Choshek victory to me.* "I hope my message got through that I was coming." She examined her armored suit. "It's never been this damaged before." She shook her head, hardly able to believe what she had endured up to this point. At least the reward for those sisters would be more than enough compensation for her troubles.

A team of Choshek militia approached her. From their midst emerged a strikingly beautiful middle-aged woman. "I am Mongsu, Dukar of the Tashmere province." Her mantle of authority and dignified demeanor was immediately apparent to Rediquin. "We know who you are. We received your message, Rediquin. You are requesting an audience with the Grand Dukar." The women's firm tone matched her steely gaze.

"Yes, I am here seeking an audience with Grand Dukar Droden Namtar. I have what he requested," she replied in a matching tone. She kept her guard up, as this could go desperately wrong in an instant. *She looks sort of like my mother*, she noted.

"Your reputation of delivering on your word proceeds you. I'm impressed and that does not happen very often. Please follow me." Dukar Mongsu turned and strode between her escorts, with Rediquin following closely behind.

Rediquin remained at the Dukar's side as they entered a well-lit chamber. *Nice, there's plenty of food and water here.* The doors closed, and Dukar Mongsu moved to stand near an oval table. She placed her hand on it, looking at Rediquin. "It is necessary for you to remove your helmet until I finish asking you some questions." Mongsu's tone was firm yet friendly.

Rediquin removed her helmet and stood looking impassively at the Dukar. Her short red hair glimmered in the chamber's light. "Go ahead and ask."

"Activate recording." Dukar Mongsu crossed her arms and looked deeply into her eyes. "We found the body of Magula Siban in the Shentar gardens. Under the Dukar oath, are you aware of what happened to him?" Avaka's expression remained impassive.

"After I entered the Shentar gardens to get a better vantage point to assist, I spotted Magula inside the hedges with his weapon pointed against Choshek defensive positions. He fired several shots." Rediquin shook her head in anger. "He was a traitor and had to die." She repelled Mongsu's intrusive stare with one of her own. "I killed him." Her voice shook with the anger she still felt.

"Yes, we figured as much. He had been demoted to a lower rank in Musterion security. Rediquin, you are cleared of killing a high-ranking Choshek officer without authorization. All traitors will be eliminated," Mongsu stated loudly, then touched the surface of the table. "Deactivate recording." She turned to face Rediquin. "I will inform the Grand Dukar what happened, and that you seek an audience to deliver what he asked for. I do not know when that will take place. The civil war is causing lots of major disruptions in every sector. But until then, please make yourself comfortable. You deserve as much for assisting. The Magolopes are delicious this time of year." Dukar Mongsu bowed slightly in respect, then excused herself. Her guards followed her from the room.

"This looks good." Rediquin's mouth watered as she looked around. She scooped up some fruit on her way to a seating area in the corner. She chose the chair with her back against the wall and sat lightly on the edge. "I hope I don't have to wait too long." She sighed with pleasure, then took a big bite. *Delicious.* She began to relax and wiped the juice from her chin. "Maybe I will take some on my way back to Ramah." She smiled, sensing some semblance of normalcy had returned to Musterion.

Now, she mentally prepared for what was to come next. A meeting with one of the most cunning Grand Dukars she knew. Thankfully, she had the one thing he coveted above all else: Cymbratar.

Chapter Four

LETALIS MOON

Zeta Three's face was cast in shadows until he leaned back and turned to look at Fay, who sat up, yawned, then stretched, arching her back. "I hope you rested well." His tone was sincere, and Fay nodded mildly in acknowledgment.

"Yes, well enough. Have we arrived?" she asked, rubbing her eyes.

"Not exactly," he replied with a wry look on his face. He entered a command on the control panel that retracted the protective viewport shield. Looming in the distance was a large mining ship. He noticed her pleated brow and she looked at him with suspicion.

"Mining ship, XP-49817, this is the *Rekullah*. I'm requesting permission to board." Zeta Three waited for a few moments, reading the sensor array data. He leaned forward and peered at the ship with a frown. "Strange, there seems to be little activity on the ship."

"Maybe they're all asleep," Fay said mockingly.

"*Rekullah*, send your traveler's identifier code (TIC)," said a hollow-sounding feminine voice.

"At least one person is awake." He darted a glance at Fay. She was now looking at the mining vessel with an intensity that he didn't understand. *Whatever. These sisters are a strange bunch. But I kind of like them.*

"I am sending my TIC to you now." He tapped the control console, then placed his right hand on the screen, which burst with a glow as it scanned his hand.

"TICs successfully received, stand by," the same voice replied.

"What are we doing here?" Fay crossed her arms and glared at him. "Are you double crossing someone?"

He decided to let her combative attitude go for the moment. "Look, I need to pick up some supplies and refuel my ship." He reviewed the sensor array data once more. Something was niggling at the back of his mind. *No mining activity. That's very odd. The captain knows me. I should have gotten permission to board by now.*

"I just want to say one more thing." Fay's voice held something that he knew he should pay attention to. A sort of knowing that he was inexplicably drawn to. He turned in the chair to face her. "I sense something is wrong. I'm not sure what it is, but I definitely sense some sort of danger." He cocked a brow in disbelief. "It's a gift of sorts." Fay returned to intensely staring at the mining ship.

"*Rekullah*, you are cleared to land in hub nine," came a hoarse female voice through the coms, followed by a loud cough.

"Acknowledged, *Rekullah* out." Zeta Three's nostrils flared, and he looked at Fay again. "See, nothing to worry about." His lips pressed together as she silently shook her head. He shrugged off her dismissal, then concentrated on maneuvering through a field of mineral silos. He pulled lightly back on the controls and descended straight to the transportation hub. *Where are the maintenance crews?* he wondered, noting how empty the place looked. There were usually work crews on duty at all times. *Maybe Fay is right. It's way too quiet.* He was troubled by the thought but set it aside.

After landing, he powered down the ship and paused, looking suspiciously around. "Warning: Trace amounts of Thamak radiation detected," the ship's automated voice announced.

He glanced at the data on the main control panel screen. "Well, that explains why no one is around. They must all be in the med bay. See, there's nothing to worry about," he said lightly, a relieved smile splitting his cheeks.

Not a moment later, the ship signaled a new message was incoming. "Priority one message… Hmmm, it's the captain. This could get interesting." He activated a private communications link. A thin transparent panel hovered above the control console.

"Greetings, I'm glad to see you. It's been too long, my friend." The captain's weary tone and pale complexion took him by surprise.

"It's nice to see you again, Captain Gwenara. If you don't mind me saying, you don't look well. I didn't see any crewmembers, are they sick?" He already knew the answer.

"Yes, we are all very sick. I need your help." A deep, hard cough underscored her plea. She struggled to draw a breath for a moment.

"Were is your physician?" He tensed with dread and fought an urge to leave.

"Mdepha, our medic died just as you arrived." Gwenara's face grimaced with pain.

"What can I do? I'm not a physician." Self-preservation warred with compassion as he watched her struggle.

"Captain Gwenara, I can help you. I have years of medical experience." Fay rose and inserted herself in the conversation.

Zeta Three pressed the mute button. "What are you doing? I don't have time for you to play physician." His eyes narrowed in a threat. "Especially given the fact the Letalis system patrol will eventually arrive. Then I'll have to fight my way out or get caught with you. That is definitely not part of my plan. Now be quiet." He reactivated audio function.

Gwenara swiped her forehead with an orange rag. "I know you're probably worried about the authorities." She coughed hard and spit into a towel, then cleared her throat. "But don't worry about that. No one will come anytime soon. Everyone is preoccupied with the civil war spreading across Letalis." The captain touched her temples, grimacing. "If you check the public transmissions you will know that is the truth," she said through gritted teeth.

Fay placed her hand on his right forearm. "No one is coming to help them." Her soft tone held an urgent desperation. "Please." She swallowed hard and bit her lip, begging him with her eyes.

"Fine, we'll help. Captain, where are you?" He shot a hard look at Fay.

"I am in the med bay along with most of my crew. The others are manning as many stations as they can." She began coughing violently again. "I am sending someone to assist you to refuel your ship and get supplies as you have requested." Captain Gwenara wiped her forehead. "I know I'll owe a favor or two but thank you, Zeta Three. I'll be expecting your associate shortly." She terminated the communication link.

He stood with arms crossed and glowered at Fay menacingly. "Just to let you know, the bounty on your head is dead or alive."

"You know this is the right thing to do. She is your friend." Fay's tone was just as firm as his.

"Hold on!" He was losing his patience. "You are no one to lecture me on what's right and wrong." His voice was getting quite loud as his index finger stopped just short of poking her left shoulder. "You were most likely responsible for killing millions on Necropis, so how dare you lecture me on morality?" he shouted, with a pause between each of the bulleted words. His face was angrily flushed with blood. Regaining control, he took a deep breath and relaxed.

"I apologize, I have no right to tell you what to do." Fay stood with her shoulders back and her chin tilted slightly up at him. "I just want to help." Her voice was soft with the heaviness of guilt.

He realized just then that this unselfish act of service was her trying to make up for some of the damage she had done. "Look, I think I understand." He pressed his lips together, then nodded his acceptance. "Come on. Let's get going before there's no one left to help." He nodded for her to precede him off the bridge.

In the cargo bay, Zeta Three tossed a suit made of a fine golden mesh to Fay. "Here, wear this. It should give you protection from the Thamak radiation. Thankfully, I have two for situations like this." He tugged his own suit over his clothing. He laughed at her, seeing how much the second suit dwarfed her small frame. "A little too big, I see. You can adjust it with these metal bands." He pointed to silver bands that he was adjusting on his own suit. "The clear visor filters out most toxic gases. Good, that looks better. Oh, and here, you are going to need this. It will show you the way to the med bay." He placed a metal disc in her palm. The cargo bay door opened, and they walked down the ramp.

The high-pitched sound of an old fueling vehicle was unmistakable. It appeared momentarily from behind a row of maintenance crafts. "Fay, the transpods are right over there. The map on the disc will help you get to the med bay. I'll meet you there when I am done."

Zeta Three didn't wait for a response. He moved immediately toward the refueling vehicle that had just arrived. *I need to hurry and get out of here as fast as possible. I have a feeling the Letalis authorities will board this ship…sooner rather than later.* His heart wrenched with concern at how sickly the driver looked.

Fay stepped out of the transpod into a wide corridor. She reached out with her spiritual discernment, searching for danger. A sense of an unseen threat hung heavy in the air. Her ears twitched as she heard a scraping noise in the dimly lit corridor. The lights flickered and then went out. She tipped her head to the side, trying to hear better, straining to see into the darkness. *That sounds like some sort of*

animal. She was unarmed. *What do I do?* Alarm flooded her body as she quietly waited.

A small emergency light came on. *What's that? Oh…* A few meters away, a corpse lay sprawled on the floor. She moved closer. *Her shoulder is badly mauled. What was she attacked by?* She snatched up an assault weapon next to the dead crewmember. *This will do just fine.* The whine of the weapon powering up echoed in the still corridor. She pressed her back against the wall, ready to fire at the source of the menacing growls growing louder by the moment. Dropping to her left knee, she pointed her weapon with nervous hands toward the clanking of claws on the metal floor.

Coming into view in the dim ring of light was a beast with long razor-sharp teeth. Its reptilian snout was stained with its victim's blood. Without hesitating, she fired, then fired again, missing both times. With no time for panic, she shot yet again and hit her mark dead on between the fiery red eyes. With a strange yelping wail, the animal crashed into the dead crewman.

But it wasn't over. She could still hear the rapid clanging of claws on the metal floor—this time from behind. With speed she rarely exhibited, she twisted sharply and stuck the tip of the weapon into the second beast's gaping jaws, firing repeatedly. The sheer force velocity of the heavy beast knocked her backward and the gun ripped out of her hand.

Fay shot back to her feet with adrenaline coursing through her veins. She reached and pulled the weapon out of its mouth, wiping the barrel on its thick spiny hide. It had a collar around its thick neck and she realized this had been some sort of pet or a guard animal.

"I was right, there was danger for me. What could have gone wrong for this animal to turn feral like that?"

The sense of danger had not abated, so she continued to follow tightly along the wall until she read the large sign above a set of wide double doors: "Medical Bay." She entered with caution.

The hissing sound of the second set of doors closing behind her indicated that she had entered an environmentally sealed room. She turned the corner and saw a dozen individuals on sickbeds. The captain lay on a metal table close by. She motioned for Fay to approach her. *She doesn't look good at all. She looks even worse in person.* "Captain Gwenara, please don't get up. My name is Fay."

"Thank you." Gwenara lay weakly back down and pointed across the room. "Mdepha was working on a vaccination but died suddenly during a test." She strained to continue to speak.

Fay helped ease the captain back down on the table. "Please save your strength. I will do what I can." With time running out, she ran to the other side of the room. "This equipment looks rudimentary enough," she murmured. She activated the universal translation on the workstation as her mind sifted through what she would need to do. "Let's see what happened here…"

Fay quickly reviewed the data logs recorded by Mdepha. *Everyone and every beast, for that matter, was affected by an unknown form of radiation.* A cold wave of shock slid over her as she continued to read the ships' logs and discovered that the ship had been near Necropis when this event happened. *Balese and Victoria must have destroyed their project's laboratories. We have struck a blow to our enemies. Let them reap what they sowed a thousand times over.* Her hatred for the Kravjin and the Necrogogs would never fade. But here she was dealing with the fallout of her and her sisters' revenge. *Nevertheless, perhaps I can bring something good out of this for these poor souls.*

Gritting her teeth, Fay focused her mind on the task at hand—saving lives. Self-condemnation would have to come later. She wasn't surprised to see this was the same type of radiation poisoning that was often treated within the Stadageo. She pulled up the physician's vaccination formulas and testing. *You were heading in the right direction, Mdepha, but you need Cymbratar-altered DNA to reverse the effects of Cremindraux radiation.* She smiled with relief. "Fortunately for you, Captain, and your crew, I just happen to know where to get some." Her softly spoken words made it all too real. She grabbed an empty flask, cut her finger with a sharp knife, and watched her blood drip into the clear container.

After a few moments, a weak feeling washed over her, and her knees felt as if they would buckle. *Maybe that was too much.* She braced her hips on the lip of the metal lab table and waited until the throbbing in the end of her finger stopped. She lifted the tip and looked to see the wound closing itself rapidly, changing from raw red to pale pink, almost completely healed. "Good as new," she muttered, then removed a flask filled with a purplish fluid from the cellular compound replicator and replaced it with her own serum. "This should work." This was how Stadageo workers were treated when they were accidently exposed to the toxic radiation. She activated the replication process to synthesize a large quantity of the Cremindraux radiation vaccine. Fay surveyed the various screens. *Looks to be working properly. It should be any moment now.*

Sure enough, the screen began to flash, indicating the completion of the replication. "Good," she said happily. She moved as quickly as she could and filled a vaccination administrator with multiple doses. She tossed the flask that had held her altered blood into the disposal bin and made her way to the bunk where the captain lay inert.

"Sorry, Captain, but this is going to hurt." She pulled down the captain's collar and injected the vaccine into her neck. Gwenara groaned with agony and every muscle in her body tensed, causing her to seize up in a fetal position. Fay cringed in sympathy and gently pushed her back down, slipping a light blanket over her. She noticed color already coming back into Gwenara's face, then sped to a row of patients. "Abba El willing, this will work on all of them." One by one, she administered the lifesaving serum.

"Good work," said a craggy voice. Fay turned to see the captain on her feet.

"Captain, it was Doctor Mdepha's solution, it just needed a few adjustments." Fay smiled, noticing crewmembers rising from the previous row of sickbeds. "Excuse me, Captain." She casually walked over to the med station and erased the key data of her blood. She motioned for one of the healed patients to come to her aid, then filled several vaccination administrators with the new serum. Looking at her name on her badge, she said with some urgency, "Nora, please take these and inject your fellow crewmembers in the neck. Right here." She gestured to the rise of flesh just to the side of her neck. A sense of gratification at instructing rather than having been commanded washed over her.

"Thank you for helping us." Nora's face was flush with emotion at her near-death experience. Nora looked to the captain, waiting for her order.

"Do what she has told you to do," said the captain. "Grundon will accompany you; it looks as if he has recovered sufficiently. Grundon, take weapons, my Jaxu guards have become rabid. There are four of them."

"Actually, I killed two of them," Fay interjected. The captain nodded, then sent the team to their critical duty. Nora and Grundon walked briskly to the med bay doors, which were already opening. Zeta Three stood there looking somewhat winded.

"Captain," he said jovially. "It's good to see you looking much better." He grinned widely at them and holstered his energy pistol.

"Actually, thanks to your associate here, I've never felt better." Captain Gwenara's face had a youthful glow.

"You can thank Mdepha for the formulation. All I did was make a few adjustments," Fay said softly, humbled by the attention.

"Did you get what you needed?" the captain asked Zeta Three.

"Yes, thanks, and for the record you still owe me a favor." He smirked.

Gwenara moved closer to him and said in a low voice, "Now that I have my mind clear, I forgot to mention that the Varkrato League is sending lots of ships to Letalis to end the civil war raging across every continent and ocean." Her brow furrowed, clearly puzzled as she examined her youthful-looking hands.

"I'm aware," he said, catching Fay's eye with a knowing look on his face. Fay flashed a frown at him, warning him to silence. "It's time for me to go, so until next time, Captain." Zeta Three bowed his head.

"Maybe next time you can visit a little longer." Captain Gwenara turned to Fay. "Thank you very much for your help. We are greatly in your debt."

"You are welcome, Captain," Fay said with deep sincerity.

"Let's go." Zeta Three cocked his eyebrow at Fay, then tipped his head toward the med bay doors. Fay trailed behind him, basking in her small redemption.

Zeta Three's hands darted across the main control panel. The lights came on in the cockpit. "Ok, all powered up and ready to go." He was relieved to see crewmembers appear on deck in the distance as his ship lifted off and glided through the atmospheric shielding of the docking bay.

"The captain was right, I don't see any Letalis system patrol ships. The government must have diverted all resources to squelch the civil war. Let's see what's going on." He switched the scanners over to listen in on the Letalis government communication frequencies.

"This is Talian sector. Rebel forces have broken through our outer perimeter defenses." The man's voice held a note of panic. "We need reinforcements immediately. Repeat, Letalis Mobile Command, this is Talian sector. Rebels…." The message abruptly terminated.

"Sounds like war to me," Zeta Three quipped. *Time for cloaking.* He activated the systems and sent his associate Raduu a coded message that he would arrive shortly. He turned to look into Fay's eyes. *I see no fear, only determination. Now I know why they are feared by their enemies.* "Are you ready for your final journey home?" His tone was lightly mocking.

"Yes, just as much as you want to see your love interest." She smiled knowingly at him, then continued, "I will gladly face the consequences for my actions."

"Love interest, what are you talking about?" His cheeks reddened.

"I saw the way you looked at her. You know…Rediquin." Her eyes sparkled.

He remained silent, not knowing how to respond to this teasing. His heart had leapt with unexpected feeling at the sound of her name.

A red beacon atop the communication screen began flashing. "Raduu." He activated the encryption function and immediately entered the new coordinates into the ship's systems. In just moments the speck in the distance grew to a large planet, and then a moon. The ship's sensor array detected many large vessels entering the Letalis system. He accelerated just enough not to overheat the cloaking systems. The moon was dotted with clouds and small bodies of water and even fewer areas of vegetation. It was currently rife with danger. He activated the manual controls and flew skillfully the rest of the way. He slowed directly over a row of plateaus. *Nice place you found here, Raduu.* He maneuvered the ship near a group of petrified trees and landed. Without a word, he powered down the main propulsion energy cores and activated auxiliary power for the cloaking systems. "Ready for a reunion of sorts?" Zeta Three got up and looked into Fay's eyes. "It's time to go home, come on," he said kindly and walked to the back of the ship. He heard Fay take a deep breath before she followed him.

Just outside the cloaked ship, they waited near a petrified tree stump. His hands rested on his still holstered pistols. Fay stood behind him. A human female rounded a big boulder. Her militaristic attire and distinct headgear marked her as a Sacarii, an elite humanoid hunter specialist.

"I am Tola. Raduu is waiting for you and your cargo," she said in a tone void of emotion, but her glare at Fay told a different story. Zeta Three felt himself bristle defensively. Without waiting for a reply, Tola turned and headed in the same direction from which she had appeared.

"Let's go." He gestured for Fay to go ahead of him.

"Long time no see, my friend." Raduu smiled widely, gripping Zeta Three's hand, shaking it firmly.

"Yes, it's been quite a while." Zeta Three turned in the direction of Raduu's gaze. "This is Fay." As he spoke, Tola and another smaller, but very hard looking woman positioned themselves behind their new prized captive.

"Where are the others?" Raduu's somewhat suspicious expression was not lost on his old apprentice. "I have it on good authority there is more than one on Necropis.”

“You are right, there are others. I had no choice but to leave immediately due to unforeseen circumstances. But don't worry, not all is lost. I have made arrangements with Rediquin. She is retrieving the others and will split the bounty with us. You know her reputation as well as me. Failure is not an option.” He was proud of her legendary exploits almost as much as he was of his own.

“Rediquin, you say.” Raduu grunted and nodded his agreement. “You have met Tola. My other specialist is Em.” He tilted his head to the other mercenary at Tola's side.

Zeta Three nodded.

“Sounds good to us, Raduu,” Em said. Zeta Three was not surprised that Tola and Em also knew of her reputation.

“Raduu, before you leave. I need to speak to Victoria, alone if you don't mind. I have a question to ask her regarding a dream. I heard she might be able to interpret it.” Raduu looked at him curiously, but Zeta Three did not feel compelled to explain.

“We leave shortly, don't take long,” Raduu said firmly. “Follow me.” He led the way to the encampment a short distance away. At the bottom of the ramp of the ship stood a woman he felt he knew somehow, along with two stasis units.

“I'll wait here, Raduu,” Zeta Three said. It was a fair distance from the ship. Raduu said something to the mysterious woman, then pointed in his direction. She looked at him then without hesitation walked to him.

"I know who you are… Zeta Three," she said when she reached him. Her voice was warm and soothing. "I had a dream and in it a divine being told me your name, Solek Modroxex. I was told to trust you. I am Victoria."

He stood shocked and speechless, as no one knew his true name. He did not feel unnerved, though, and put his hands on his utility belt. "Greetings, Victoria. I was visited in a dream by a divine being also. I was instructed to meet you at this very location." He paused for a moment. "I did not know exactly who my forefathers were until it was revealed to me in a sequence of dreams… I am a direct descendant of the patriarch Barabba Nobiveth Modroya. I was instructed by two luminous beings to bring the remains of the matriarch Sarai Chawah Modroya back home, and told you were a key to my quest." He gazed into the lovely eyes of the mature woman. A sense of reverence fell over them that he could not explain.

"I know where she lies. I was blessed to find our matriarch's body within her ambassadorial ship, the *Kirjath-Arba*, in an oddly shaped ravine directly across from here." Victoria pointed toward the matriarch's tomb. Zeta Three looked off in that direction, swallowing hard at the unexpected feelings of awe and wonder that were filling him.

The sound of Raduu's ship engines powering up signaled that their time was up. Over Victoria's shoulder, Zeta Three saw Em and Tola loading the two stasis units on to the ship. Fay was nowhere in sight.

"Don't tell anyone what you know about me. I will bring Saria back home," he said, firmly looking at Victoria's glowing face. He imagined that his looked much the same. *There is so much of my past that is missing from my memory. But this helps put some of the pieces back together.*

"I believe you, Zeta Three. May Abba El continue to guide your steps. One more thing, Solek. That which was lost will be restored…a family." She bowed her head and scurried back to the ship.

He watched the ship lift off the plateau, then vanish. *I'm a direct descendent of the great patriarch Modroya? That's intense. A family lost, and a family restored? More mysteries.* He began to jog-walk, breaking through dried-up branches, before stopping at the ledge. The dim light of sunset highlighted the odd shape in the ravine directly across the valley floor. He thought for a moment he saw a glow in the form of one of the luminescent beings that had visited him in a dream standing next to a dark shape.

"That has to be it. My ship is just small enough to land down there." He turned and darted back to it.

Chapter Five

REDIQUIN

Rediquin opened her eyes, stood up, and stretched her arms forward, then relaxed. Just then the door opened, and a male humanoid guard entered. "The Grand Dukar Droden Namtar is ready to see you now. Come."

Perfect timing, thought Rediquin as he pivoted to lead the way. She followed him to a wide-open space deep within Musterion. To her left a platoon of heavily armed Necropis soldiers and Choshek mercenaries were heading out. *Looks like the Grand Dukar has more influence in the Necropis military than I suspected. I'm impressed.* She ignored the curious stares of two sentries as she entered a well-appointed chamber. Her escort pointed to the floor just inside. "Stand here and leave your visor retracted," he commanded loudly, then moved across the room and stood near a platform.

She did as he requested, standing loose and relaxed, sensing no danger. A bluish beam scanned her from the top of her headgear to her boots, then vanished. *Must be some sort of new security measure. Times are changing fast. I don't blame Namtar for that.*

Movement from the far side of the area energized the room. From behind a shield emerged a red- and yellow-skinned, striking figure. He sat atop a large chair on a platform that was moving toward her. "Welcome back home, Rediquin." His uniquely rich, deep baritone voice highlighted his alien roots.

"I am pleased to see you unharmed and well, Grand Dukar," she said with some surprise that she really felt that way.

"Yes, those usurpers will pay for their treachery. Now, what is it you have for me?" His golden yellow eyes fixated on the small box she held.

"I have your trade tax." Rediquin extended her hands to hold out the box. He gestured to her escort to bring it to him. The lanky but strong Extomek male placed it on the table next to the Grand Dukar, who rubbed his palms together with what looked almost like childish glee and opened the box. His leathery-looking cheeks split into a wide grin, revealing his white fang-like teeth.

"Good, very good," he said happily, then closed the box. He leaned forward and braced his forearms on the armrests of the chair. His face became stern. "Now about the other matter." He lifted his right hand, and from the shadows appeared two Extomek and a Phemaux like Grand Dukar himself. *Witnesses, no doubt.*

Rediquin palmed a metal cube and her demeanor matched his. "I have this to give you and about that matter…" Her voice trailed off.

"Bring that to me." His almost sad, somber tone reflected the seriousness of what the cube contained. The Extomek grabbed it out of her hands and placed it next to the box. "Now tell me… everything."

"It contains a recording of payment received for services to a Muak'Xod Dukar named Tabor Gwauth. The details for the traitorous services rendered are contained within the cube, as well as the code to access the payment received. This happened not more than two days ago, Grand Dukar." She remained starkly composed as Namtar activated the visual and audio stored in the metal cube.

"Very generous payment for services to be rendered," the Grand Dukar said as he deactivated the device. He placed his long, steepled fingers pensively up to his chin, resting his elbows on the arms of the chair. The silence in the room loomed darkly as the Dukar continued to look at her.

"As you can see, it is Dukar Gwauth who conspires against Ormaz Bharata," she said in the same tone. "So, I forfeit payment made into that account and give it to you as a pledge of my allegiance to you, Grand Dukar." She placed her closed right hand over her chest. No one could tell that her heart was pounding fast in her chest. Her demeanor was as calm as a still pool of water.

"You are wise and bring honor to the ways of the Dukar. I appreciate that you eliminated that traitor Magula for me. That says a lot about who you are." He leaned forward. "It was Overseer Gandu Khanon who ordered Grand Dukar Ormaz Bharata to Ramah to personally place and activate agents within the Ramah government. He never intended to betray the Gandu Khanon. Now Dukar Gwauth will meet his fate as a traitor." With that he returned to his previous commanding posture. It was clear to her that he believed her now, which emboldened her.

"I have a request," Rediquin said confidently. "I need to capture certain individuals and bring them back to Ramah to earn a large bounty." Her voice remained very controlled and spoke volumes of the restraint she always maintained over her emotions.

"Yes," he drawled, clearly anticipating her request. "I am aware of them. They are out of harm's way. The problem is that one of my senior operative, Medon Sotasen, wants to interrogate them and take the bounty himself. You may know him by Crexex Voordesh." He grinned.

Her eyes narrowed as she remembered that Zeta Three had told her about him hunting the sisters back on Necropis as they were mining the Bordroxium ore. What she had not known was his other operative name, Voordesh. It was all making sense now. Dukar Namtar leaned forward, looking intense. "Yes, it seems that he had great interest in wresting my trade in Cymbratar away from me," she said. "And in doing so, Voordesh has violated one of our laws by assassinating one of our most important allies whom we gained at great expense. Senator Gemina Tmatjar of the Wufong Federation. It seems that Voordesh tortured her to death in his attempt to persuade her to betray me," she said angrily.

"What?" he roared, rising to his feet at this. "Do you have evidence?" The Grand Dukar was clearly not pleased that one his rising stars had committed such a blatant blunder. He sat back down hard, upset.

"Yes, I have irrefutable proof that he perpetrated the deed. I can try to secure another ally within the Wufong Federation, but that will most likely cost more than the first Senator." Rediquin glanced meaningfully at the box of Cymbratar. She understood he could not deviate from Choshek protocols, especially given the fact that the prominent network of mercenaries known as the Jinhadeem would seek revenge for one of their leader's assassination.

"If you have evidence, then I am sure that the Jinhadeem are also aware of this." The Grand Dukar placed his hands together, anticipating her next words. His face remained hard and his eyes narrowed in waiting. He gestured to an agent standing in the shadows. "Contact the leadership of the Jinhadeem and inform them that we will pay a truce tribute," he said in a calm but deadly voice to the narrow-faced, slender agent.

"I will give you the evidence and I claim the Askari right to challenge to the death on Crexex Voordesh, for breaking Choshek ally protocol as well as the right of bounty on the two fugitives," Rediquin said loudly. She knew the Grand Dukar had no choice if he wanted to avoid retribution or a turf war with a well-established organization in the neighboring Wufong Federation.

"Excellent, he is close by waiting for me to release the rogue sisters to him, so yes, I grant your claim of Askari on Crexex Voordesh for breaking prominent Choshek protocol and for the bounty on the fugitives," he said, raising his right hand.

"We have heard and seen an Askari between Rediquin and Voordesh. He who lives will inherit the wealth of the other, including the bounty on the rogue sisters," the others who were standing around Namtar's seat echoed in unison.

"I hope you prevail. The public exhibition of the corpse of

Crexex Voordesh and the truce tribute would stop a war between our organizations." Rediquin bowed as the others behind the Grand Dukar vanished into the shadows. "An escort will take you to the Askari chamber. May the gods give you victory, Rediquin." He extended his right hand as if to impart a blessing of favor.

Let's do this. Long held injustice and rage hardened into the brutal coldness of a killer as she accompanied the escort, who was dressed in the traditional assassin's attire, from the room.

Rediquin stood at the edge of a circular stone platform with an Askari blade in her right hand, just inside the well-lit Askari chamber. Behind a wide stone column across from her was her opponent, Crexex Voordesh, who over the years had repeatedly tried to wrest the Cymbratar trade from her. His presence was cold and menacing. Her nostrils flared, then she closed her eyes. *I will avenge all those you killed, Voordesh. Your treachery knows no bounds. You will die by my hands.* She became both observer and participant, ready to engage her adversary.

Focused now, she moved fluidly through a short Kohyim regimen, with only the sound of the blade whipping through the air. *There is only one way out now.* She knew that one of the Askari death match laws was that the victor had to exit the gate from which their opponent entered the chamber. *I am an Askari blade. I am victorious.* The wide column in the center of the circle descended with a grinding noise, allowing the combatants to engage.

"I really wanted to test my fighting skills against those rogue sisters." His rather high-pitched voice held a sneer. "The bounty is dead or alive." He laughed as he looked her up and down with a curl of his lip. "But, I suppose you will have to do for now, and besides, your Cymbratar trade will finally be mine," he boasted with his hands on his hips in challenge.

"Just so you understand why you are going to die today." Her voice rang with cold, deadly purpose. "I know that you have been actively after my trade for quite some time, but you have not succeeded. But even more, Senator Gemina Tmatjar of the Wufong Federation was an ally and a friend." Rediquin bent her knees in anticipation that he would make the first move.

Just as she expected at the taunting, Voordesh came rushing at her like the large beast in the Kritokhaan jungle had charged at her. His grunts echoed in the chamber. *Does he really think his sheer size is an advantage?* She stood motionless until he was an arm's length away. Her body moved in a blur as his blade sliced through her left sleeve, then she used his forward momentum to trip him. He crashed heavily to the ground.

She violently kicked the blade out of his hand with her left boot as he tried to turn over, then slammed down on his hand with all of her body weight focused on her right foot. He yelled in agony. Still in motion, she jumped away from his right leg sweep.

Voordesh got to his feet again, quickly regaining his balance. "I'll kill you!" he roared. His face was twisted with rage now and his bald head was red and wet with exertion. His left hand darted out to try to grab her and she pushed the blade through it, then head-butted him. The momentum of his backward stagger removed the blade.

Half his hand now hung loose, and blue blood began to gush. She vaguely noted her blade dripping with it. He looked dazed. *I am the blade that seeks vengeance upon the guilty. The recompense for treacherous deeds.* She rushed into a death charge of her own for the kill before he could regain his wits. With a high leap, she came down on him, driving the blade deep into his neck.

"This is for my associates you killed and for breaking the Dukar rule." Grasping his throat, he fell to his knees then folded onto his back. "You wanted to fight a rogue sister?" Rediquin let all of the wealth of her rage be spent on him now. She spat in his face, then leaned close as he lay gasping with his life rushing out of him. "I am a rogue sister." Her words bulleted at him with a slight pause in between each one.

His dimming eyes looked at her with what seemed to be some respect. His mouth moved as if he would speak, then slacked in repose.

"Now, according to Askari rules, what was yours is now mine," Rediquin said triumphantly. With the coldness of a seasoned assassin, she removed her blade from his neck and wiped it on his sleeve. She froze for a moment, noting a necromonic symbol on his forehead. It seemed to have just appeared right after his death. The mark seemed to by a styled dark speech letter used by sorcerers Guilds.

The rush of victory was quickly replaced by apprehension as she stood looking at the widening pool of blood. She had to step to the edge of the combat stone to avoid it. Her head whipped around as she saw dark shadows flying around and a sort of shrieking noise filled the room. Just then, a translucent portal appeared near Voordesh, blocking her escape. "What is that?" she said in awe.

An oblong object emerged from the multi-dimensional opening. Hues of blue energy cascaded downward from its onyx surface as it hovered just above his lifeless body. She could just make out a fine golden mist that emerged from his corpse being swept up into the bottom of the mysterious object. *What are you? Am I next?*

She was relieved when it vanished. *Back to the dark realms of Creminmorta, no doubt. It must have been the mythical soul collector.* Memories of the stories of it filled her mind with fascination and dread. "Serves you right, Voordesh. Eternal damnation in the realms of Creminmorta." She inspected the cut on her forearm. "That looks to be healing nicely," she said, then moved briskly to where Voordesh had entered the Askari chamber.

Now I'm like my clients who have plunged the blade of vengeance into my enemy's heart with their own hands. I have come full circle. Her dark muse broke as she inserted the tip of the bloodstained blade into the center of the gate. The clanging of mechanisms rang in her ears as the gate opened. The rush of the cool subterranean breeze and bright light welcomed her. Glad to be out of the menacing darkness, she stepped out of the chamber and breathed freely for the first time in a short while.

A masked individual motioned with his weapon in the direction she should go. She walked up a steep, winding ramp to a narrow platform where a small shuttle transport was being attended to by a maintenance crew. Rediquin entered a series of commands on her forearm's control screen, which activated her ship's auto retrieval systems, bringing it to her location. A green-skinned Extomek holding a short metallic cylinder stood near one of the transports. The short yellow horns atop its head and its large yellow reptilian eyes denoted its female gender. "Congratulations on your victory." She greeted Rediquin. "As is customary, you are now the sole possessor of your adversary's trade network and half his wealth." The Extomek placed the brushed bronze cylinder in her waiting hand. "In this cargo box is all of your gear you arrived with." She gestured to a metal box resting to the side of the transport. "It has been refurbished as ordered by the Grand Dukar."

Rediquin nodded her head. "I receive what is rightfully mine, but I have decided to give this as an homage to the Grand Dukar." She handed back the metallic cylinder with a slight bow.

"The Grand Dukar accepts your gift." The Extomek took possession of the cylinder, looking genuinely surprised at the unusual return of the victory spoils. "This disc contains the location of the two individuals you seek," the stoic Extomek said and handed it to Rediquin. The woman then excused herself and entered the transport.

Rediquin wasted no time opening the container and donning her combat gear. She peered into the distance, resting her hands on her holstered weapons and enjoying the view of endless seas. The glowing green beacon on her armored forearm made her smile. The *Furies Scepter* was here.

"Open cargo bay door," she said and jumped into her ship, striding immediately to the cockpit. "Now let's get those two rogues and get out of here. I have no time to waste."

Deep inside one of Necropis' most hostile environments, the Kellmesh Desert, a massive sand storm had reached the barren Saubon mountain range. Orisa Sotasen and Mirinda Kuffa, rogue sisters and saboteurs of the Stadageos, were scrambling to escape and disappear to start a new life. But first, they had to complete a mission given to them by the Choshek organization in order to earn a ship for the long journey back to Ramah, their home.

"Hold on… compensating for wind velocity," the pilot shouted. Electrical sparks cascaded across the control panel. The ship's hull scraped along the jutting cliff walls, causing violent vibrations.

"We aren't going to make it!" Mirinda wailed.

"At the very least we'll eventually get buried by sand storms," remarked Orisa, wryly rising from where she had fallen from the impact of hitting the cliff. "I better get strapped in it looks like this will be a bumpy ride." Orisa said. The ship they were riding in broke away from the cliffs and headed into a narrow gap between the mountain peaks. The pilot followed the curved path cut away by an ancient glacier. The shuttle slowed as it approached a sheer rock face. The pilot entered a series of codes. A moment later, a wide section of camouflaged wall retracted into the mountainside, revealing a transportation bay.

"We have arrived at your destination. You will wait here. Your leader will be here shortly to pick you up," the masked humanoid male commanded.

"Who will we meet?" asked Orisa.

"You must leave the shuttle now," he said, ignoring the question.

Mirinda and Orisa looked at each other, released their seat restraints, and exited the shuttle. Mirinda adjusted her scarf over her mouth and nose, as fine dust swirled around the transportation bay.

"I hope the person we are meeting comes soon, or I'll evaporate in this heat." Orisa wiped the beads of sweat off her forehead with her sleeve, then looked at a red marker they had been given. "So, this guarantees our safety. Interesting. I never knew the Choshek had a code of honor." She tucked the marker back in her vest.

Mirinda began to pace. "Even so, who knows who will betray us, kill us and collect a reward," she spouted.

"There's nothing to worry about. We are going off-world on a new mission, remember? Eventually we will make it back to Ramah, and that's all that matters." Orisa's tone was warm and reassuring.

"To be truthful, that's not what's troubling me—it's the civil war that has spread across Necropis. And we both know who really started it." Mirinda clasped her hands behind her back and paced along the ledge of the old abandoned transport hub.

Orisa stood facing the barren landscape, then removed her headscarf. "What matters to me is that we will return to Ramah. I made an oath to myself that I would rebuild my family's legacy and have a family of my own one day." Her voice filled with determination. "And now, after all this time, I'm so close to fulfilling that promise." The longing of her heart was clear. She lifted her hands to cover her face momentarily as if to gather her emotions from the depths of despair and longing. She swallowed hard.

Just a few short steps away, Mirinda came and hugged her, then gazed into her moist eyes. "One way or another, let us hope Abba El will make a way where there seems to be no way." Mirinda's hope was firm and Orisa couldn't help but agree. She nodded, and a small smile appeared on her face.

A wave of dust swept across the floor. "I think it's a cloaked ship landing." Orisa tapped Mirinda on the arm and darted behind a guardrail for protection. "I wonder what kind of mission this is," Orisa said quietly. "At least my ankle is completely healed, and we will be able to go together this time."

"Whatever it is, they'll provide the necessary tools to accomplish it." Mirinda's irritable tone reflected her distaste. "I hope we can make this our last mission. I'm more than ready to go home." Mirinda caught Orisa's approving nod.

A light thump heralded a sleek ship's landing and appearance, seemingly out of thin air. The ship de-cloaked; its cargo bay door slid open. With heavy, purposeful steps, a lethal looking individual came down the ramp with gloved hands on both holstered pistols. Unafraid, Orisa and Mirinda came out from behind the guardrails to meet her.

"Greetings, Orisa and Mirinda. My name is Rediquin. I have been given charge over you by the Grand Dukar Namtar. Here are the orders." She showed them the holographic instruction, then quickly slid the device back into her utility belt.

They were taken aback momentarily. Orisa frowned. "You have

been given charge over us? Why is that?"

"I don't have time to explain. Please follow me." Rediquin's cape swayed as she spun around and headed back up the ramp. Mirinda and Orisa, sensing no immediate danger, followed her into the ship. The cargo bay doors slid closed as they boarded.

"Sit down, and don't touch anything," Rediquin ordered. "Engage protocol Rediquin 1." She retracted her visor, then turned to address them. "If I don't disengage that protocol, within the calculated time we are to reach our destination every mercenary in this region of space will come looking for you... Escape is futile." Rediquin's expression was hard.

"Why would we want to escape? We will do our best to complete the mission." Orisa's voice was filled with uncertainty.

"You are now my captives. There is a bounty on your heads." Rediquin rose with a pistol in her hand. "I know who you really are and what you have done." Her narrowed eyes held both strength and threat. "You would do well to come along peacefully. Or we can do it the hard way with restraints."

Rediquin stared hard at them. "You are not going on a mission. I'm taking you to Ramah." She looked pleased and a little smug.

"What is going on? Did Fay send you?" Orisa felt bewildered, but a relief began to come over her.

"No, Fay did not send me, but she should be there by now." Rediquin continued to look at them sternly, clearly ready to force them if necessary. "My mission is to bring you back to Ramah. The why and how is not your concern," she said coldly.

"We will go…willingly," Mirinda said, and her body visibly relaxed.

"Good. Now, I want you two to stay in the cargo bay. I'll join you soon enough to make sure you are comfortable enough for the journey." Rediquin reached under her seat and tossed each of them a TEPPs.

A sense of betrayal burgeoned in Orisa's heart at the Dukar for selling them out. She was sick of the constant lies and subterfuge. She stared at Rediquin who did not back down. Orisa decided they would trust her for now. Besides, what other choice did they have? Giving in, she nodded her agreement. She could feel Rediquin's piercing gaze drilling into her back until the doors sealed shut behind them.

"I knew we would be caught. The bounty for anyone who worked at the Stadageo must be large," Mirinda said once they reached the relative privacy of the cargo bay.

"I don't think we will need this." Orisa said, removing the red maker from her vest and threw it toward the back of the cargo hold. "So much for the Choshek code of honor." She bit out folding her arms across her chest.

"Let's be thankful that this mercenary will deliver us to the Ramah authorities instead of Necropis military, or worse yet, Khanon," Mirinda said as she slid to the floor with her back braced against the wall. She then stuffed the food ration into her vest. "What do you think will happen to us when we arrive? What if they know we destroyed the Stadageo and caused a global civil war." Her somber tone was clearly shared by Orisa, who rolled her head to the side to look at her. She lay across the top of a long containment module.

"I don't think this bodes well for us." Orisa swallowed the lump in her throat and continued fatalistically. "At least we will die back home. Hopefully they will bury us alongside our real family.

"Does it even matter at this point what happens to us? We have avenged our family's murders. My only regret is that there were so many unintended casualties caused by the destruction of the Stadageo. As for the civil war, we know from the Choshek network that it was only a matter time before the separatist's rebellion to break away from the Varkrato League would start." Mirinda's voice held the weight of the burden of responsibility for so many deaths.

"Yes, I feel the same, but I suppose you are right," Orisa replied, then closed her eyes, forcing herself to focus on the faces her family. *Oh, how I have missed you.* She embraced them with her heart. *Maybe I will finally get to say over my family's graves, I have avenged you and your legacy will begin anew.* She allowed herself to slide into a meditative state.

The ship lifted off, and ascended high into orbit. Rediquin was not pleased to see a large armada of ships approaching Necropis. *They look to be Varkrato League ships sent to put an end to the civil war. I'm glad I made it out in time.* "Now I have to go around those ships," she said, annoyed, and adjusted the flight path. *Time to collect my bounty and return these wayward sisters back home.* "I wonder if Jazrene will recognize me. I don't know if I am ready to see her."

The stars slid out of focus, replaced with enveloping space displacement travel. Sometime later, Rediquin scratched the pink almost healed wound, then rolled her sleeve back down. "Ramah, Mother." She removed her helmet, then reached under her seat and retrieved a thin crystal wafer and placed it on the armrest, activating it. *It's been so long since I've done this.* She tapped the communications screen, now filled with recent images of an elderly women walking in a lush garden. Spreading her index and middle fingers on the screen, she focused in on a more detailed image of the stately woman. The close-up shot revealed the signature silver eyes of a Marium Kahnet elder. Her gleaming white hair was elegantly styled and accented with a golden brooch. The next image ripped her heart out, as the woman was kneeling at a grave marker, wiping tears away with the sleeve of her robe. Rediquin clutched her chest in pain and unexpected grief. "How I've missed you, Mother."

Something changed in that instant. She felt her resistance to seeing her mother break away in her spirit. She began to weep softly, releasing long held emotions. "I am ashamed of what has become of my life. I won't blame you if you reject me, then I will be truly dead." She wiped her own tears with her sleeve, then replayed the images once more.

Yaqal 30

He ascends from the depths of the bottomless pit. He torments the hopeless. He clothes them with shame and feeds them misery. Anguish is their bed. They are bathed in bitterness. He gives them desolation as their inheritance. But I am redeemed by the radiant beauty of HIS glorious love and the light of HIS majesty parts the path to peace. I sing HIS praises forevermore.

Chapter Six

KHANON

Aboard the military capital ship *Aurgog*, Khanon peered through the viewport of his quarters. "The Fiero system. Why has Abaddon sent me there?" he wondered aloud, his brow creasing. All he knew was he had to eliminate the new religion on Shalem, no matter the cost. He had barely escaped with his life as punishment, because he had failed to discover the Marium Kahnet rogue sisters before they destroyed the Stadageos. He shivered thinly, remembering the threat on the face of Chi Ku Ren, the Kravjin supreme leader, at their last meeting with the Spectrarex and his longtime spiritual guide Abaddon.

The room in his quarters was very quiet. *No visitors today, I guess.* He did not miss the intrusive Nossorads. He sneered at the thought of them. They were Abaddon's eyes and ears from the realms of Creminmorta.

A notice of an incoming message beeped, suddenly, on his desk. "Now what?" Khanon grunted as he stomped to his desk and sat heavily in the plush chair.

"Let's see, hmm, a coded message from Ramah." He grinned. "Receive incoming message." He leaned forward and read it quickly, then once more to be sure.

```
Sender: Agent Medrassa

Message: Identified corpses of two Stadageo workers
returned to Ramah for a bounty by mercenaries. End
of message.
```

"The other infiltrators must be dead as Abaddon told me on Tartarus." Khanon smiled, then laughed in relief. "Death is too good for them. After they destroyed the Stadageo and Leviathan complex, I wanted them to suffer and beg for death. But, now because of their actions, many neutral governments are set to join the Varkrato League. All to our benefit." The screen split in two.

```
Incoming Priority One Message

Sender:  Krauvanok Alliance Supreme Council

Message: Effective immediately, Krauvanok Alliance
Command has been given complete authority over the
Augatar region. Your position as Senior Overseer in
that sector is temporarily suspended until further
notice by the Krauvanok Alliance Supreme Council. End
of message.
```

His smile faded. "No surprise." Khanon had anticipated this would happen, given the severity and scale of the civil wars on Letalis and Necropis. Nonetheless, his pride had taken a blow. "Message received. Close it," he said, somewhat disheartened. The first message vanished, then was replaced with another.

```
Sender: Agent Ammadax

Message: The Mantis Alliance is sending massive
military convoys to build up its Guardian bases on
Ramah's moons. End of message.
```

"What, why would they build up bases there?" He frowned, thinking hard. "I'm sure it has to do with that blasted Mantis Messiah on Shalem!" He slammed his fist on the desk. "I will crush and obliterate that upstart religion. Their leader is dead and now all who follow The Way will perish," he said through gritted teeth. "Interesting that some of those executed have stated that their Messiah was resurrected...rumors for sure."

Straightening, he ordered his ship, "Send a priority one message to the Grand Dukar, Ormaz Bharata… Recall all agents from Ramah and send them to Shalem. Report to Praetor Inquisitor Mindendra for reassignments… End of message." *They should have eliminated every single Marium Kahnet when they had the opportunity thirty years ago. They believed they had killed the so-called Messiah then, but obviously not. Well, he is dead now.* The screen indicated his message was sent.

Now, let's see exactly where I am going. "Terminate communications links and display general data on our destination," Khanon said calmly.

```
General Information of Fiero Prime

Governing regional body: Langorra Regional Authority

Primary industry: Mining of common and rare minerals
```

```
Most valuable mineral: Barraxium ore

Number of mines: 66

Mines operational: 65

Mines closed: 1 [*]
```

Khanon examined the location of the mine Abaddon had instructed him to enter. "Of course, it's the one that's closed," he muttered. *Let's see why it was closed.* "Open the annotation on the closed mine," he said curiously.

```
Closed mine: Langu 2

Quarantined: Indefinitely

Cause: Unknown

Fatalities: 1,332
```

So many deaths…and the cause is unknown? *What is this?* He shook his head in disbelief. Abaddon had apparently forgotten to mention the mine was basically quarantined forever. "Looks like I might've been given a death sentence, after all." Khanon sighed.

A familiar sibilant voice swirled in his mind. *"You will not perish."*

Khanon quickly looked around his quarters. Seeing nothing, he shrugged it off. *It's just my imagination.* A green beacon lit his screen. *We must have arrived.* "Open bridge link."

"Lord Khanon," said Captain Tshera. "We have entered the Fiero system and will be in Fiero Prime's orbit shortly. I have contacted and informed the Langorra Regional Authority of our arrival and instructed them as per your orders not to interfere with your inspection of the mines."

"Good, I will be ready to disembark as soon as you land, Captain," Khanon said with a small, appreciative smile. "Close link." *I guess I will find out soon enough why Abaddon wants me here.* "Deactivate my station." He swiveled his chair 90 degrees to the left, stood up, and made his way to the disembarking section.

Captain Tshera barked orders to a nearby officer: "Send a battalion to escort Lord Khanon and secure the perimeter around my ship!" Her battle-hardened expression commanded respect.

Khanon sensed that his destiny would change with this journey. His train of thought was broken as he felt the thump of the ship landing resonate in his calves through his boots. He stood to the side, waiting for the deployment of the battalion of soldiers to precede him down the ramp. A mobile communication drone hovered next to him.

"Lord Khanon, we have secured the perimeter around the mine's entrance," said Captain Tshera.

"Excellent, Captain. I am going alone. If I do not return by nightfall send help for me," he said with a sense of doom weighing on him.

"As you command," the Captain replied.

Khanon's steps were heavy as he walked down the steep ramp to the dusty parched ground, heading directly to the sealed gates of the main entrance to the Langu 2 mine. His eyes quickly adjusted to the bright lights along the curvature of the wide hallway. Musty and stale air. Judging from the dust on those rails, this mine had been closed for quite some time. *What do I do now?* He knew an answer to this puzzle would present itself. "Ah, here it is." Just ahead was a semi-polished silver wall. He could see himself in the reflection. He stepped closer. "Mullgoth!" he shouted with all his might. He could hear his bellow echo in the distance.

The silver wall rippled, then a gate opened in the center. With confidence, he stepped through it. "It's colder than I'd like, but the air is definitely clear of contaminants," he noted. Cautiously, he stepped closer to the rails along the edge of a precipice. *What am I looking at?* He surveyed the massive cavern. It seemed recently excavated. He frowned deeply, then peered into the distance where three massive, partially constructed towers stood. "Those look like metallic plateaus. What are they for?" His voice echoed in the distance. Leaning forward, he stared straight down. A wide circular platform adorned with an intricate Toxrokk design lay invitingly at the bottom of the steep ramp a few hundred meters away. He felt a compulsion to go to it and did so.

As he reached the center, he strongly felt the presence of his master.

Khanon knelt and braced his arm on his left knee. "I am here, Master, as you commanded." A slight sound caught his attention and he looked up to see two tanzanite obelisks rising from the floor. They emitted tendrils of blue and red energy that danced invitingly. The golden luminescence of the Toxrokk hieroglyphs was mesmerizing to behold. Suddenly, a golden serpent's eye appeared suspended between two monoliths. With a rush of wind, it transformed into a multi-dimensional veil from which Abaddon emerged.

"Rise, my loyal subject." The booming voice of the maleficent being rolled over him. Khanon rose with renewed security and awe of his guardian. "As I informed you on Tartarus, those responsible for the destruction of the Stadageos and the Mecropex are dead." The loathing and hatred laced within Abaddon's deep baritone voice was not lost on Khanon. "I have commanded you to travel here for a purpose that far surpasses your understanding. I am eternal, a day for me is a thousand of your years." Hot spewing plasma and smoke erupted from his mouth as he spoke.

"What does my master ask of me?" Khanon bowed his head obsequiously, determined to gain favor.

Abaddon extended his clawed hands toward Khanon. "Kresh ~ Sheku." His voice sounded more reptilian than humanoid. A soft glow rose in front of Khanon, who quickly slid away from it. Rising from the floor before him was a crystalline column. Atop it were dozens of Nazar amulets and a Nazar ring was partially imbedded in its gleaming surface. A Gwesha blade was in the very center.

Guided by the necromonic essence within, he stood and strode forward and removed his gloves, dropping them to the floor. Khanon reached for the Gwesha blade and gripped its handle tightly with his left hand. He lifted the hefty blade. Intuitively, he knew what to do next. "Saungra ~ Topesh." He spoke the incantation loudly. Blue energy engulfed his hands. He moved his right hand over the objects, then pricked each finger with the curved blade. "The blood speaks," he said as he sprinkled his necronos-infused blood on the Nazar amulets and ring. He returned the blade to its previous location.

Coming out of the necromonic trance, he felt the sting of the open wounds on his fingertips. The power of the moment spun around him like a cold wind. He quickly donned his gloves for protection and watched the bloodstained column descend back into the floor. He stared at a sphere that appeared in Abaddon's palm. It was made of rotating bands of gold and silver with swirling black clouds inside them. Each band had necromonic symbols hovering within that glowed blue and green. A Creminsphere, the device that allows access to the realms of Creminmorta. *Why does he have one of those? Is he sending me there?* He swallowed hard, deeply troubled. He looked up into his master's face.

The enigmatic device shot out of Abaddon's hand and stopped a half-meter from his face. It took everything in him not to jerk his head back. A stream of crystalline onyx matter touched Khanon's forehead. Immediately, he felt his spirit be transported through a trans-dimensional vortex and into another plane of existence. His momentum soon ceased, and his eyes adjusted to the bright red rays from the large sun above. "The Creminsola sun," he marveled. "It has been blue since the end of the age of Kelkabara." Below him were the craggy plains of Barracura, and at their center was the Abyss of Barracura. He dared not say the name aloud lest he be thrown into its lifeless maw. "This is the dominion of Prince Saurcine," he said, astonished.

Fear assailed him as he looked upon an Oglok that was gorging on the remains of its prey. He had read about the large, heavily horned, bipedal beast in the Maveth Codex. "This is definitely the realm of Grythinmor," he said. He took courage that the beast seemed to not notice him. A cloud of sulfuric mist wafted up against him as if it was trying to permeate his spiritual body. He could almost taste the acidity of metal. At that moment, the cloud gained substance and his spirit was taken up along the mountain range and came to a stop near a wide plateau. From this vantage point he could see the large, powerful, and deadly multiphasic necronos stream. "The mighty Creminmorta River." His heart swelled in pride and awe at this rare privilege, but then he cringed as he heard shouts of anger and agony coming from it. He put his hands over his ears and looked away. "It has separated the five realms for six thousand years. I wonder if the changed color of the sun marks the beginning of another battle between the five realms; the Krauvmesh war." He tried to imagine such a sight, to no avail.

He leaned forward to try to see into the distant adjoining realm. That had to be the realm of Haxadrene. *Just look at those majestic mountains. That must be where our supply of precious metals and minerals come from, the famed mines of Daugravog. I wish I could see the throne of Prince Augergesh. I'm sure it's constructed with marvelous materials the likes of which have never been seen by mortals.* Khanon's thoughts were interrupted by a sense that he was not alone. Just below, on another plateau, stood a willowy human female dressed in strange clothing. The clothes were whipping around her body and yet there was no wind. His spirit was inexplicably drawn closer to her, just fifty short meters away, and he waited to see who she was since he was positioned behind her. An open silo in the style of a necronos pod, with the dome half closed, was beside her.

Just outside of the silo was a winged being, who sparkled like a gem. His beauty had no equal. "I am Navmolek," the being said loudly in a rich baritone voice. He stretched his hands toward the human female. Khanon couldn't help but gasp in surprise. *He is one of the five spirits of Spirradeus. The god of all religions.* "Be fruitful and you will bring forth the Krevomax at the appointed time." Navmolek lifted his large hand and in it was the dagger that was stained with Khanon's own blood. He felt an urgent fear for his very life as the god imparted the essence of his spirit around the blade. The blade then transformed into a Kravjin ceremonial consecration wafer.

Khanon watched Navmolek place the empowered wafer into her body. She didn't seem to be resisting, as her body gently turned and then was deposited into the pod. He could finally see her face. "Avisha Khanon." His mouth dropped open in surprise.

The dome closed and descended into the ground now covered by the Tisrad Dragon's seal. In the distance, he saw a thick mass of root-like tubes racing toward Navmolek from the Hauskavesh mountains. The roots embedded themselves into the ground around Avisha's pod. Khanon tried to fathom what this meant. Above, a shooting star was streaking toward where Navmolek waited with crossed arms. The trail of energy from the star grew larger until it was clear it was yet another celestial being that landed, making a great crack in the ground. "Krauvmesh, god of war," Khanon muttered fearfully, watching this large bestial looking god standing near Navmolek. Within his wings were grimacing faces. His forehead was sealed with three necromonic numbers that glowed red.

"The time for the five realms of Creminmorta to battle for supremacy has arrived." His powerful voice was thundering and sounded omniscient.

Khanon was ripped back into the vortex just then, and his spirit slammed back into his body. He grabbed his head, which felt as though it was about to explode, and grunted in agony. He wiped his eyes and saw a black viscous substance on his hands, which must've been the effects of multidimensional travel to Creminmorta. Then the necromonic substance was absorbed back into his body. *I knew that's why their sun changed from blue to red. Now, after millennia, the five lords will battle each other for first position. They will have even more influence in the five galaxies of the Quintástraya.*

"Your bloodline has been one of the chosen to fulfill what is needed in lengths of time you cannot fathom," said a voice.

Khanon looked, startled, at Abaddon, who was standing waiting. Still wrapped up in the experience, he had not realized it was not over yet.

"I am honored and fortunate beyond measure, my Lord and Master." Khanon's voice was harsh with the pain that was pounding in his head. He sank to his knees and bowed his head to the floor.

"You must continue your journey to the Thrakonan planet Gerobon and bind your bloodlines in the customary blood ceremony with the new Order, Saurcine. Once that is completed, I will instruct you as to your next task." With that said, Abaddon vanished into the mirror-like veil.

The piercing pain in Khanon's head lifted as soon as his dark master was gone. His mind raced. *Maybe my lineage will produce the Krevomax. He did not say specifically, but what else could he have meant? I am after all the most deserving among all the Kravjin. Who better than myself? Abaddon is wise to have chosen me.* His heart swelled with pride. He slowly got up and brushed the dust off his clothing.

"I feel stronger than before. The Bisgabeth gateway to the Kilodromus galaxy is very close. I should make good time to Gerabon," he said and quickly returned to his ship.

Back aboard the *Aurgog*, Khanon continued to pace along the bridge of his ship, watching Fiero Prime vanish out of sight as the ship entered the Space Displacement Stream (SDS).

"Captain Tshera, we have intercepted an emergency communication between several mines and the Langorra Regional Authority," a senior communications officer said in a firm tone.

"What is the emergency, Captain?" Khanon could not help but be curious as he'd just left those mines. "Inform Lord Khanon."

She nodded respectfully. "Lord Khanon, nine mines have reported thousands of casualties. The cause is unknown," she stated with a frown on her face.

"Interesting," he said somberly and cocked an eyebrow. "Very sad. I trust they will find the cause." He nodded his head, dismissing her. *Must be the Tisrad Dragon's will.*

"Lord Khanon, we are approaching the outer perimeter of the Bisgabeth neutral zone," said the captain.

He made his way to the main viewport of the bridge and became utterly mesmerized at the creative omniscience of the builders of the Bisgabeths. The massive structures were impressive to behold, to say the least. He would never get tired of seeing them.

"We have set a course to the Kilodromus galaxy, Lord Khanon," said Lieutenant Trebba.

Khanon acknowledged this with a nod. Turning back to the viewport, he marveled at the vast and mysterious transparent nebulas clouds. *We were once like gods, to build such wondrous constructs.* Lost in the moment, he reflected on the time of Kelkabara when all creation was in a state of perfection. The unmatched time when man had expanded into the stars and created the Quintástraya. *One day from my lineage one will come as a god. Avisha, my niece and blood relative, has been chosen to be the fertile soil of the Krevomax. My brother will be proud to know that his daughter is not dead but is now seated in the realms of power and destiny.* His heart swelled with importance at the future glory to his family name.

Lost in thought, he never felt the shift as the ship vanished into the outer dominion of the omniscient-like power of the Bisgabeth.

Chapter Seven

RAMAH

Jazrene Vallo savored the cool spring air, which carried the joyful sounds of children chasing Pumgaroos in the nearby gardens. She reached down and took off her shoes so that she could enjoy the dew on the lush, vibrant grass as she leisurely strolled off the path. A dozen meters ahead, a small white-furred Womtat scurried between decorative shrubs, pursued by a potential mate. *A time of renewal and the rebirth of things once dead.* She crossed the soft grass and climbed to the top of the hill that separated the main Monastarium from the ancient Mevaseret mines, which came into view as the low-lying fog evaporated. Leaning down to put on her shoes, she enjoyed the warmth of the sun on her face. *The time of my departure will come shortly after the Barayalad is completed.* That was what she had been told. Her mind raced with wild speculation as to how it was to come about.

Shadows dotted the ground and her brow pleated curiously, because the sky was cloudless. She shielded her eyes with cupped hands and looked up. "Another convoy of Mantis Alliance cargo ships." A joyful smile lit her face at the sight of ships carrying skilled workers and materials to complete the restoration of the

Monastarium. *Yes, Abba El, I am so grateful. Will I see it?* She made her way down the slope, then around the curve of the mountainside and through a narrow crevasse.

The entrance to the mine was just ahead. To the left was a cluster of Pangaboon nests clinging to thickly intertwined vines. *A time of renewal.* The recurring thought emerged again. She knew that it meant something. *I will pray on this.* She could feel the heat emanating off the bronze floor from the mine's refining processes.

The lone humanoid security guard who was in a meditative Kohyim position suddenly came to attention at her approach. "Good morning, Mother Vallo." His voice was gentle and serene.

"Good morning, Jetek." She responded in kind with a genial smile, then continued past the DNA bio-security scan at the main entrance of the mine. Just ahead were the newly expanded sections of the mine. The pleasant odors of mining wafted into her nose. She entered the brightly lit jeweler's crafting room, which was filled with activity. To the right behind a thick protective transparent wall were the Goelyakar, the items associated with the Mantis Messiah's death and resurrection. All of the jewelry for the order of Marium Kahnet hierarchy was being fashioned from these sacred items. The jeweler's table in the very center was where the Yoke of Kahnet necklaces were being wrought. *They are so beautiful. Those appointed to the newly created office of Sharath will be blessed to wear the sacred necklaces.*

"Welcome, Mother Vallo," said Dugra Atta reverently. Jazrene turned to look at his maroon face. His large beautiful translucent opal eyes were glowing with excitement.

"Greetings, master jeweler." She nodded with a wide smile. The matching swell of emotion in her heart threatened to choke her up. *This is a historic moment. The fulfillment of so many prophecies coming to pass is not a burden to be taken lightly, and that I'm part of it is almost overwhelming.* She lifted her hand to her mouth to contain the rise of joyous tears.

"Come, let me show you the rings before they are placed in their respective boxes," Ada said, gesturing toward a row of six-meter-long white tables.

The glittering highest quality gems were separated into three piles: blue, red, and purple. *The Mevaseret gemstones, the rarest in this sector of space.* "Our matriarch Sarai would be pleased," she whispered around the lump in her throat. Atta slid a mobile gold column to her, atop which sat a golden platter containing one of the five unique rings.

"What do you think, Mother?" His voice was filled with genuine pride and satisfaction at a job well done. He lifted the ring gently between two fingers of his white-gloved hand.

She palmed the precious ring. "The symbol of the authority of the Hadassah." He nodded, accepting the weightiness of the statement.

"How beautiful, Master Atta. The material from the Goelyakar really brings out the brilliance of the three gemstones… Truly Abba El has bestowed you with exceptional craftsmanship. Just beautiful!" Jazrene handed the ring back to him and looked over his head at the intricately designed gold and silver ring boxes a few meters away.

His gaze followed hers. "Those were finished yesterday, along with their matching tiaras," he said proudly, then activated a protective shield around the golden column.

She was drawn to the sparkle of the multicolored gems of the tiaras that lined the shelves of the ornate armoire. Her face glowed with a rare joy that she had not experienced in her life to this point as she stared at them.

"As you can see we have designed tiaras for the new office of Modroya, as you instructed." It was clear he was excited.

She smiled at him and his face split into a wide grin. The toothy smile was somewhat intimidating because his teeth were so big and stark white against his skin tone. "What about the Semsa rings and Késefs?" she asked.

"We have the initial amount requested and will continue to craft them in regular allotments as you have outlined." Atta's tone was somber now. *Most excellent. I could have not prayed for a better outcome.*

"May I ask you a question?" His voice was meek and quiet, almost a whisper.

Something in the spiritual atmosphere shifted and she felt a swell of warmth for him. She let it show in her eyes. "I will answer your question in a moment if I am led by Moshiach to do so." She paused and opened her spirit to Moshiach. "Atta, like your forefathers, you have conducted yourself with honor and integrity in the office of master jeweler for our Order. I will answer only that the Moshiach has showed me your question. I only ask you tell no one." The seriousness of her hushed tone emphasized the weight of what she would share. "I will soon depart." She said it calmly, but his response was dramatic as his face crumpled and he sank to his knees.

"Mother Vallo…" He could not hold back his emotion and tears dripped down his cheeks. She placed her hand lightly on this top of his wiry hair and waited for him to get his composure back. "I will tell no one, as you have asked me," he finally said. He looked up at her pleadingly and swallowed hard. "Please impart a blessing upon me and my family, Mother Vallo." His voice trembled with grief.

"Do not be sad, my dear friend. I am going to the divine realm of Bayit El." She stretched her hands over him and a brightness entered the room. She sensed several divine beings in the room but remained focused on Atta. "I bless you, Dugra Atta, that you and your family have a prosperous life's journey. May you be kept safe under Abba El's mighty wings and be guided by the hand of Moshiach." Her voice resonated into the atmosphere. She felt the gaze of the master jeweler's trusted apprentices, who were coming in from another part of the workshop. Atta reached out, cupped her right hand, and drew her fingers to him, then reverently kissed her hand.

She smiled and bowed her head to Atta and the apprentices, before leaving the shop for the last time.

Jazrene Vallo stared at one of the moons from her balcony. The night was clear and crisp. She breathed deeply, enjoying her solitude. *Now the citizens of Ramah will feel safe with large Mantis Alliance bases on our moons. So much has happened in the past several weeks. Our Matriarch is returning home.* Her spirit swelled with joy. She had just received the message of Sarai's homecoming today. *More prophecies will be fulfilled now.* "It's time to meet our guests." She glanced up at the beautiful sky, then headed toward the main reception hall.

"Mother," said Adah, coming to attention. Janan, Kalani, and Wen bowed their heads, then opened the doors to the main hallway. *I've never seen so many guests and dignitaries from the Grand Assembly.*

"Welcome," she said as she greeted her honored guests from the Galactic capital of the Mantis Alliance. She sensed her escorts followed closely behind her. All eyes were riveted on her as she continued to greet everyone on the way to the main platform. Her escorts peeled away and took their place among their peers.

With the grace of royalty, she made her way up the steps, then turned to address them. It was silent in the room. She clasped her hands to her chest and bowed her head. *Bless them, Moshiach.* She let her arms drift to her sides. "We are honored to have you all here." Her voice easily reached every corner of the large hall She looked at the two highest-ranking members of the Grand Assembly present. "Your Honors, please come and address our guests." She gestured for them to join her, then moved to stand by her chair. They mounted the platform, bowing their heads in acknowledgement to her.

"I am Semera Amavesha, a senior Librator representative in the Grand Assembly… We declare as of this moment, the Order of the Marium Kahnet is officially grafted into the Grand Assembly of the supreme councils of the Mantis Alliance and their representatives will be called Modroya." The mantle of her authority rested easily on her slight shoulders. She was a middle-aged humanoid woman with an impeccable record of service. "With that said, we declare that all restrictions placed upon the Marium Kahnet prohibiting assistance from their peers in Kilodromus, Malgavatta, Praxvarna, and Vlberium galaxies are permanently lifted. And to leave no doubt, those who dwell in the Bisgabeths have blessed this transition by placing a matter displacement portal (MDP) within the newly constructed Monastarium's auxiliary complex." She nodded firmly. With the matter settled, she walked to the side of the human man waiting for his turn.

"I am Tphu Tgesh a senior Magos in the Grand Assembly…an invaluable member. Safety and security is of the utmost importance; hence we have begun to build a Class 1 Mantis Alliance military base on Ragoon Two and a second base on Ragoon Three." His rich bass voice matched his well-muscled body. He was a renowned Mantis prophet warrior and was well respected. Sounds of excitement filled the grand hall. The air hummed with it. He waited until they quieted a bit before continuing. "As of today, the Ramah government will undergo a transformation to better reflect the authority of the Holy Order of the Marium Kahnet. This will transpire under the guidance of the Grand Assembly. This transition will take place over the course of three months. Within that time, the sisterhood's Grand Assembly representatives called Modroya will be ready to travel to Mantacletos to begin their duty." The fierce conviction in his unwavering tone left no doubt that this would be accomplished. A loud roar erupted in the room and people began to rejoice. "We thank you all for your attendance in this historically momentous occasion." The room erupted again in excitement as the guests began to talk loudly amongst themselves.

The two turned to the elder sitting just behind them. "Congratulations, Mother Vallo," said Amavesha with warm respect.

"On behalf of the sisterhood, thank you." Jazrene clasped their outstretched hands.

Tphu turned his back toward the crowd and leaned in. "One day, I will go where you are going… Congratulations, you have finished your race well," he said in an undertone.

Jazrene smiled up at him. She was not at all surprised that he knew she was leaving to Bayit El. He was among the most gifted Mantis prophets of his generation. "Thank you, both of you, for your support all these years." She beamed with joy at them. They excused themselves and rejoined their respective groups. She caught the eye of the Prime Minister of Ramah and gazed deeply into her narrowed eyes as she returned to the podium. *I pity your anger against us, but Moshiach moves me to compassion and mercy for you.* Jazrene lifted her hands, calling for silence. "I would like to thank our Prime Minister Nephera Tam Samgasat for her support during our times of great distress." She gave her a genuine smile of affection. With all eyes on her, the Prime Minister had no choice but to return the smile and nod in acknowledgement.

Jazrene knew the Prime Minister blamed the Marium Kahnet for the massacre thirty-some years prior. The hatred burned in her eyes.

"Thank you for attending this momentous occasion," said Jazrene. "Honored guests, I invite you to join me in the next room for a meal. For those of you who cannot stay, may Abba El and Meshua richly bless you." She gestured to her right, where a wall retracted, allowing the aromatic odors of prepared foods to waft into the room.

As expected, most the guests headed over to eat. Jazrene stepped down to the floor and made her way to where Amavesha and Tphu waiting for her at a reserved table. She looked across the room to the tables set up with bright white cloths, where mounds of luscious fruit and vegetables harvested from the garden were set on silver platters. The sisters assigned to cater to her and the high-ranking officials approached with genial smiles.

"We are honored to serve you and your guests, Mother Vallo," said a young woman, sliding Jazrene's chair out so that she could sit.

"Thank you. I'll have the usual, Sister Aurie." The supreme councilors re-seated themselves on either side of her. Instrumental music played in the background. Jazrene looked quietly around the room, watching her guests deeply engaged in conversation. *This is going very well indeed, better than I expected. Even the Prime Minister seems to be enjoying herself.* She listened with half an ear to the conversations going on at her own table. It was so good to hear the pockets of laughter that rang out in the room. Aurie was making her way around the table taking orders.

"What are you having, Mother Vallo?" Amavesha asked.

"Solmar fish with Thamus rice is so delicious. It is one of my favorites," she said happily.

"I would like to order the Solmar dish as well please," said Amavesha. It was a well-known fact that the Emecemian race preferred an aquatic diet.

"I'll have the same," Tphu quickly chimed in.

"Would you like anything else, your excellencies?" Aurie waited with the data pad held up nearly to her face.

"No, thank you," they all said nearly in unison.

Aurie laughed lightly. "Well, that was certainly easy. I will be back shortly with your orders." They all laughed with her.

"The Barayalad is going well, don't you think?" Jazrene turned to Tphu and waited for his full attention. "Is it true that the Watchers appeared to the Grand Assembly?" She was curious about the sequence of events that precipitated the decision to graft the sisterhood into the Grand Assembly. Up to this point she had only heard rumors.

"Yes, it was a sight to behold, like nothing we have ever seen." She could see the wonder dawn in his eyes as he spoke. "They told us to graft the Order of the Marium Kahnet into the Grand Assembly immediately without delay." Jazrene noticed that he had commanded the table, judging by everyone's rapt expressions as they heard him speak about the beings that resided in the Bisgabeths. *I wonder what it's like inside one of those constructs and how they were actually built.* She, like everyone else, often speculated how the Kelkemek forefathers were able to build those massive structures, which allowed travel between the five galaxies.

"Mother Vallo, I am going to remain here to witness the ascension of the new Hadassahs. I look forward to meeting with them," Tphu said. "I must sincerely congratulate you. It seemed to me an almost impossible task to refashion the sisterhood. But we know that with Moshiach all things are possible." Everyone drifted back to their conversations and he picked up a piece of fruit and took a bite. A look of bliss accompanied the juicy mouthful.

"Mother Vallo, I hear that you will not take a leadership role. Is this correct?" said Amavesha.

"Yes, that is so," Jazrene said in a low voice and took a bite of Oranga fruit.

"I am sorry to hear that, Mother Vallo. You will be missed." Amavesha's voice held a note of disappointment. "I do understand though."

"Thank you." Jazrene smiled graciously at her. The table servers arrived with silver trays. "Let us eat, shall we?" Jazrene quickly blessed the food and began to eat. After the meal, she excused herself and visited every table, personally thanking everyone for attending the Barayalad. Then left to attend to the next matter, one that was of most urgency.

Jazrene caught the casual gazes of a few sisters before she vanished through the cloaked entrance that led to the mountain complexes. Her thoughts troubled her as she continued to make her way to the deeper sections of the caves. *I pray that the rumors are not true. If they are, they would pose a large threat to the Sisterhood and the Grand Assembly. A group of women mimicking the Mariam Kahnet. It is just like the enemy to copy what Abba El does.* The doors to a room slid open. She walked in.

Those in the room bowed their heads "Greetings, Mother Vallo. It is good to see you again," said Jaya, a senior Semdressa leader in the Kilodromus galaxy.

"It's good to see you too, Jaya." Jazrene smiled.

"This is Somae, senior Semdressa operative, Tollerron sector," Jaya said.

"I am blessed to meet you, Mother Vallo." Somae nodded in respect.

"So, what is the word concerning this new religious Order?" Jazrene asked.

Jaya glanced over to Timnah then back to the Jazrene "We have verified reports that a Thrakonan Princess, Rishna Atharva, is also the high priestess of the Order of Aggrevox that is forming a new religious Order in the similitude of our own called Saurcine. Among those in attendance are several wayward sisters." Jaya's stoic demeanor was typical of those in her position.

"Are they the same sisters who killed several bounty hunters that had captured them?" Jazrene asked.

"They are," Jaya responded.

"Then they have chosen to walk in the path of darkness. I will not risk any more lives in the efforts to restore them back into the sisterhood." Jazrene's spirit was saddened by this news. "Where are they gathering?"

"On the planet Gerobon, near the capital city of Attomayo." Jaya glanced at Timnah.

"My spirit tells me there something else that I should know." Jazrene cocked her eyebrow and waited.

"Yes…several of the sisters who have come with me have had disturbing dreams. One of which involves the dragon's seed. The others, eerily enough, are of a new bloodline for a conqueror of the Mantis." Jaya remained stoic as she spoke.

"I see in the spirit a clue to the Saurcine Order…Sanctaurus 5 ζ 3: *The daughter's womb turns into darkness and the spawn of the Dragon is birthed.*" Jazrene's recitation echoed in the room. The darkness of this prophecy coming to fruition was daunting.

"These dreams are a warning to us that a new and dreadful threat will appear," Jazrene said. "We must see more clearly before we can decide what to do. Timnah, you and Jaya call on the other Semdressa leaders and those of the Veth'Shar. Tell them I will have a meeting in the Sanctus Opalarium tomorrow, early afternoon." Her words inspired confidence in her strong leadership and inherent knowledge of what to do. "And if led by Moshiach, the Mantis Prophets will join us." With her mind already miles away, Jazrene excused herself. "Now onto my next task." She headed back to her quarters.

The light in her library turned on as Jazrene entered. She purposely leaned forward and peered into a small display screen on the wall. "I will see you soon, my beloveds," she whispered to the holographic images of her dearly departed family. "Time to remove this," Jazrene said then tapped the surface of the image. *I will see you shortly.* Her thoughts made her smile as she erased the family image.

She headed down the hallway and stretched out her hand toward several flowerpots and gently, with her fingertips, brushed the silken flower petals that lined wall, enjoying the moment. *I love the smell of Jumsom blossoms.* The wonderful refreshing smell lifted her spirit.

The lights in her office automatically turned on as she entered. Her low heels sank into the plush Callamus crafted rug. As was her preference, the window shades were open, allowing an unobstructed view of the snow-covered mountain peaks. She looked at the cleared surface of her once cluttered curved desk. *Only one more thing to do.* "This is my last official act from this room," she said somberly. She placed her hands on the crystalline surface of the desk. "Jazrene Vallo, activate Marium Kahnet Class 1 directives." Her resolute tone resonated in the room.

A screen popped up and a moment later, the right corner glowed green. She reached under the desk and retrieved a thin crystalline sheet and a silver quill. "I, Jazrene Vallo, Mother of the Marium Kahnet, authorize activation of directive MKD523-19-61. This is to take effect immediately." She carefully wrote out the order and laid the quill to the side. "Archive and send a copy to Director of Orphan Advocacy Uma Semoa," she said and placed the sheet onto the screen, which absorbed it. "I am discreetly going to visit the Amatat orphanage tomorrow early morning. Send message to same. Send same directive to the Marium Kahnet administrators throughout the Quintástraya. End session." With that said, the screen descended back into the desk. "Now with that done, the sisterhood can adopt orphan girls once again."

She smiled widely, closed her eyes, and began to meditate.

The soft tone from her wristband woke her, giving notice to her that the new Hadassah had arrived. She glanced out the window. The orange glow around the snow-covered mountains told her it was dawn. Jazrene stood, did some Kohyim body stretches, and headed out to meet her appointment.

Time to meet with my replacement. This should be interesting. She left the office and outside. *How am I leaving? I was told in my dreams that when the five sisters ascend to the office of Hadassah only then will I leave.* She walked across a small patch of grass then straight to an auxiliary landing platform where her guest would be waiting.

Just as she had expected, sitting on a round stone was Karina Calero, the chosen Hadassah for the Zhanifra galaxy. *She looks so young, but she was chosen, so I have to trust the outcome of the new tests and trials.* Her face was serene, giving no clue to Karina of her internal misgivings. Jazrene reached out with her spirit, testing. *She is wearing casual clothing, like myself.* Karina, who was looking intently at her as she approached, smiled. Karina's perfectly smooth hazel skin glistened in the moonlight. Her large silver eyes met Jazrene's with warm transparency. "Greetings, Mother Vallo."

"Greetings, Karina." She lightly touched Karina's right shoulder. "Are you ready?"

"Yes, I'm eager to learn and meet them," Karina replied happily.

Jazrene turned toward the shuttle. "If you don't mind I will fly the shuttle." Her firm tone left no room for argument. They entered the small craft and settled into the pilot's seats.

"I see you have a lot of experience at this," Karina said, observing her elder deftly activate the power core and navigation systems.

"Only out of necessity. There were only a few experienced pilots left after the Kravjin attack." Jazrene's voice was matter-of-fact.

"Which orphanage are we going to?" Karina asked.

"To the town of Meoglitto," Vallo said.

"May I ask you a question, Mother Vallo?" Karina seemed hesitant.

Jazrene pondered the request then looked piercingly at her. "Yes."

"Why are you not taking a leadership position…are you dying?" Karina seemed genuinely concerned.

Jazrene smiled reassuringly and shook her head once. "No, as you know, once you have eaten Victus, our body's DNA is altered to a state that it is almost impossible for one become ill." She looked at the young woman. "Since you have been chosen to become the Hadassah of this galaxy, I will share with you a secret… I have had dreams of my time of departure and was visited by two Malakphos, who told me that my time to leave this realm is at hand. How that is to come about is a mystery. But I am not concerned about that. My work is finished." She smiled contentedly.

"I see. I sense a lot of peace about that. Moshiach is well pleased, Mother Vallo." Karina's voice held a note of wonder and joy. She nodded at the sweet-spirited woman with a gentle smile.

On final approach toward the lower plains of Jaussa, Jazrene adjusted the ship's altitude lower.

"I am glad that the adoption ban is now lifted," Karina said.

"Yes, I am too, as you know this is a special visit. Those we choose will take part of the new lineage adoption celebration." Her tone was filled with optimism.

"This is a rare occasion indeed." Karina paused, considering, then said, "Does this have anything to do with the wayward sisters?"

She had only heard of these ceremonies recently during her secret ascension classes.

"Yes, when any wayward sister returns and wishes to live a new life, this is what must be done. As it is written in our tenets." Jazrene paused for a moment while she maneuvered the ship along the string of towns that dotted the borders of the Gecca Desert. "I want to ask you for a favor. When you officially take my place, please consider relocating the orphanages to more pleasant environments…say… the Phauna Enoki plains."

Karina's response was immediate. "That would be an excellent choice!" The connection between them was strengthening. The young Hadassah seemed to be a lot like herself. *Thank you, Abba El, for this special young woman you have raised up.*

"Who is returning?" Karina sounded intensely curious.

"Those names no longer matter. What is important is that they will start a new life, with new names, and you will be there." Jazrene pushed the ship control stick forward, smoothly guiding the ship to the edge of a large town. She leaned back then continued, "We will choose human male and female children ages three to five." She stared at the dilapidated buildings below. The town was blighted, rife with squalor. "Phauna Enoki will be a nice place for the children."

Dust erupted around the ship as it touched down. "Don't worry, Karina, Moshiach will guide your steps as he has mine." She reached over and softly squeezed Karina's hand. "Let's find the children for the new lineages, shall we?"

Their faces were hit with the hot air once they left the shuttle.

Heat and malodorous smells wafted off the rocky surface. *A time of renewal. A time of new beginnings.* Jazrene stooped down and picked up a tiny girl. Karina did the same. Xoll, the orphanages' administrator, and a few of the staff came out to meet them.

"Welcome Mother Vallo," said the male Tekramok humanoid, bowing his head, as did his assistants.

"It's good to see you again Xoll. This is Karina, the new Hadassah." Jazrene felt a little boy tugging at her vestments. She gazed at him with a wide smile. One of the staff picked up the boy in her arms to stop his pestering.

"Greetings Mother Karina." Xoll nodded his head once more.

"We are here to choose children for adoption," Jazrene said.

"Yes, of course Mother, as you wish," Xollo said gladly.

Jazrene spotted a young human girl with long curly red hair. *She reminds me of Thya, I will see her very soon when I leave this plane of existence.* Jazrene's thoughts were interrupted by a strange vision of a being birthed from the Tisrad Dragon. It darkened everything for a moment, including the calm center in her heart. But the vision vanished as quickly as it appeared.

"This way please," said Xollo.

Jazrene nodded, forcing her worry aside for the moment. She and Karina followed him, and the children all around them did too.

Chapter Eight

CRISS LUMBRA

Jazrene replayed the vision she'd had just moments ago. This one was much clearer than the one she'd had at the orphanage. *A human birthed, and those strange tubes attached to his abdomen. Strange, very strange.* She dreaded the thought that some of her daughters had gone astray, following after the prince of darkness. *A new prophetess Order in the similitude as our own. Now, a new enemy will emerge, one that will threaten the sisterhood and the Mantis Alliance.* And here she was being called home. *Why now? I don't understand. My work seems unfinished somehow…*

Shaking her head, Jazrene turned her anxious thoughts toward seeing her beloved family in Bisgabeth and continued her way to the oldest section of the Monastarium. She entered through the center of the thick doors, which closed behind her. Standing in the room before her, in front of their seats, were the five Hadassahs and their respective Semdressa senior members. They all acknowledged her with a nod.

"Please be seated, the Veth'Shar will be here shortly," Jazrene announced. Their clothing rustled as they took their seats. No one seemed to have a need to speak.

Is it true that the one who anointed Meshua with Nardos oil for his burial will be here? She was excited by the prospect of speaking to someone who had blessed the Messiah. She stayed seated as Tham Saullus and four other senior Veth'Shars from their respective galaxies entered. "Please be seated, brothers." Jazrene gestured for them to sit on the right side of the room.

"Moshiach guide our meeting," she pronounced. Then looking around the room, feeling the weightiness of the atmosphere, she proceeded. "As you know, we are here because of recent revelations of a new religious Order and prophecies regarding the Dragon's seed. Mother Amadi, will you please tell us your dream." She turned to one of the Hadassahs.

Amadi's long white-streaked hair accentuated her silver eyes. "I had a dream about a woman dressed in regal blue raiment. Her eyes were luminescent blue. There was a birth. She held a curved onyx blade dripping with fresh red blood after she cut the umbilical cord. Then I heard a newborn's cry."

"What type of blood was on the blade?" Jazrene looked intently at Amadi.

"It was human blood." Amadi's voice was calm—she did not seem frightened—but Jazrene looked around the room and saw concern in everyone else's eyes.

"I had the same dream, Mother Vallo," said Hadassah Tkeva. In quick succession the three remaining Hadassahs confirmed the same dream.

"My dream is somewhat different, but I will reveal that a little later. Does anyone have any clue as to who this woman is?" Jazrene could see the pieces coming together now, and the reality chilled her to the bone.

Senior Semdressa Qadir stood up from her seat and walked to the front, addressing the room. "I strongly believe that Princess Rishna Atharva, who serves as the High Priestess of the Order of Aggrevox, is the woman in these dreams. Over the past several days she has received prominent royals at her residence. This has occurred five times over the course of a year, but this marks the first time that wayward sisters are attending. I have irrefutable evidence that in a few days they will participate in an unspecified ceremony." Her steely tone resonated as truth. At Jazrene's nod, she returned to her seat.

"Who are these sisters?" asked Vallo.

"They are some of the daughters who repeatedly failed the Aletheia." Amadi's somber tone reflected her disappointment that they had left the sisterhood.

"The test indicated that their hearts are not pure, even after several prayer sessions. Disappointing," Jazrene said sadly. *They could not pass the testing of truth and faithfulness, and now have turned to the ways of darkness by joining this new sect. Why must I leave now, Abba El? I sense that this new Order will pose a great threat to the Mantis Alliance.* Jazrene's spirit groaned at the coming darkness. She deliberately turned her attention to the matter at hand.

"We earnestly tried to bring them back. But obviously, I failed." Amadi's stark tone held self-recrimination for her inability to re-assimilate the wayward daughters.

Just then, all eyes were drawn to the front of the chamber, where two Mantis prophets entered. Jazrene recognized them from their visit last year. "It is so good to see you again, and welcome, Masters Jiang and Azad. I was praying that Moshiach would send his prophets. Please join us," she said warmly. They remained standing silently in front of her.

"Congratulations, Mother Vallo, on the Marium Kahnet's representation in the Grand Assembly." Jiang's smile vanished as he addressed everyone in attendance. "Sons and daughters of Abba El, we are here as a confirmation that the bloodline of the Dragon's seed is at hand," he said.

"Mother Vallo…you had a dream of a newborn, the seed of the Tisrad Dragon." Prophet Azad gazed directly into her eyes.

"Recall and tell us the number of umbilical cords the newborn had." Jiang lifted his right hand toward her then let it fall back to his side. The tension in the room mounted.

Jazrene stared into the near distance, looking into the spirit. "I had a dream of a woman dressed in the regal blue robes that my sisters saw. I also saw she was giving birth to the Dragon's seed. The seed transformed into a two-legged dragon with a large horn on its head, and with it the dragon destroyed many stars." She paused as she focused on the dream that was replaying in her mind's eye. "The newborn had twelve umbilical cords." Her voice held a note of curiosity about what she was seeing.

Then it came loud and clear. She spoke aloud, feeling the weight of the culmination of prophecy being woven together and manifesting in the natural.

"Sanctaurus 5 ζ 2

"The vanquished daughters have brought forth the seed of the Dragon.

"And

"Sanctaurus 5 ζ 8

```
The bloodlines of dark essence will bring forth a
man child who destroys the stars."
```

Prophet Azad looked around the chamber and began to pace in measured steps. "They will call him the Krevomax, and from among the twelve bloodlines he will come forth. He will win many battles for his father, the Tisrad Dragon." Azad paused and stared hard at a large crimson stone appearing above them from multiphasic folded space. It transformed into a reptilian eye. Jazrene's whole body stiffened.

"In the name of Meshua we close the portal to the eye of the Tisrad Dragon from this chamber and the Monastarium," commanded Jazrene loudly. The others echoed the same command.

"The enemy acknowledges we are a threat to his plans. We must act quickly to destroy those bloodlines." Jazrene firm tone was resolute.

The silence that fell in the chamber was interrupted as Sisters Timnah and Jafari entered the chambers, accompanied by a petite woman with thick wavy black hair. The Késef she wore sparkled briefly in the sun's light before the doors shut behind them.

"Please come in. Who is our honored guest, Sister Timnah?" Jazrene said, feeling yet another spiritual shift in the room. The three women came to stand between the two prophets.

"This is Sister Bethany from Shalem." Timnah signaled for her to speak with a nod.

The woman bowed low to the floor. "Thank you, Mother Vallo, and all highly-esteemed servants of Abba El and HIS Meshua." Her high-pitched, light voice was pleasant.

"I was told in a dream to give this to you, for you will have need of it." Bethany removed a white marble vial from the side pocket of her skirt and palmed it for everyone to see. "This is the vessel and the oil that I used to anoint Meshua for his burial, after which he blessed me." Her face beamed with the radiance of her encounter with him.

Jazrene gladly received the vial from Bethany. "Thank you. We would be highly honored if you stayed here in the Monastarium for a few days. We would love to hear accounts of Meshua from you, as a witness of him and his resurrection. You are welcome to stay for a few days if you would like."

Bethany instantly returned her warm smile. "Yes, Mother Vallo, I would be honored to do so." She nodded her acceptance of the invitation. Jazrene was drawn to the serenity and humble authority this small woman wore comfortably.

"Sister Jafari, please show our honored guest her sleeping quarters."

"Would you please bless me and my family, Mother Vallo?" Bethany dropped to her knees with her hands clasped together.

"Yes, of course." Jazrene smiled at her, then gazed upward. She placed her hand over Bethany's head and recited the Ruahnaush. "Be at peace, Sister. Your family will be safe from the civil war on Shalem. You have heeded Meshua's words, to flee your city and head into the villages within the mountains." Her Seer gift at times surprised even herself. "Do not be afraid. The Mantis Alliance has sent a battle fleet to bring order and stability." She held out her hand and helped Bethany rise from the floor. "Jafari, enable Bethany to communicate with her husband."

Jafari replied with a nod. "This way, Sister," she said, then led Bethany out of the chamber.

Sister Timnah nodded to Jafari before taking her place among the other Semdressa members. Jazrene stood between the two masters and held the vial in the palm of her right hand.

"Mother Vallo," said Jiang, drawing her attention. "To cut off the bloodlines. The sacred oil must be applied to the source where the essence of the Tisrad Dragon flows into this realm."

Azad lifted his hands into the air. "Moshiach, will you tell us from where the source of this ungodly bloodline is established?" He, like everyone else, remained in a trance-like state, waiting for the information to be revealed.

"I see the gates of Creminmorta and one of its five lords…" said Jiang. His nostrils flared as if he had smelled the vile smoke from it.

"He is Prince Saurcine, ruler of the realm of Grythinmor and gatekeeper of the abyss of Barracura. He is the foundation of the daughters of the blue flame… They are called the Saurcine," proclaimed Azad.

"An Overseer named Khanon is called to be among the first to establish the Dragon seed bloodline for their messiah... the Krevomax," said one of the Hadassahs.

"The Saurcine are the instruments used to create the bloodline. The first lineage ceremony will commence shortly," said Amadi.

"The Saurcine have been given a multiphasic portal to the realms of Creminmorta. From it, tendril-like umbilical cords connect to a golden statue of a woman," said Azad.

A rush of sound drew everyone's eyes to the center of the room, where a pedestal ascended from the marbled floor. There was a blast of bright light, then appearing on the top of the column were two long blades. A loud rumble of thunder accompanied a second flash of light in the room. "You must use these weapons forged by your forefathers, for conventional weapons will not prevail against the beasts that protect the blood eggs of the prince of Grythinmor. They are hidden in a lair deep within the mountains of Hauskavesh… Destroy them." The omniscient loud voice shook the chamber, and everyone bowed their heads. Standing above them was a powerful warrior, a Pheragim, a gatekeeper of Bayit El.

"We will do as you have asked," they all said in unison.

Jazrene marveled at the Pheragim. *This must be a key to stop the Krevomax bloodlines from forming, but who will be chosen to journey to such a place?* Her muse was broken when she felt the thick presence of Moshiach lift. For a moment, there was silence in the chamber.

"The blades are to remain where they are. It is for the chosen to remove them," Azad said.

"Yes, there are two who will make the journey to Creminmorta. One from the Semdressa, and one from the Veth'Shar." Jiang stood next to the pedestal. "These were given here on Ramah. So, shall the chosen come from Ramah," he stated with certainty.

"We pray that the chosen be successful according to Meshua's perfect will." Azad's voice was heavy with purpose.

"Then let it be as you have said, Master Azad," Jazrene said. The others nodded in acceptance of her statement.

"The crimson stone, the eye of the Tisrad Dragon, must also be destroyed," Jiang added.

"Agreed," Jazrene confirmed. It became clear to her that there would now be more than one mission.

The two prophets surveyed the room. "We must travel back to Mantacletos and give a report to our elders. May Moshiach always guide your steps, Mother Vallo," Azad said.

"Be blessed in your travels," Jazrene responded in kind.

The two prophets bowed their heads and left the chamber.

Jazrene turned and gazed at her empty seat, then looked at Sister Karina. "Those chosen to wield the blades will need help from our elite units, the Criss Lumbra, to traverse the plains of Creminmorta. As such, I authorize the activation of all Criss Lumbra units. The Saurcine Order no doubt has a similar network of highly skilled agents. We have to be ready to defend and fight." Jazrene surveyed everyone in the chamber.

"We agree, Mother, the Criss Lumbra as of this moment is activated," said Karina.

The other Hadassahs repeated the statement.

Jazrene then made her way over to the pedestal. She placed the vial in the center between the long blades. The crackling sound of electrons was followed by a purple transparent canopy that enveloped the pedestal after she stepped away. *My journey continues on a new path, as all previous Mothers have gone before me, to Bayit El.* She stood with her head bent, then lifted her eyes to them once again.

"What I tell you is for your ears only. I am to leave to the Bisgabeth shortly. I do not know exactly how it will happen, but it will be so." She distantly heard the sisters' hushed astonishment. "Karina will need not only your prayers, but your assistance in this new quest to cut off the Dragon seed bloodlines." She glanced over to Mother Amadi, who nodded in acceptance of the commission.

"We are now part of the Grand Assembly, and this is the beginning of a new chapter of the sisterhood." Jazrene welcomed the four sisters who had entered the chamber, carrying trays of Prosphora bread and cups of grape effervesce. "Let us celebrate together the new covenant between man and Abba El."

Jazrene partook and enjoyed the fellowship. All the while struggling with the fact she had ordered the activation of the sisterhood's lethal agent network. She kept reminding herself that she had no choice.

Chapter Nine

BOUNTY

Raduu rubbed his nose with the back of his hand and glared at the two rogues. "You two, activate the hover systems on those stasis units and place them right over there," he barked, then stepped away from the ship's ramp. Em and Tola stood in the rear of the cargo bay, derisively watching Fay and Victoria work as instructed by their gruff mercenary leader. Tola's face had a slight sneer on it.

Victoria ignored the pair and concentrated on her tasks. The slight figure of Nia, who looked peaceful in death, was visible through the square, synthetic polymer window. She swallowed hard with grief, then placed her hand on the window, leaning down. *She looks so serene, so content. Nia, we are home… I am home, yet I feel so strangely out of place. The sisterhood must be involved in bringing us back here. But for what purpose, to punish us for our crimes? No matter, I will deliver the sacred tomes and the Leviathan data. My fate is of no further consequence. My life is forfeit.* She could feel Raduu's impatience and guided the capsule's motion to speed up a bit.

She noticed Fay gazing intently into the capsule containing

Taona. Victoria caught Fay's eye and nodded, commiserating. They deactivated the forward motion of the stasis units and stood quietly. The expanded Monastarium main transportation hub bustled with ship traffic. A steady stream of Mantis Alliance military cargo ships descended from a low mountain range five kilometers away. Victoria was fascinated by the sight.

"Well, judging from the large presence of Mantis Alliance military here, the reports must be true that the Marium Kahnet are now officially part of the Grand Assembly," said Raduu. "Maybe I should ask for a reward commensurate with your Order's new influence and authority." His wide grin revealed his chipped yellow teeth. Victoria quickly looked away. His ignorance was almost unbelievable. She decided to ignore the remark of the unruly mercenary.

"After this, we go to Dossel…oh, our bounty is at hand." Raduu rubbed his hands together. The roughness of his palms made a loud scuffing noise. He haughtily crossed his arms.

"Victoria, we kept our word…to bring you back safely, did we not?" Tola said. It was clear she was reminding Victoria of her pledge not to inform anyone of the treasures she and Em had recovered from the ambassador ship, the *Kirjath-Arba*. The matriarch Sarai Chawah Modroya's ship would remain hidden to all but Zeta Three, who had been given the task of bringing her back to Ramah. Not even Raduu knew of it.

"Yes, I remember." Victoria understood, and would keep her word not to mention it to anyone. Her word was all she had now.

All eyes focused on seven women coming out of the large cave. Four of them wore physician's insignias on their collars. A tall one wore a thin silver headband and the two others carried an ornate wooden box.

"Greetings, Raduu, Em, and Tola," said the tall stern woman. The mercenaries acknowledged her with a nod. No introductions seemed to be forthcoming.

"As I stated in my last message, those two are dead," Raduu said into the somewhat tense atmosphere and pointed to the stasis pods. His tone was hard and uncaring. Two physicians with medical devices in hand began scanning the corpses. Fay and Victoria were also scanned with similar devices and carefully examined.

"Trace elements of necronos plasma are present in both Fay and Victoria. They are a match to all bio-identifiers that verify their identity," said one of the doctors. He kindly patted Fay's upper arm and smiled at Victoria.

"There is too much multiphasic radiation to properly identify these two," said a physician, scanning the stasis pods.

"I can tell you for a surety who they are." Raduu bristled, then continued aggressively, "They are Nia and Taona."

"Take them to decontamination," said the tall stoic sister, ignoring Raduu's posturing. Fay and Victoria watched the pods carrying Nia and Taona until they vanished around the corner, into the depths of the cave.

The sister motioned for the other two holding a wooden box to lay it at Raduu's feet. They opened the beautiful lid for him to see its contents. "Here is your payment for services rendered, Raduu." Her tone was flat and emotionless. She signaled for the box to be relinquished to him.

Raduu, Em, and Tola stared at the rare Mevaseret gemstones inside the box, which were highly valued for their brilliance and ethereal qualities. Stacked alongside them were ingots of gold Kelkatanium. A look of greed slid across Raduu's face. Victoria was not surprised. She imagined he was rubbing his hands together, itching to play in the box as if it was a pile of leaves. *He would sell his family to get his hands on the source of those ingots, I am sure.*

"It seems to all be here." His tone was smug, and he looked at the tall sister. "Tell your superiors since you are now representatives in the Grand Assembly, the price for recovery services will increase accordingly. Besides, you wouldn't want to have rogues like these two traveling the Quintástraya tarnishing your image, now would you?" He bared his stained teeth in a semblance of a smile and curled his lip at Fay and Victoria. Raduu spun, closed the treasure box with a snap, and barked, "Let's go." Wordlessly, Em and Tola picked up the heavy chest and followed him onto the ship.

Fay and Victoria were silent as they watched the energy signature of the mercenary's primary thrusters lighting up. It lifted off, swiftly disappearing into the low-lying clouds.

"Welcome home," said the tall sister. "I am Timnah." Victoria looked back at her. "Do not be afraid, no harm will come to you. The first order of business is that you will undergo a debriefing. Please follow me." A gentle smile softened her stern countenance.

Timnah turned and led the way into the center of the cave, and the wayward sisters followed.

Fay and Victoria looked with great curiosity at the brightly lit interior of the cave. A small complex of buildings constructed of hewn white stone stood in the middle. *Why have we not seen this before?* Victoria wondered. *Wow, this is magnificent.* Her heart quivered with guilt and shame at how warmly they were being welcomed. *Surely, I don't deserve to be treated like this.*

"This was built not long after we were attacked," Timnah said, discerning their hearts.

"That's what I thought. I've never seen this place before," said Fay. She wobbled a bit and Timnah reached out a hand to steady her. Fay appeared even more disoriented than she had moments before.

"You will stay in that building for a short period to re-acclimate to our gravity and the current state of Ramah society since your departure. You will be prepared for assimilation into the Marium Kahnet, but first you must be debriefed." Timnah pointed to a single-story building to their left. The building had no doors.

They don't trust us not to try to escape. Maybe it's better this way. Victoria swallowed and resigned herself to this thought. It was hard to believe that they would just accept her into society. Surely, they were just lying to her to get her cooperation.

As they turned a corner, Victoria was surprised to see a dozen Mantis Guardians in full battle gear stationed around the building. She saw Fay's matching look of surprise. *I guess whoever is doing the interrogating is a high-ranking military officer. Maybe they are here to execute us for genocidal war crimes.* Victoria's heart was heavy with thoughts of the devastation they had wrought on millions of innocent civilians. She would never be released from the prison of all of the horrors they had caused.

The sound of a door opening broke her dark muse. "Sister Timnah, we are ready for the debriefing to begin," said one of the two human males standing just inside.

"Good. Fay, you go with Master Sergeant Kang. Victoria, you go with Major Zanyu. I will see you shortly after." With that said, Timnah left.

"Please, this way, Sister," said Master Sergeant Kang to Fay. He led her down a narrow brightly lit hallway.

"Sister, please follow me." The Major's facial expression held a sort of curiosity. Victoria felt heavy weights dragging at her spirit. She glanced one last time to where Fay had gone, then followed the officer.

Fay and her escort stopped at a closed door. The, Master Sergeant knocked hard once, then briskly opened it.

"Welcome, Sister. Please come in and have a seat," a tall Auxomox humanoid said. He wore a uniform similar to that of the KMI; it was clear he was a high-ranking officer of some kind. "I am General Thabus of Mantis Military Intelligence (MMI). I am very interested in your journey from the time you left until now. Don't be alarmed; we have most of what we need. But we would like to hear your firsthand experience of the events that took place on Necropis." He laid a small bronze disc on the small table in front of her and took a seat behind it. She stared fixedly at the disc. "Don't worry, Fay, you are safe here." He waited. "Shall we begin?"

She looked at the row of large windows behind the MMI Officer. They made the room much less threatening.

"I have nothing to lose," she said, looking him straight in the eye. He nodded his head encouragingly. Fay began to quickly summarize how they had traveled to Gahenna and how she and the sisters had used the Mantis Alliance to attack Gahenna as a cover to infiltrate a secret project hidden under a vast battle testing ground called the Stadageo. The events leading up to and the destruction of the Stadageo and the devastation to the people caused her to pause once or twice, overcome with sadness.

"Where are the others you mentioned helped you?" General Thabus asked kindly. "Somehow I believe they will be here soon."

"They will confirm what I have said is true." The conviction in her voice was not lost on the MMI Officer.

"Just a few more questions and you can go. You don't look older than twenty. Can you explain this?" He shifted in his chair and looked intently at her.

Victoria waited in a soft chair for her debriefing. Her eyes darted to the door as it opened. *Intelligence, Science, and Military Command,* she guessed as the three individuals entered.

"Sister Victoria, or should I say more appropriately Vivika Nefrisunni, your birth name. I am pleased to meet with you. I am Admiral Anaka Haussa of MMI." There was no expression on the officer's face that gave Victoria a hint of what she was thinking. "I know you worked on a secret project deep in the Rakia expanse. Can you tell me more about the project and the vortex anomaly near the Tartarus system?" The hazel eyes of the female Admiral pierced deeply into hers. *I wonder if she has the gift of discerning one's soul.* Victoria wanted to repel the intrusion with everything in her, but then decided to just get it over with.

"Admiral, how about this instead?" Victoria removed the pendant from around her neck and placed it on the table. "That is actually a data chip, disguised as a decorative pendant. It contains all the detailed plans of the secret project named Leviathan." She took her hand off of it and felt triumphant that she had accomplished her mission. The human male science officer retrieved the pendant and placed it on a thin crystalline plate. He activated the decryption. A moment later, a 3D holographic layout of the Mecropex and Pratheous appeared. Above it, detailed information scrolled quickly.

"Stop search," the science officer said. "Is that what I think it is?" His eyes widened as they all read the data.

"Yes, those are the Leviathan races, now sealed in hibernation in their respective vortexes," Victoria somberly stated.

Suddenly, the MMI officer who had been silent to this point leaned forward and removed the data chip. "I cannot emphasize strongly enough that you erase any knowledge of your past. This will ensure your safety and the safety of those around you… Do you understand?" His stern face and glaring eyes forced a response.

"You're not going to execute me?" She waited tensely for his reply.

He looked taken aback at this and then his expression gentled. "I can understand how you would have come to that conclusion, but no we are not."

Victoria swallowed hard and closed her eyes, hardly believing her ears. The room was silent. "Yes, believe me, those memories will remain here, buried in a cave, never to be retrieved…and one more thing, it took two of us. The other person who helped destroy the lab was Balese Thanas, but her real name is Mila Geodora. She died on the moon called Pratheous during the mission," she said. Her body relaxed, and she was surprised to find a sense of spiritual release beginning to happen. She gasped as she felt a weight lift off her shoulders. Her past truly had begun to leave.

"We cannot absolve your conscience from the consequences of your actions. That task is given to the sisterhood." Admiral Hausa was gracious enough not to speak about the death toll she had caused. The MMI officer looked at the other two. "We have what we need," the admiral said.

"That concludes this debriefing. You may leave us." The MMI officer touched the cuff of his right sleeve. Victoria guessed it was a signal of some kind. *I guess I am free to leave.* She stood up, bowed her head, then left the room, strode down the hallway and out of the building.

Timnah and another sister stood waiting for her. "Are you ready to begin anew?" Timnah asked warmly with a big smile on her face. Victoria began to believe that this was real, that she was being given a second chance. She looked with an unexpected fresh hunger at the Kodashah—the Holy Book of the Prophets—and a data pad the other sister held in her hands. "Take these items and read them in your room," Timnah said with a look of compassion in her eyes. "You are required to remain here in this place until you are ready for your transition to your new life. Also, you may not contact anyone outside this place for now and no one is to know about this place. The others will also have the same asked of them. Trust us, this is the best way for all sisters who return home. There are many who have returned like yourselves who now have more joyful, fulfilled lives… Come now. Sister Acelia will accompany you to your room."

"Thank you, Sister Timnah." Victoria was humbled, and it was clear in her voice.

"Come, Sister, this way," said the elderly Acelia, leading the way. There was clearly safety here amongst the sisterhood. "Rest well, Victoria. Abba El has it all well in hand."

"Thank you, Sister Timnah."

Just as Victoria entered one of the buildings, she glanced back and saw Timnah standing with another young woman. *Must be waiting for Fay*, Victoria mused.

Victoria was surprised how spacious her quarters were. She could smell the delicate fragrance of the flowers planted in the window box in the bright room. The sister placed the Kodashah and the data pad on a nearby table and quietly left.

"Time to explore." Victoria walked through every room. "Good, this has a shower," she exclaimed "What's this?" A small stack of neatly folded garments was on a chair. She picked them up one by one and held them to her body. "These will fit." She sighed with pleasure. "No time like the present." She quickly pinned up her hair with a silver ornamental clip and set about washing away the tumultuous journey back home.

"I feel so much better now. I can't believe I am home, yet something seems unfinished." She sat in the plush chair next to the table that held the book and data pad. "Ramah government and the state of society. Well, sounds interesting enough." She quickly delved into all the pertinent information.

Some time later, she placed the data pad near the Kodashah. She hesitated, contemplating reading the Holy Scriptures. *I am too tainted from all that I have done to read that.* She lay back in the soft cushions of the oversized chair and dwelt on the Hoshkadish and the three-day planetary observance and remembrances of the tens of millions slaughtered more than thirty years before. And the death and resurrection of the Messiah.

A rhythmic knock pulled Victoria out of deep sleep. Her eyes opened but she remained motionless. "Someone is at the door," she muttered, still thick with sleep. She woke with a strong sense of fear. She would think of the nightmares later. Another set of soft thumps brought her to her feet.

"It is I, Timnah," said the familiar voice.

"Just a moment please," Victoria said, wiping her eyes and stretching as she walked to the door.

Timnah wore the distinctly darker vestments for the Hoshkadish.

"Please come in." Victoria felt that she could trust this sister and stepped back, allowing her in.

"It is time for you to take the next step in your new life. But first you must change into something more appropriate. In the back room, in the top drawer of the chest, you will find perfectly fitting clothing like my own. I will wait for you outside." Timnah's face beamed with a happy smile.

"Very well, I won't take long," Victoria said and darted to the back room. *My new life? What exactly does that mean?* She decided to withhold judgment, very much afraid to be disappointed. She changed swiftly and returned to the elder.

"Let's go," Timnah said. "We are going to go down to the valley." Soon they were boarding a hover glider.

The moon's light was just visible through the high wispy clouds above. The glider was quiet save their light breathing. *How late is it?* Victoria wondered. She watched Timnah maneuver around groups of trees.

"Victoria, this is a step in your new life. The beginning of your new family lineage is to pay homage to your past in order to embrace your new life and family." Timnah was looking at her, seeming to try to gauge how she was accepting her new environment.

Victoria looked blankly at the sister, keeping her face impassive. Her thoughts raced. *Should I tell her about my dreadful dream about a woman engulfed in light with a blade dripping blood in one hand and a fetus in the other?* Victoria felt something she could not identify welling up. It threatened to overwhelm her.

They landed a few meters inside the forest. "Come." Timnah's gentle voice dislodged, then shattered something in Victoria's heart. The elder sister lit an oil lamp and led the way out of the craft. "You will need this memorial stone." Timnah handed it to her. It was too dark to read what was on it, so Victoria just clutched it to her chest and followed.

The grass is so thick and lovely; it smells delicious and untainted. Grave markers dotted the small, gently sloping hills. Timnah stopped at one of the white markers, set the lamp down next to it, then stepped away. Victoria stood at the foot of five stark white markers grouped together. *Here lies the beloved of Abba El, to whom the promise of HIS resurrection he shall call.* She read her family's names aloud. Her lips parted just enough to allow the whispered pronunciation of each of their names to escape.

The dam broke with a vengeance. The inconsolable grief she thought she had dealt with so long ago returned and drove her to her knees. Her forehead bent to the ground and a fiery wave of emotion rushed out of her. She was vaguely aware of the damp fecundity of the soil beneath her face. She tightly gripped the memorial stone and lifted herself up a bit. She knew that she was to place the stone on their graves, joining with the others placed there by surviving

Nefrisunni family members. She began to rock back and forth, and she whimpered. "Oh, Dad…Mom." The names of her siblings were incomprehensible through her deep groans and sobs. A torrent of warm tears ran down her cheeks.

After a time, Timnah bent down and gently touched her shoulder. "You will see them again one day… When you are ready, I will be waiting for you in the hover glider, do not rush to leave." She waited for Victoria to look at her. "When you take the lamp, you leave your past life behind. Know this: the light of Moshiach will guide the rest of your life." Timnah placed a tender kiss on the top of her head, then left.

Victoria sprawled onto the grass spread-eagled and gripped the mound as though she would bring her family back by the sheer force of her will. After a time, she felt the last vestiges of the raw emotion leave. *Forgive me for not honoring you.* She sat up and slid her hand over each grave marker. "I will see you in Bayit El." She placed the memorial stone with the others left long ago by surviving Nefrisunni family members.

She stood up and lingered, now able to remember wonderful moments she had experienced with her family. Like the time the whole family went to Mantanok sea park to ride Longfin seahorses for her fifteenth birthday. *I can still feel the cool turquoise water splashing on my face.* She smiled when she remembered plucking her youngest brother out of the water after he fell off his Longfin seahorse. She laughed, glad she was beginning to remember the good times too.

Eventually, she picked up the lantern, ready to continue her journey, and headed back to Timnah.

Chapter Ten

ZETA THREE

Zeta Three heard the ships monotone voice announce he had arrived at his destination. He quickly gulped down his flask of Kravajava and took long strides to the bridge. He sat hard in the pilots' seat and stared at the large blue planet of Ramah in the distance. A sense that he should remember something tugged at his spirit. It was a sort of niggling sensation that he had been in this place before. *Why can't I remember?* He'd felt these same sensations of his soul resonating with a hidden truth of who he was before he encountered Raduu many years ago. *The dreams I've had…* A Malakphos had visited him recently in dreams and told him he was a direct descendant of the Patriarch of Modroya. *Yet, even after all this time I still can't recall my past before I encountered Raduu.* "Maybe my next mission will be to find out more about my past."." He said.

"Remember," a supernaturally strong voice said. His eyes darted about the cabin, looking for the unknown person who had spoken. No one was there.

Remember? I don't understand. His heart searched desperately for any clues. *Is this in reference to the missing pieces of my past?*

The divine voice repeated the word. *Remember.*

"Internal sensors have detected an encrypted signal emanating from your holster," the computer female voice said.

"What?!" he shouted, then stood up and examined his holster. "I don't see anything." He removed it then laid it on the control panel. "Did Rediquin plant some sort of tracking device on me?" He felt the prick of betrayal from his love interest. *That can't be, think, think…*

He took a deep breath, then relaxed. "Let's see what happens if I squeeze these two ends together… Nothing. How about this then?" he said as he tested the cylinders he thought added to the holster's strength and durability. "Hmmm, this is interesting." His curiosity piqued as a part of the cylinder popped open, revealing a green metallic pin. Zeta Three removed it and placed it into a data socket on the control panel. "Verification needed. Oh?" He placed his hand on the lit screen.

```
Identification Verified
```

Where have I seen that?" He frowned, straining to recall where he had seen the stylized Reshmek letter that was displayed on the screen. *Remember.* The word swirled in his mind and heart. Then, like a key to his past, the ancient letter unlocked the door of his hidden memories. He leaned back into his seat and sifted through the torrent of images scrolling on the screen. One right after the other.

"That's my father, mother, and my brothers." He had dreamed

about them. "What happened to me? What's going on? Who am I really?" At that last word, a memory of a tale told to him by his old mentor Raduu came to his mind. *"I was passing near the Chemma asteroid belt when I saw a fading energy signature."* True to his opportunistic nature, Raduu had gone to investigate and found a badly damaged shuttle.

"I was on it," murmured Zeta Three. "He said I was found crumpled on the floor, half dead, the lone survivor in a crash. I was in a coma for many months and my body and brain had sustained major trauma. My long-term memory loss would likely be permanent. Now it all makes sense." He leaned forward and held the sides of his head, willing more memories to come. Raduu had taken him in and in payment for saving his life had required him to help on a few missions. Those few missions turned into several years of dangerous escapades before Raduu felt he was paid in full. It had been truly the school of hard knocks that Raduu laughingly called "training."

A sense of excitement began to build. *Remember.* The word still rang in Zeta Three's ears.

He stood up as something welled up out of his spirit. He looked at Ramah in the distance. "I stand as a light against the darkness. A keeper of secrets. A steward of the sacred. I am a member of the Veth'Shar." The declaration was loud and clear. His spirit stood tall and immovable. *Now I remember everything.* More memories came in a flood, filling in the remaining gaps of his past. Even the murderous rage he experienced when his family was mercilessly slaughtered. Although just a junior member of the Veth'Shar, he'd requested to join the strike force comprised of elite Veth'Shar military. He had known at the time it was highly unlikely that any of them would return alive. Their strategy and mission had been to use mining ships in the Augatar region to get as close to the Necrogog base in the Chemma asteroid belt as possible, and destroy it. He truly had been the lone survivor of the hugely successful mission. But he could find no joy in that.

"My compatriots died in honor." He gasped as the memory of the experience flooded over him. The station he had manned on the ship had exploded. Strangely, there'd been a bright white light all around him. His body had been in midair from the force of the explosion when he saw the outline of a large hand around him shielding him from certain death. "Abba El, it must have been… But how did I end up in a shuttle? I don't understand." He shook his head and let the mystery go. "I just have to accept it as miraculous." He felt strong and whole.

He activated the ship's archival data core. "Computer, display relevant data of the past thirty years on Ramah," he commanded.

"Data now ready," said a very familiar voice. He stiffened in shock. The computer's voice had completely changed, apparently with the insertion of the data pin. It was the voice of his mother, Audrina Modroxex.

"Computer, from now on identify yourself as Mother."

"Command is now in effect," said the well-loved voice.

Emotion gripped him as he envisioned embracing his mother and family. "I've been living and thriving in my enemy's territory for all these years. But now I will return and uphold my Veth'Shar oath." He turned to face the module that contained the precious remains of his ancestor matriarch Sarai Chawah Modroya. He stepped forward and placed his hands-on top. *I was imprisoned in the mask of a false identity, but the hand of divine providence has set me free. Now I see clearly my life's path.*

"Warning, Mantis Alliance armada detected," announced the ship's automated voice.

Zeta Three deactivated his ship's masking drives. *No need to draw unwanted attention to myself.* The Mantis Alliance military possessed the technology to detect any ship, cloaked or otherwise.

He looked at the scores of Mantis Alliance capital ships positioned around an orbital shipyard, and his eyes widened. "The reports are true. The Marium Kahnet are now part of the Grand Assembly," he murmured. "Incredible, I've never seen a fortress that size move before." He was amazed watching the forty-kilometer-wide military base descending from orbit to its new moon home. He activated the Veth'Shar signal to Ramah. "I'm sure someone will receive this." He grinned with joy. "I am home."

"Mantis Alliance patrol ship approaching. Three hundred kilometers and closing," said Mother. He remained calm and maintained the ship's course and speed. "Incoming coded message."

On the screen, the center of the Reshmek letter swirled then transformed into a live communication feed. A middle-aged human male with white hair appeared.

"Greetings, I am Tham Saullus. Please place your finger on the glowing Reshmek symbol," his elder said politely. Zeta Three did as he was instructed.

"The DNA profile matches your data file. You don't look that much older than the image I see. But I know it is you. Welcome back from the dead, Solek Modroxex. I am a senior Veth'Shar. Our records indicate that you volunteered for the Chemma mission. Are there other survivors?" Saullus waited with raised brows.

"Not that I am aware of." Zeta Three chewed on the name that had not been spoken in so many years. Solek Modroxex.

"Tell me, it's been over thirty years since the Chemma mission. I am interested to hear how you managed to retain your youth," Saullus said.

"I will inform you of what I know regarding that, but first I have to deliver something." He felt like someone released from prison just coming out into the light. A part of him cringed, though, as the darkness of his jaded past mocked him.

"Yes, you are fulfilling your oath. You are returning our most precious cargo back home." *The Veth'Shar know about the matriarchs return home.* He was greatly relieved that his task was close to completion. "We have your landing destination secured. No one outside our high-ranking members and Mother Vallo are aware of your arrival. We will meet after you complete the mission. It's a great honor you have been given, Solek. Again, welcome back home, son."

"Thank you. I will wait to be contacted. Until then," he said, deactivating the live feed. He was pleased to note that the Mantis Alliance patrol ship had turned from its intercept course.

He stood up and placed the pin back in his utility belt, wrapped it around his waist, and adjusted it to its previous length. His stomach grumbled with hunger. He quickly reached over to the adjoining seat and ripped open a TEPPs and devoured it.

A message came in on his secure contact link. "Hmmm, wonder who it is." He took several large swigs of Kravajava. "Ah…that tastes so good," he said vigorously then sat back down. "Now then, let's see what this is all about." He pressed the hidden button under the control panel. A message popped up on the screen.

```
Sender: Rediquin

Message: Arriving with cargo shortly. End of
message.
```

His heart warmed with feelings. *She will be here soon, with the wayward sisters. Hopefully they are all alive. I can hardly wait to see her.* He thought about the beautiful woman he believed was more than what she presented herself to be, a cold calculating Cymbratar trader. He turned his attention to descend into Ramah's orbit.

"I'll just travel along the mountain ridges." The feeling of freedom at not having to hide was good. *Must be spring,* he thought, looking at the glowing amber horns of mating Swaugu rams dotting the lower regions of the mountain range. His eyes followed a luminescent multicolored river of hundreds of thousands of migrating Emshi butterflies. He slowed as he flew over one of the Hoshkadish memorial fields, spotting a single light. A single soul stood over a grave. He turned slightly away as if to give them their privacy. *Only fifty kilometers to go and I will have honored my sworn oath to Victoria, and my ordained destiny.* "I wonder what will happen to the sisters once they are returned," he murmured, his concern for them putting a frown on the edge of his mouth.

He landed his ship on the neatly clipped grass near the center of the Monastarium. Through the cockpit, he saw a lighted pathway created by a dozen sisters holding lamps, leading the way to a magnificent building. A lone dignified figure came through the double doors holding a lamp. He moved to the cargo hold. "Time to bring Sarai home." The solemn weightiness of the moment hit him. He quickly made sure the hover pod was ready for removal, then opened the cargo door and dropped the ramp.

A rush of cool mountain air brought back memories of when he and his family would come to play in the gardens and chase Pumgaroos. He took hold of the hover pod and carefully moved Sarai's remains down the ramp. *My task is now complete. My ancestral mother is home.* The thought resonated that he had accomplished something prophetic.

"I am Mother Jazrene Vallo. Thank you, Solek, and be blessed for this act of kindness." The sister who greeted him had a voice that was tender and sincere. She fluidly bowed to him. She placed her right hand on the pod and took a deep breath. "*Yaqal 130. I am sent by Moshiach to travel and sojourn among the stars with the lamp of truth and at the appointed time HIS hand will bring me home to give rest to my bones.*" Her voice was filled with great authority and power. The sound of the wind seemed to pick up just then, and with it was a presence of holiness that swirled about them all.

"Please follow us," she said with a gentle smile. She seemed to understand what he was experiencing. He felt a strange need to cringe or revel in the holy presence around them. Mother Vallo turned and led the way into the Monastarium. The sisters guided the hover pod into the building.

Zeta Three silently followed her into a science laboratory where the hover pod was engulfed in a green plasma field. His eyes darted everywhere, greedily drinking it all in at once. Two senior biomolecular engineers of the Monastarium, who identified themselves as Sisters Yolinda and Omeko, examined the remains. He found himself staring at Mother Vallo. She reminded him so much of Rediquin somehow. *Everyone knows Jazrene Vallo's whole family was wiped out by the attack. She was the lone survivor.* Jazrene seemed to sense his intent look and looked at him. He wiped the frown off his face.

"What is it, Solek?" Jazrene said.

"Not exactly sure, but you remind me of someone," he said quietly so no one would hear.

"I can discern that you are in love with her." Jazrene smiled.

"Mother Vallo, we have confirmation that the remains in the hover pod are that of Sarai Chawah Modroya," Yolinda said with excitement. Omeko nodded her agreement.

"She is home!" Jazrene's voice was filled with measureless joy. She raised her hands in praise. Everyone else joined her, offering praises to Abba El and HIS Messiah for her return. The sound of rejoicing filled the sterile room with loud laughter and warmth.

Zeta Three was unaccustomed to this form of celebration and raised his hands. "Praise Abba El and HIS Redeemer," he said sheepishly.

"Please take Sarai and prepare her for a proper burial next to her beloved husband," Jazrene directed Yolinda and Omeko after the room quieted. They bowed their heads and moved the containment pod, vanishing through a Nano wall.

"Follow me, Solek, please," Jazrene said. He acquiesced immediately to the spiritual leader of the Marium Kahnet.

The brightly lit room they entered reminded him of the large library he'd played hide and seek in as a child. Just inside were two women who looked quite older than Jazrene. Witnesses, no doubt. He nodded warmly to them. They dipped their heads in unison, remaining silent. Jazrene picked up a colorful wooden box and handed it to him. "This is for you." Her tone seemed to indicate her instinctive knowledge that he would reject the gift. Her hand stayed on his that was cupping the box. She squeezed his hand lightly. "Please honor us by accepting this meager reward in light of this action." She stepped back and waited. "Inside is a message from Tham." She looked deeply into his blue speckled eyes and an intensity came into her gaze. "I can see that you have consumed that which makes you younger and stronger. But you did it out of ignorance. You did not know who you were. I knew there was something about you in the spirit when I first set eyes on you. You have direct lineage to the Matriarch. Even now you doubt your future as a Veth'Shar. The pull of your previous life as a mercenary is strong in your heart. But more clarity of your true destiny will come very shortly, and so will your true love." Her face glowed in a similar fashion to the Malakphos he had seen in his dreams.

How does she know these things in my heart? He dared not to dismiss what the holy woman said.

"I pray a blessing of favor and prosperity over you." She smiled. "Welcome back home, Solek Modroxex." She turned to the two witnesses. "Sisters, please escort him back to his ship."

"Yes, Mother Vallo," said the one closest to him.

"Of course, please lead the way, Sisters." Zeta Three turned one last time as he reached the door, still baffled. Mother Vallo was still looking at him with that piercing gaze, a bright glow around her.

Aboard his ship, Zeta Three pondered what the Mother Vallo had said about his divided mind. Should he continue living as a mercenary or become fully committed as a Veth'Shar? "Why can't I be both? Who said I can't be?" he shouted defiantly. "I'll ask Tham, maybe he has some answers." He laughed derisively. "My love is coming… What is that all about? Is she referring to Rediquin?"

Shaking his head, he activated the ship's power cores to start the engines. But he had to admit he was really attracted to her. It was so strange that she and Mother Vallo looked so much alike. The way Jazrene had cocked her eyebrow was the same mannerism Rediquin had.

"Alright, time to see Tham." He opened the wooden box and whistled. "Look at those beauties." The gorgeous Mevaseret gem stones lay glittering in the dim cabin's light. He plucked out the disc and closed the box. "Where am I going?" He placed it on the armrest and decoded the location of his destination. "Off to my new destiny I guess."

Inside her private quarters, Jazrene reviewed the announcement of the return and burial of Saria Chawah Modroya to the Grand Assembly that she had just written. "This is excellent."

She left immediately for the Monastarium's new Grand Assembly auxiliary complex. *I'm not surprised at how busy it is. It looks like everyone is holding meetings.* She couldn't help the smile of pleasure those thoughts brought. The burgeoning possibilities for Ramah to become the center of commerce for this sector of space with the Marium Kahnet now holding seats in the Grand Assembly flooded her mind. *At the very least the orphans of Ramah will have a better chance of a normal life. They might even want to be adopted into the sisterhood. As many pilgrims come to visit the Marium Kahnet's founder, and the matriarch and patriarch of the Modroya lineage from which our messiah had come, many will no doubt want to be blessed by the sisterhood.* She nodded in acknowledgement to the few who noticed her walk by. *The interior is magnificent. Those pure silver and gold accents are stunning.* Three of the largest ever cut Mevaseret gem stones were set above the entrance of the Maxum Administrators' Office in a perfect trio.

"Good evening, Mother Vallo," said one of the two Veth'Shar sentries on duty.

"Good evening, gentlemen," she replied. The wide double doors slid open then closed behind her. The large space was humming with a bevy of activity, as the Order prepared for official business in the next few days. Most of the workers were the older sisters. Some of them had come from the other four galaxies. One by one they stopped what they were doing, noticing that she was there. Soon she had their full attention.

"I just wanted to personally thank you for your diligence and faithfulness through the years." Jazrene raised the document she had just written. "I am about to send this announcement of the return of Sarai Chawah Modroya to the Grand Assembly and to our allies. She will be buried with a simple ceremony tomorrow." She could not have been more content as the whole room erupted in elated rejoicing. She felt as though she was walking on clouds as she went to her office.

Jazrene placed her hand on the flat surface of the desk, and a half-meter square lit up. "I am Jazrene Vallo. Prepare to send a priority one message to the Grand Assembly." She placed the announcement on the lit surface. "I authorize this message to be sent and then stored in archival records." She watched the handwritten document sparkle, then be absorbed into the surface of the desk.

After deactivating the link, she moved over to the large window and marveled at the site of the Mass Displacement Gate (MDG). She had always wondered why she'd been instructed by Moshiach to leave such a large empty space. Now she knew. "Those are Chayots, I need to speak to them!" The silver metallic, sentient droids had just emerged at the entrance of the gateway below. She stepped half a meter closer to the transparent metal window. "Take me to the MDG control center," she said loudly.

The floor around her lit up with a green light, then a moment later the platform she stood on smoothly descended. *This semblance of the omniscient technology our forefathers possessed in the time of Kelkabara is beyond our comprehension. How great was our fall.* She had never before been mesmerized by technology, but the large pentagon gateway that enabled one to travel far distances in just moments was impressive. Looking at it was a vivid reminder that the legends and myths of the ancient gate wars were true. The Watchers referred to as Prespators had won control of the Bisgabeths, the unimaginably massive gateways that enabled travel between the five galaxies of the Quintástraya.

"Greetings, Mother Vallo," said the Bisgabeth representative.

"Greetings," she replied to the highly-advanced android. *I wonder why they have no hair.* "Have the Watchers given the other Monastarium's a MDG?" she asked.

"Yes, and they have been calibrated for exclusive use by the sisterhood. The Marium Kahnet will now have the ability to travel to each Monastarium and the five galactic capitals," a male Chayot said.

"When will the gate travel controllers be ready?" she asked.

"The sisters are being tested for DNA compatibility and light spectrum cognitive acuity. I believe we should have the first group of MDG controllers shortly." The Chayot's voice sounded like a real human.

"Where are they being tested?"

"Inside." The Chayot looked over his right shoulder toward the large gateway.

"Well, then, I will let you continue with your work." She nodded her head, satisfied.

"Have a pleasant evening, Mother Vallo." He bowed his head and moved back to his workstation.

"Thank you," she replied, already ascending.

The melody of songbirds in the morning echoed through Jazrene's bedroom window, announcing the dawn of a new day. She sat up and stretched, enjoying the quiet and peace. *No dreams,* she noted. *I thought I would have one since I was told I am departing soon.* Soon, her thoughts turned to the duties of the day and she began her morning Kohyim routine.

Some time later, after taking her last bite of Victus bread, she left the rest on her private patio railing for whatever animal might have need of it. Walking in the cool grass in the garden, she heard the commotion of multitudes of people throughout the extensive additions to the Monastarium. She paused, breathing deeply in the solitude of the moment. *Mother Sarai, it's just about time you lie next to your beloved husband, but first things first.* It almost choked her up to see how many had become Marium Kahnet members. For the first time since she was a child, the hall was filled with new faces she knew came from every sector of space. *The manifold manifestation of HIS hand upon the sisterhood is clearly evident and undeniable.* Her muse continued along the same vein as she walked past rooms filled to capacity by Marium Kahnet daughters, on her way to see the new Hadassahs.

"Good morning, Mother." Her daughters Jada and Sonja hugged and kissed her cheek. Their faces were beaming with pride of her achievement and her part in a Kodashah prophecy.

"Good morning, daughters," she said, looking around at the

gleeful expressions on every face. She stared into the silver eyes of the sisters who had ascended to the rank of Hadassah, then into those of her replacement Karina. *They look so young. But I know that they have successfully passed every test and ceremony as required by the new governance laws of our Order. Thank you for your leading, Moshiach.*

"As you are aware, the official burial of our matriarch Sarai Chawah Modroya will commence later today. Although it will be a simple burial procession, there will be many dignitaries and Grand Assembly members present. I must prepare the burial site for Mother. If you wish, you may come with me right now to assist."

Jazrene turned and headed toward the outer courtyard, nearest the eastern gardens, and was pleased to hear the sisters talk amongst themselves as they followed behind her.

Chapter Eleven

SAURCINE

Deep inside Varkrato League of Worlds controlled space, on the planet Gerobon, the Saurcine's unchallenged leader often referred to as Queen Mother Rishna Atharva was preparing to depart from her home in the capital city of Attomayo.

"All is ready for the next phase to complete the coupling between my daughters and the powers of Creminmorta," Rishna said with a loud voice. "I will be the mother of many sons, and one day, one from among my daughters will bring forth our messiah, the Krevomax. He will conquer our enemies and crush the Mantis Alliance into the dust of history."

She looked over her image in the wall mirror with approving, luminescent blue eyes. *I look like my mother… beautiful, but I also possess more power then she or Father could ever dream of. No matter, my time to reign will soon come. It's a shame that my last suitor did not survive the Kauxog Mulud. But oh well. If they can't subdue me in combat, how can they be worthy to marry me?* Rishna's thoughts were interrupted by a soft tone in the room. She turned to face the entrance of her sleeping chamber.

"Enter," she ordered clearly.

A familiar, slender woman wearing the deadly assassins' vestments of Tregoon entered through the open doorway and bowed her head. "Queen Mother." Her tightly pinned-up silver hair glistened in the room's light. Rishna felt a cold presence behind her. The Tregoon's spotted luminescent eyes darted to the back of the room, and she immediately reached for her holstered weapon.

"Mekka, don't be alarmed. That is the Surapharin, but we call them Tisrak… Wait outside," Rishna said firmly.

"As you wish, Queen Mother," Mekka responded and left the room.

Rishna turned. The middle of the back wall, which was constructed with materials from Creminmorta, warped and transformed into a multidimensional communications link. She stepped forward, completely unafraid of the deathly pale black hooded being. A white cloud of condensation formed in front of her face. She then took shorter, measured breaths as the frigid cold enveloped around her. *I wonder if a permanent solution has been found.* She hoped there would be.

"Rishna," the macabre being said. "The solution to completely restore and sustain the Tree of Knowledge is to saturate its soil with the blood of the innocent." Its reptilian tone resonated around her. It was as if he had heard her thoughts.

"Any particular race or age, or gender?" Rishna responded coldly.

"The Tridents of Hades were created for humans, and so it must be their blood. Gender does not matter." The black hooded messenger of death peered into her luminescent blue eyes.

"Age?" she asked.

"For now, a steady supply of infant children is required," he said and seemed to grin.

"The quantity needed?" Rishna continued to press for more specifics.

"Several thousand to restore, and a continued supply of hundreds to maintain it," it said with flaring nostrils.

"When will I get to partake of the Tree of Knowledge, as I will be the one supplying the sustaining life substance?" Rishna strongly coveted the information said to be contained from consuming the fabled tree's fruit.

"When we deem it so. But first, bring us the blood." Its voice increased in intensity and power.

"I will do what is necessary," Rishna said, pressing her lips together. A wave rippled across the surface of the communications link, then transformed back to its previous state. She grinned widely, an idea of how to achieve this already coming to her mind. She turned away from the communications portal and headed out the door.

A stream of water cascaded along the edges of the canopy that covered the walkway to her shuttle. *I just love winter storms; there is something about the sheer power they unleash.* She surveyed the downpour and out of the corner of her eye she saw a lightning bolt streak across the thick darkened clouds. She enjoyed the soothing rumbling sounds of thunder. Mekka and three other Tregoons stood by the shuttle's open door, waiting for her to board. Wordlessly, she made her way to the back of her shuttle. Its opulent appearance was deceptive, as it had been retrofitted to her specifications and included high-energy weapons.

"Queen Mother, welcome aboard. We are ready to leave as soon as you give word," said Captain Tregga.

"Proceed Captain," she said loud and clear.

Then, as she had done on many occasions before, she activated the privacy force field. There was a crackling sound as it enveloped her plush seat. The Tregoon remained standing near the two doors.

Rishna tapped the left armrest, lighting a crystal panel. Her slender fingers deftly entered a series of codes. A half-meter rectangular holographic display appeared a meter away from her face. "Activate communications," she said. A green bar lit up at the top of the screen. "List the individuals that are in charge of the orphanages in Gerobon."

Dozens of names popped up with very lofty titles.

Interesting, did not realize there was so much bureaucracy. "List only human females."

The display did so.

"This won't be too difficult a task. There are only a handful." Rishna touched one of the names. "Regenta Austallar, age 63, no children…widow. Yes, I believe she will be perfect for my needs. Who can resist the rejuvenating effects of Cymbratar?" Speaking of that, she needed to check on the progress of how the development of Nembratar was going. Rishna tapped the orphanage's headquarters in Attomayo communication link. "This is Queen Mother Rishna, I am coming to see Senior Administrator Regenta Austallar first thing this evening. She will be notified when I will arrive." She tapped the name once more, then tapped the top of the flat panel on the armrest. The display screen vanished.

She felt her spirit grow cold. *We must have arrived.* She deactivated the privacy shield and readied herself to meet the menacing being from Creminmorta.

The shuttle landed, and the Tregoon guards immediately exited to secure the perimeter.

"All is ready, Queen Mother," said Mekka.

Rishna sat up and quickly exited. Even in the storm, she admired Augrapinna, the beautiful Amphosar sanctuary fortress. Its, tall proud spires defiantly jutted into the skies. Rishna acknowledged the guards at their stations by lifting her right hand toward them, and continued her way through the open archway. Tanzanite obelisks lined both sides of the main hallway. The gold symbols and letters of the Toxrokk language that covered the obelisks glowed brightly at her passage. It did not frighten her, as she was comfortable with the spiritual power around her. *A strange gift from Lord Saurcine, maybe. I should remember to ask him why or what causes them to glow.* Rishna dismissed the muse and stepped onto the center of the hover platform. Once she held onto the silver railing, the platform lifted and skimmed across the open ceremonial parade grounds.

Waiting on the landing platform were high ranking Saurcine sisters. Princess Themma Hansu, Larina Bea Sallan, and Xi Cheelu. The others gave her a satisfying sensation of victory—the ladies Kim Sumvesh,

Cora Sandor, and Vellina Besseret. These had turned from the Marium Kahnet and had given themselves wholly to Lord Saurcine. Rishna's expression remained stoic, but inside she was jubilant. *You are just the beginning of what we will take from the Mariam Kahnet.*

"Greetings, Queen Mother," said Xi, as the others bowed their heads.

"Let us complete the Garden of Eden project, shall we?" Rishna's voice was laced with anticipation.

Once inside, the light from the Thakus crystals imbedded in the walls also emitted a welcome warmth. Even so, the impressive space was cold. The ladies followed Rishna across the white marble floor to a set of closed double silver doors. She reached out and placed her hand on the center ring of gold. The doors slid away, revealing rows of rings, various types of necklaces, and tiaras.

"Daughters, please stand here." Rishna gestured with her hand. The women lined up in front of her.

"Queen Mother, I have a question. Where are the new recruits? I thought they would be here." Vellina's voice was soft and she looked puzzled.

Rishna gazed into her blue eyes. "The Sybleths will be appointed soon. As for you, since you have successfully completed all necessary testing to become a Mother in our Order, I hereby bestow upon you the rank of Veshtep. Now, you will be among the first to have the office of administrator of the new Amphosars." Rishna placed a golden choker with a tanzanite cut gem in its center in Vellina's outstretched palms.

Vellina took it and placed it around her neck. She lifted it up and watched the sparkling of the tiny jewels in the light.

Rishna continued down the line, doing the same for the rest of the women. "Once the Amphosars are completed you will be summoned accordingly to meet your Superiors, the Sybleths." She touched the side of the jewel-encrusted vault and the doors immediately closed.

"Now, my daughters, you will be part of something much greater than you could have ever imagined." Rishna grinned. She turned, gesturing for them to follow.

In front of them was a ten-meter-tall wall. She looked back and saw their curiosity in their blue eyes, then smiled wryly as the panic dawned on their faces. "My dear ones, that is a Nossorad. As you have read in our holy tome, the Ambatanok, witnesses and enforcers of the Chomtheke binding of the Varkrato League of Worlds are all a part of this ceremony." Rishna turned and saw the ghastly-looking creature's head protruding out from the wall. Venom from its fangs sizzled as it hit the floor. She lifted her hands palms toward the wall and chanted. "Dugra~Shantalla~Umesh." Rishna's voice was infused with necromonic power. Blue and red tendrils of energy lashed out of her hands crashing against the wall. A moment later the wall warped and rippled. "Follow me," she commanded and walked through the wall. The others followed closely behind.

Rishna stopped at the edge of the crevasse, then turned to face her daughters. "This place is sacred. Keep it to yourselves. What you sense is the power of channeled necromomic energy. It will allow you to use your gifts more easily. Follow me." She turned to face the chasm. "Edak~Shallah." Her authoritative tone resonated in the large cavern. The mantle of authority she wielded underlined the power of her lofty position. Her body levitated half a meter above the ground and she proceeded to walk across the crevasse. Rishna heard the others pronounce the same invocation and sensed they were right behind her.

Just ahead was a wide stream of a bright, shimmering metallic liquid. Without a word spoken, Rishna glided over and on to its surface, and flowed with it as it cascaded in a gentle slope deep into the mountain. She breathed deeply, engulfed in the moment. *The stream's aroma is sweet, but I'm sure it's not pleasant to drink. The ladies must be very curious as to what lies ahead.* About a kilometer into the mountainside, three hundred meters ahead, the liquid metal stream disappeared under a rock portion of a landing platform. She led the others out of the stream.

"It is ready. Now we must do our part to ensure that our messiah comes in his due time." She confidently strode to a red marbled stone floor a hundred meters away. Glancing back at the group, she was amused by the wonderment in their eyes, as they surveyed the massive cavern. At the other end of the marble floor she saw the multiphasic portal several hundred meters away. The others obediently joined her.

The center band that made up the ten-meter-tall oval portal pulsed with purple and green lights. The center warped outward as it expelled necromonic energy.

"We are ready, Master Abaddon," Rishna shouted into the portal. As soon as the words left her lips, the portal sparked with blue and red tendrils of energy. A massive being stepped out of it. Its wings expanded as it emerged and veins on its body pulsed with red light. It let out a breath of plasma and pitch-black smoke.

They all bowed low to the ground.

"Rise," the mighty being commanded. "This is will begin the process to ensure the Master's messiah, the Krevomax, as you call him to come forth. As you have been informed, the Tree of Knowledge will require the sacrifice of scores of human infant children to repair and human fetuses to maintain it. If you wish to taste of its fruit, so shall you provide."

"Master Abaddon, I have indeed been informed by the Tisrak. Should I prepare the place of transference near the Eye stone?" Rishna asked.

"Yes," he responded with a loud voice. The malevolent being lifted its clawed right appendage. "Thrag~Noos~Comm." Rishna knew that they all were feeling the power of these words penetrate their bodies. It was painful to say the least. She held back a groan. She could hear the others panting at her side. Then a single large winding tube, similar to an umbilical cord, shot out from the portal and into an adjoining tunnel. The tunnel led to the hidden section temple of Saurcine on the other side of the Shanga Mountains. "Once you return to that sanctuary, you will see how the sacrifices must be done," he stated plainly. Then he moved to the side and repeated the command. This time, twelve tubes just like the other shot straight under the marble platform Rishna and her group stood on. Abaddon stretched his hands toward Rishna. "Immus~Consu~Errata." A sphere of purple and red shot from his hands and before she could react, it enveloped her head. The necronomic sphere of knowledge evaporated.

"I understand what must be done next, Master," Rishna said in a state of serene peace. She felt distant from herself almost as if she was coming out of a trance.

"I will return, but if not Lord Saurcine will arrive at the sanctuary. Prepare for the first bloodline. Gandu Khanon will arrive shortly." His sulfuric breath wafted over them. The smell was acrid. It was hard for Rishna to not cough.

"Yes, Master. I am honored to serve you." Rishna bowed, as did the others. She looked at them and noted that they appeared anxiously silent. Just as quickly as Abbadon had appeared, he vanished back into the realms of Augranash, the preeminent realm of Kravanoblus, the Tisrad Dragon.

"Let us finish, shall we?" Rishna looked at the others. Twin looks of awe and fright covered their faces. She would soon see if they remained steadfast.

"Do we just drop our blood onto the tops of those tubes?" Cora asked.

"Yes, the edges of the tubes are sharp. We will all take turns on each root," Rishna stated. *They look like unbiblical cords of some type. Fleshy, yet not. Strange.* As the leader, she would be first. Rishna held the sharp edges of the first tubes. She winced as the edge cut deep. Her blood dripped down into the purple tunnel.

The others one by one mimicked her actions in quick succession at each of the tubes. Then, as instructed by Rishna, they consumed a necronos-infused communion wafer containing the same necronos properties as Cymbratar. Even with those wafers, it took some time for their cuts to heal and replenish the blood they sacrificed. Cora, Themma, Larina, Xi, Kim, and Vellina stood in a circle holding hands. A small drip of blood slid from their noses to their lips. They all touched the metallic tasting liquid of life with their tongues. Images of infants crying as they were being sacrificed flashed through everyone's mind. A river of the comingled blood of the innocent began to flow, seeming without end.

They began to chant necromonic harmonies around the group of tubes protruding a meter out of the opening in the marble floor. Rishna stood in the center with her hands raised, chanting a variation of their chant. With all eyes open, they witnessed the tubes become tightly packed together, then from their tops forming a single object. A stunningly beautiful woman of gold emerged. From her upper thighs down was formed of the deep purple tubes. The rest of her body from the hips up looked like a curvaceous pregnant woman with long silver hair and eyes of luminescent blue.

"All worship the mother of many sons and the mother of the messiah, Chavah, the mother of life," Rishna pronounced loudly. They dropped to their knees in unison and prayed to Chavah.

Chapter Twelve

REUNION

Rediquin disengaged her cloaking systems. It was pointless to keep them up, since she was certain a Mantis Alliance patrol ship had most likely detected her already. *I hope they will not want to inspect my ship.* After a few tense moments, the *Furies Scepter* arrived at Ramah without incident.

"Look at that orbital shipyard," Orisa said in amazement.

"I wonder what has happened since we've been gone, Orisa," Mirinda said quietly.

Rediquin ignored the excited banter between them and adjusted course to descend to her destination. "Disengage protocol Rediquin 1," she said with force. "Please be seated." She turned the ship to follow a convoy of civilian ships headed toward the Monastarium. They'd not only rebuilt it, but it was greatly expanded. *Those towers on the east side are very beautiful.* Her heart leapt with trepidation at the possibility of seeing her mother for the first time in decades. But she quickly set that thought aside to concentrate on the task at hand.

She broke away from the convoy and maneuvered the *Furies Scepter* along a narrow gorge to a cave hidden from view below, and landed on the dusty natural lip. "We're here, Sisters."

"Do you know what they will do with us?" Orisa's nervous tone reflected the expression on Mirinda's face.

"What I know is that you will not be executed. Count yourselves fortunate." She didn't mean to be so cold; it was the only way she could cope. Rediquin powered down the ship and rose. "Time to go." She motioned for the rogues to exit.

Just outside, she stood next to the ship with her hands resting on her holstered weapons. She retracted her visor and drank in the unique color of Ramah's dusk. *Just as I remembered.* A flood of memories assaulted her mind. She gritted her teeth, trying not to be overwhelmed. *Stop, just stop.* She became aware of Mirinda quivering next to her. She turned to look at the sisters. They seemed to be experiencing the same feelings she was. *I wonder if I knew them as children.* She frowned at the unwelcome thought. Then her mind swirled with the images of her mother. *Should I? I don't know.* She struggled with the decision to meet her mother now or another time. *What if she rejects me? I'll die a second death if she does.* She swallowed hard and moisture filled her eyes.

"*Meet with your mother,*" said a voice she had not heard since her youth.

She tested the suggestion in her spirit. "Yes, I will see Mom." As soon as she whispered those words an invisible weight lifted off her. Just then three women appeared from the shadows of the cave. The tall one looked like the one in charge. One of them was a physician.

One of the others held a box.

"Welcome home. I am Timnah," the tall, stately women said. Her demeanor gave them a sense of calm, which was greatly needed.

Mirinda and Orisa folded their hands over their chests and bowed their heads with deep respect for the elder. Timnah stood staring at Rediquin with a look of recognition on her face. Rediquin felt a strong compulsion to run away from this emotional wrenching and turmoil.

The physician scanned the two women. "These are the rogues. They have small traces of radiation but nothing lethal," she said to Timnah.

"Here is your reward," Timnah said, motioning for her companion to open the wooden coffer. The glittering contents of the reward were much larger than Rediquin had been promised. *The ingots of gold Kelkatanium are worth more than dozens of Cymbratar. Where did they get it? Is it mined here somewhere?* She took the box and closed the lid. "Seems to be all here. I have not seen the Mevaseret gems in person before. They are beautiful." She looked slightly upward into Timnah's eyes. "These two are all yours." She took a step away from the rogues.

"Please follow me," said Timnah in a cordial tone, and Mirinda and Orisa did so, looking a little less afraid.

Rediquin watched them vanish into the shadows of the cave, then proceeded to secure the valuables inside of her ship and get some intelligence reports on the current state of Ramah.

Rediquin enjoyed the cool fresh air as she walked briskly toward the ledge of the cave. She could see some of the boundaries of the Monastarium clearly marked by infinity flames. Her mind recalled the major event she'd learned from her intel network had taken place earlier this day. *So, the Matriarch of the Modroya family was laid to rest today. I'm sure that fulfilled a prophecy or two…well at least that's my guess anyway.* A scuffling noise drew her eyes near her feet. A Mocau scorpion searching for a mate displayed its purple and yellow luminescent body. It must have thought she was an enemy, as it was poised to strike her with its nasty tail. She crushed it under her boot before it struck.

The crunching sound caused her to reflect on her work as a mercenary. *The sisters and I have wrought a crushing blow to our enemies. Should I continue my quest to avenge my family?* She began to struggle with her vow to bring retribution on those who'd caused the Ramah infanticide long ago. She weighed the knowledge of the tens of millions who were killed by the actions of the rogue sisters. Testing her spirit, she decided it had quelled her appetite for more blood. "What should I do? I don't know any other life," she whispered. She sensed someone approaching but remained relaxed. *It's probably Timnah.*

But a moment later she knew she was wrong.

"I am glad you are still here." The well-loved, familiar voice of her mother broke the silence. "I apologize for not being present when you returned Mirinda and Orisa back to us. I was preoccupied with other pressing matters." Jazrene's voice was firm and kind.

Rediquin braced herself. *She might hate me for what I have done.* She swallowed hard and gracefully pivoted to her right side, meeting the silver eyes of her mother.

"Do I know you? You look very familiar." Jazrene's voice was puzzled.

The instant recognition broke Rediquin. Her eyes began to water, and tears broke through the long-held barriers to trickle down her cheeks. "I am Minna Lavine Vallo," she solemnly choked out between gasping breaths.

Jazrene took a step forward with a searching look on her face, peering deeply into her eyes. Rediquin stood still, stoically ready to accept what would come.

"I am so sorry, Mom…so sorry." The repentance was so much more than just this reunion. It drove her to her knees. The force of regret and unspeakable grief poured out in uncontrollable torrents of cries for forgiveness. She was unaware that on some level she was responding to the love of Abba El that emanated from her mother.

Jazrene immediately sank to her knees to embrace this poor soul that was so broken. Her arms wrapped around the hard mercenary as if she was a child. Her sobs immediately began to subside.

"It will be all right," Jazrene murmured, patting her back.

"I remember when you took me to my first class in the Monastarium. You wore a blue dress that Father bought you for your birthday the day before. You told me that out of all your children I was special." Rediquin's head was still bent with her chin nearly resting on her chest as she spoke. Her mouth opened to say something else, but just then the soft hands of her mother cradled her cheeks and lifted her chin up.

"Minna?" Jazrene gasped, wide-eyed. "Minna, it's you? You're alive!" she cried and embraced her daughter tightly, rocking them both. Unmitigated love and grace began to pour a healing balm into Minna's spirit, along with a multitude of loving kisses Jazrene bestowed on her daughter's face.

"How is this possible? Where did you come from? I don't understand..." Jazrene closed her eyes and squeezed her tightly once more before releasing her.

"Mother, I will try to explain," she said as tears continued to run down her cheeks.

"Minna, please come with me." Jazrene rose to her feet and helped her daughter off the dusty floor. "We are going to my quarters, we have much to talk about." Jazrene wrapped her arm around Minna as they headed back into the cave.

A short while later, Jazrene sat and listened to her daughter tell the story of her life's journey and how she ended up as a mercenary. It was not unlike her own story, which began shortly after the time of Hoshkadish, the global infanticide and murder of tens of millions on Ramah. She was amazed by Minna's sheer determination and will to survive on her own within the outlaw regions of the Rakia Expanse. *Those blue eyes have a translucent quality. Her skin is flawless, she looks so young... My spirit discerns she has used a substance tainted with necronos. What have you done, my dearest daughter?* Jazrene's serene countenance did not reveal the thoughts racing just beneath the surface.

"Enough about me," Minna said and reached for a cup of water on the table near them. She stood, restlessly took a sip, reseated herself, then held the stone cup on her lap. "Mother, I am so proud of what you have accomplished. It's a miracle. Because of you the Marium Kahnet is now part of the Grand Assembly. It must feel incredible to have laid the Matriarch to rest. Did that fulfill any prophecies?" Her expression was filled with admiration.

"Yes, the return of the Mother Matriarch has fulfilled a prophecy," Jazrene said with a broad smile.

"As leader of the sisterhood, what will be your title or office?" Minna asked.

Jazrene noticed the green light blinking on the metal band on her daughter's forearm. *Must be a notification of some kind.* "Minna, you have overcome much adversity. I'm very blessed that one of my children has survived. Timnah is right; she said you looked like me. I should have listened, then I would have been better prepared." She smiled with all the relief and joy she felt. In the spirit, she saw something dark break and drift away from Minna. She immediately knew that the constant taunting sense of isolation and loneliness Minna had been feeling was gone.

"Mother, I'm sorry for not letting you know I was alive. I didn't know until recently that you were still living." Her large blue streaked eyes held a sort of plea. "You must know by now that I have done things you wouldn't approve of." Her eyes now held a look of reserve as she waited for the judgment that might come.

"I am well aware of the recent events that took place on Letalis, Necropis, and Tartarus." Jazrene paused for a moment, gazing into her eyes discerningly. She waited to see where Moshiach would take this. "As you well know, the Marium Kahnet does not condone such actions. Taking a life, especially of the innocent, is contrary to everything we represent. We care for the wounded, even those who oppose us." Her statements were factual, but her gaze was warm and open, inviting confidence.

"That's exactly my point, Mother. You hold the highest office in the sisterhood and having a daughter who is a mercenary would only help those who oppose you. I know Prime Minister Samgasat blames the Marium Kahnet for what happened thirty years ago. It was wise of her not to try to harm you, or I would have had to step in." Minna stopped speaking and stood. "Do you see, Mother? I am not ready for the Konia Berit conversion. I know you want me to but it's something that I cannot do at this time." She frowned and looked somewhat guarded.

Jazrene knew that her daughter had spoken what was in her heart. She rose and placed her hands on her daughter's shoulders and stared lovingly into her eyes. "I can see you have lost your purpose and direction. But I'm comforted to know that you will continue in your life's journey as Abba El has ordained it. But know this, because of Meshua's death and resurrection to redeem us, there is no condemnation, trust HIS love for you."

She then placed her right hand over on her head. "Ruahnaush." This was the mother's blessing of peace and protection.

A firm knock on the door broke the weighty moment. "Please

enter," Jazrene said loudly. The door opened and Sister Timnah came in.

"You two have met, I understand," said Jazrene. She paused for a moment, then coming to a decision, she said, "Timnah, as you have correctly assumed, please meet Minna Lavine, my daughter."

Sister Timnah smiled and said, "Welcome home, Minna. I look forward to getting to know you."

"Thank you, Sister," Minna responded quietly to this unfamiliar situation. Jazrene knew she was still undecided as to which direction she would take. She also knew that most everyone would unreservedly welcome her into the fold, which could change everything for them both.

The elder bowed her head. "Mother Vallo, the four sisters are ready."

"Thank you, Sister. Inform them I will attend to them at dawn's early light tomorrow," Jazrene said. "Keep the information about Minna's return between us and the elders, please. At least for the time being. I will let you know if anything changes."

"Agreed. Also, those you asked to meet with have arrived," Timnah said.

"Inform them that I will be there shortly." Jazrene nodded her dismissal.

To her daughter she said, "For now, until you have time to decide what you want to do, we will keep your identity secret." She removed a silver wristband from her arm and lifted Minna's slender wrist and put it on. "This will allow you access to my quarters. I have a large bedroom that you can use. Come, let me show you. Please make yourself at home. I want you to stay with me for the ceremonial conclusion of the Barayalad that will take place in a few days. You'll be provided more appropriate attire for the occasion." Jazrene hoped Minna would take her up on the offer.

"It's beautiful, Mother. Yes, I will stay." Minna continued to stand quietly as if she did not know what to say. "How did your eyes change color? I hear rumors…"

"It is the Victus that we use in our ceremonies. Minna, the beginning of that is a long story from when the attacks happened so many years ago. I will have to tell you later." She could see a curiosity in her daughter's eyes that was so much like her own. She had to try. "Minna, you can leave your old life behind and begin a new life's journey."

"I've been through a tumultuous time recently." Minna crossed her arms and frowned lightly. "I need time to gather my thoughts and decide what I want to do. But for now, I need to take care of a matter."

"Is it in regards to the bounty?" Jazrene tilted her head to the side and waited.

"Well, yes, I have obligations to that effect," Minna replied. "I won't ask how you know."

"Moshiach told me. You must be going to Dossel then. It's not a safe place," Jazrene said with concern. She squelched the thought that she might lose Minna again so soon.

"Mother…really, I can take care of myself, I have survived for all these years on my own." Her self-reliance was evident in her firm tone.

"I don't dispute that, but there is a place for you here, Minna. We have need of such talent in the Semdressa, our own intelligence agency." Jazrene smiled. Minna's vast experience and knowledge of the Rakia Expanse would be invaluable to them.

"Can you trust them?" Minna frowned lightly with a long-held mistrust.

Jazrene reached out and cradled her cheek. "I ask Meshua to watch over you." Her unmeasurable gaze of love broke through her daughter's stoic demeanor. The spiritual atmosphere shifted subtly.

Minna swallowed hard and lifted her mother's soft hand and kissed it. "Mother, it's safe, I know them. Both Zeta Three and Raduu. I can trust them, especially Zeta Three," she said with a reassuring smile.

"I have met with Zeta Three. He seems to be an honorable young man. I can see why you are attracted to him. Handsome." Jazrene stood up before Minna could deny her feelings.

"Mother let's not talk about that right now." She rose with a determined air. "Right now, I have to take care of business in Dossel."

"When you return, come through the eastern gardens and ask one of the sisters where my quarters are located. Or you can use the map on that wristband. I will see you soon, my beloved Minna." Jazrene kissed her on the forehead, then gave her a long embrace and left the room.

Rediquin stood there a moment longer and felt her mother's embrace cracking the protective metal around her heart, then smiled and shook her head. "How did she know? Even I didn't know I have feelings for him… But I suppose I can't deny I have become fond of the rascal. Well then, I'd better get going."

Chapter Thirteen

REDIQUIN

Rediquin maneuvered her ship into the main flight path to the sprawling metropolitan city of Dossel. It was time for the others to receive their share of the rogue sister's bounty. "I hope for Raduu's sake, he doesn't try anything funny. Regardless, even if he an associate of Zeta Three, it will be the end of him." Her threat was as hard as her tone. She sensed that her life was about to be changed by an unseen force she could not escape. *What is this feeling I have? My love for Mother is much stronger than I thought it would be. I will do almost anything to make her happy. She deserves no less than that from me.* Her spirit darkened with regrets that almost brought her to tears. *I should have come back when I discovered she was alive. Maybe I could have helped her in her time of need.* Her heart stung even more with these recriminations. *I feel so terrible that I didn't. But now, how can I reconcile my mercenary life and the sisterhood?* "Mother I swear on my life that I'll make it up to you. How, I don't know? But I promise I will try, even if it takes the rest of my life," she said resolutely. She firmly put aside that dilemma for later.

"This is transportation hub control to *Furies Scepter*. You have access to Bay 39A. Transmitting coordinates now. Please confirm," said a raspy humanoid voice.

"Coordinates received," she responded. The city of Dossel was a sprawling mosaic of Ramah communities, diverse in every sense of the word. Most of the occupants were employed in one way or another by the mining industry. Every transportation hub on Ramah was filled to capacity now that the sisterhood was part of the Grand Assembly. She squeezed the ship between two larger ships. Powering down, she braced herself to go out among the bustling crowd. Rediquin found herself staring fixedly at the wristband that her mother had given to her just moments before. Curiously, she squeezed the edges of the silver flex metal and a luminescent map of the Monastarium appeared.

"Mother Vallo's quarters," she commanded. In a quick sequence of images, it zeroed in to her mother's location. She memorized the location, then deactivated the map. The elegant wristband was delicate and very feminine. "Silver, the sisterhood's primary color," she said, smiling. For the first time she felt a sense of being home. "Wait a minute. Where did I put that?" She jumped up and raced to the back of the ship.

"It's not here… how about here?" she mumbled as she scrambled to find what she had hidden long ago. A stash of mementos from her past. Frustrated, she dropped to her knees and sighed. Tilting her head back, she closed her eyes, then opened them, immediately noticing a piece of metal decking between the power core regulators. "Ah, I remember now," she said triumphantly. She wedged herself into the gap, grunting with the effort as she extended her arm as far as she could and lifted the metal plate with her fingers. "Got you!"

She slid the metal box out and backed out of the narrow space.

Crouching on her heels, she eagerly opened the box. Her fingers rummaged through items not seen for decades. "Here you are," she exclaimed. She picked up the tiny wristband her mother had given her when she was a little girl. *Mother gave me this on my first day of school. How old was I…eight? Nine?* "Let's see here…it should have power still." She squeezed the edges. "Mother," she said loudly. A series of lights appeared on the metallic surface, then the face of her mother. "She had thick auburn hair and green eyes back then."

The well-loved voice of her mother began speaking the familiar message of encouragement. "Don't be afraid, my dearest Minna. Moshiach is with you. Of all my children, I have dreamed that you are destined to have a special journey." Rediquin drank in the soothing words and tucked them away in her spirit.

"I am not afraid anymore, Mother." She felt a new sense of strength and endurance wash over her. She had overcome countless obstacles and perils way beyond her mother's imagination. "Mother, you were right. I have had a unique journey. But I am pretty sure it is not the one you thought I would have." She looked at the box, considering tossing the contents, but then something stopped her from such a thoughtless action. "Time to rebury this." She placed the contents neatly back in and hid the box back under the plating.

"Time to go." Rediquin got up, dusted her gloves off, and checked her gear and weapons. She took the agreed upon amount of reward from the chest the sisters had given her and stuffed it into her overcoat. "Secure ship, level 2." The cargo door opened, and her visor immediately closed over her face. Her cape swayed in the breeze as she stood for a moment, taking stock. "That was not there when I landed," she said, puzzled. A flat panel kiosk sat a few meters from her ship. She went to investigate.

"What's this? Official government markings," she said, annoyed. "A transportation hub meter with a fee of 125 Mantis Alliance Credits." She wanted to blast it to bits with her weapons. But as tempting as that was, she had more important things to attend to. *Of course, the economic ripples of the Grand Assembly on our home world have begun.* Grudgingly, she placed her Omni currency disc on the meter's screen and removed it when payment was transferred. She quickly left the busy transportation hub.

Nightfall added to the seediness of the Wukuza sector of Dossel that many nefarious individuals called home. Rediquin was not surprised to see her visor display a lot of small arms' energy signatures as she walked down the busy merchant-lined streets. *Strangely enough, this place feels more like home than the Mon—*

Her thought was interrupted by loud sirens and flashing multicolored lights. There was some sort of commotion just ahead. It looked like a raid on one of the ramshackle establishments, but in this instance, dozens of heavily armed military personnel were aiding the local civil law. Rediquin recognized the insignias on their shoulders and chest. *Regional Tactical Force.* The RTF was the Grand Assembly's civil law enforcement branch. The locals would have to adapt to the increase of scrutiny from those in lofty towers of authority. *Every society casts a shadow, and in it, the nature of fallen creation thrives.* Just short of the conflagration, she turned into an alley and examined the entrance to her meeting, then entered.

Her visor quickly adjusted to the dim lighting of the small warehouse. She removed a thumb-sized disc from her utility belt and swiped it across her visor. "Activate," she commanded, and flung it into the air. Immediately after leaving her hand, two life forms were displayed on her visor. *That must be Raduu.* Rediquin slipped one of her weapons from its holster and moved cautiously toward the back of the warehouse.

Stopping short of the last stack of crates, she saw a weapon's energy signature fire up. "Raduu, I am here to make a delivery." The loud, eerie, synthesized voice was her preferred mode of communication these days. Especially with new contacts.

A husky, unkempt, burly man with his hand on his holstered weapon stepped into view. "Don't shoot. I'm Raduu." He approached confidently, almost strutting like a male animal in a courtship ritual.

"That's far enough, Raduu," she said when he was a just a few meters away.

"Fine, as you wish." He hitched up his sagging, dingy-looking uniform pants and crossed his arms. "You must be Rediquin. I have heard so much about you. Mostly good of course." He blustered with a flash of his yellow-stained teeth showing through his black wiry beard and mustache.

"I am here to fulfill my contract with you as negotiated by Zeta Three. Here is your share of the bounty." She removed the reward from inside her overcoat and tossed it to him. With remarkable dexterity, he caught it with both hands. "Look inside and see for yourself that it's all there," she said sharply.

He obliged her request and opened the slender box. Judging by his wide-eyed look and large grin it looked like he was satisfied with the take. He slid the box into his thick coat. "It's all here. You have honored the contract. Say, how about joining forces with me and my crew? With you we could get enough riches to start our own colony." He stood, waiting.

She imagined what a rowdy bunch they were. Unsavory to the last. "I don't know you, but I will remind you to pay the bounty tax on that, especially since I previously discussed this bounty with Grand Dukar Namtar." She stood with her hands resting on her utility belt.

"What about my offer of a partnership?" Raduu's voice had a hint of a whine to it. He looked as if he wanted something else entirely.

Rediquin's visor turned crimson red. She placed her gloved hands on her holstered weapons and moved her right leg back slightly in dramatic fashion, ready to fight. "Leave!" she grunted harshly. He must have believed her as he spun and left without another word. She could hear him muttering violent threats as he went.

Sensing another presence behind her, she whipped out her pistol in a blur and spun.

"Don't shoot—it's me, Zeta Three!" His hands shot into the air.

She waited for him to remove his helmet just to be sure. *Must be using identity dampening body armor. Nice, maybe I should upgrade and get that ability. It could come in handy one day.* He stood staring at her as she took off her helmet. Her vibrant red hair glistened in the low light. "It's good to see you, Zeta Three." He still said nothing, just stood looking intently at her.

"I like your hair," he said finally. His voice held a caress as if he had touched her silky strands. *What has happened since the last time we were together? And what about me? I feel, well, I don't know what I feel. What is going on here?* He smiled at her like a love-smitten youth.

She hiccupped a little laugh and felt a blush heat her cheeks. "Stop, just stop, okay."

He chuckled and moved closer to her.

I think I could drink this in for a while. She coughed then abruptly changed the subject. "I just gave Raduu his share of the bounty. Did you change your mind? Do want your share?" she asked with raised brows.

He moved within an arm's length away from her. "No, I just wanted to inform you that I have destroyed the Stadageo plans you sold me," he said, expressionless.

"That's good to know." Her breathy tone was uncharacteristic of her during conversations with her peers.

"If you need to redeem that red marker I gave you, you might have to wait for some time," he murmured, leaning forward. His eyes held a look of desire that was new to them both.

"Why?" She felt the strong draw and breathed in the pheromones in the air. *I've never felt this before with anyone else.* Her wall of resistance cracked further. *He is handsome…but I don't have time for this now.* She took several deep breaths, trying to regain control.

"I trust you, so I can tell you that I recently discovered I am a member of the Veth'Shar," he said. "Since I have experience operating in the Rakia Expanse, I was chosen to lead a group to establish a mining site in the Fiero System. Well, that's my mission as it stands for now. But the way things are going that could change." He looked probingly into her eyes as if he was reading her soul.

"The Veth'Shar? I've never heard of them." She could not dispute their mutual attraction. *I wonder if he senses it too? He must.*

"It's a secret religious order of mostly human males," he said.

"Why are you telling me this confidential information?" She was genuinely curious. She found herself hoping that he trusted her not to betray him.

"Simple really. When I brought the matriarch of the Marium Kahnet home, I was met by Mother Vallo. She wore a silver wristband like the one you have on now." He stopped talking and looked at her wrist. "Can I tell you something?" he asked softly. He looked vulnerable and open.

Suddenly, she yearned to know more about him. She looked at him curiously and smiled. "Yes."

Zeta Three placed his right hand on her left shoulder and leaned in close. She quivered, feeling his warm breath on her neck.

"My name is Solek Modroxex. I am a direct descendent of the Modroya bloodline." His hand lightly pressed her shoulder, urging her to come closer. She didn't know what to do; her heart was pounding.

"Solek," she said warmly, feeling herself relax.

His face grazed her cheek as he pulled away just enough to gaze deeply into her eyes. She sighed and saw that he breathed her exhalation in through his nose. He leaned forward and touched his lips tenderly to hers.

Rediquin knew now that this was the beginning of something.

Unwittingly, she broke the intimate moment as she pulled out the red marker he had given her on Necropis. His arm drifted to his side and he smiled at her.

Zeta Three looked at the red market in her hand.

"Do you go around and kiss every woman you meet?" She lightly challenged with her eyebrows raised.

"To be honest, from what I can remember, you are the first in many years." His tone was uncertain and had a childlike, lost quality.

"What do you mean you can't remember?" she asked, concerned for him.

"I had an accident many years ago. It's a long story. One I would like to share with you one day," he said.

"Look, I don't need this. I want you to have it back. You owe me nothing." She slid the red marker into his vest pocket. She felt very vulnerable yet excited at the same time. *I wish he would kiss me again… Am I losing my mind, what's wrong with me?*

"Am I wrong to assume you feel the same about me as I do about you?" He waited, looking intently at her.

"Things are changing so quickly for me it's difficult to know for sure," she said with an uncertain transparency.

"I understand, particularly in light of your situation," he replied, seeming to invite her confidence.

"What do you mean by that?" she asked.

"I know you are Mother Vallo's daughter. You look so much alike. I knew it when I met her bringing my great grandmother home," he murmured.

She stared at him for a long moment, then acknowledged it with a nod, looking at him wordlessly.

"You can't go back to the Augatar region. Your identity as her daughter will eventually reach every network in that sector of space. It will compromise your safety," he said with caring eyes.

"I appreciate your concern." The weight of it hit her. She was relieved that he knew. "You are right, going back would be foolish. On the other hand, I can't see myself tending to the Monastarium gardens for the rest of my life either." She frowned at the thought of that demotion.

"Why not join the Semdressa?" he asked.

"My mother mentioned them to me. But I don't' know anything about them." Her calm demeanor hid the internal conflict that threatened to surface. It was a bright future she didn't deserve.

"It's the sisterhood's intelligence network. I'm sure they would love to have such an experienced and talented sister in their ranks." Zeta Three's tone filled with optimism and his eyes were bright.

But Rediquin shook her head. "I don't feel like I'm a sister. The term seems foreign to me. Besides, I don't believe they would want someone with my dark past as part of their holier-than-thou organization," she said glumly. "I think I should leave now. I don't want Mother to worry about me." She wanted to get away from the uncertainty of him and her future.

"I understand. Can I assume that you will be here for a few more days until you decide what you are going to do?" he asked quietly. His eyes seemed to plead with her.

"Yes." She stared into his eyes, trying to discern what he felt. She swallowed at the longing that was rising in her heart.

"I want to see you again, in a more pleasant environment of course," he said with a gentle smile.

"I would like that." She nodded.

He leaned forward to kiss her once more. She darted her lips to the side and gave him a peck on the cheek. Without another word, she quickly left.

Rediquin was cleared by ship traffic control to approach the public landing platform on the north side of the Monastarium. After setting the ship on autopilot, she changed into civilian clothing. *My old life is fading away. What awaits me now, I do not know. If only Moshiach could hear my prayers. HE would answer me and direct my steps.* She touched her lips with her hand, thinking of Solek. She wanted to see him again very soon, she couldn't deny it. *Semdressa, the sisterhood's spy network… Who*

would have thought they would have need of such a group? Maybe they could use someone with my experience. I could see myself being sent out on one of their missions. "Rediquin, we need to send food and medicine to a colony inside the Rakia Expanse." She laughed at the thought. *That's better than tending the gardens for the rest of my life.*

The shuttle landed just outside the gardens, and she made her way along with a few others down the wide path lit by luminescent Bulba Toolla flowers. Her gaze followed the purple eliminated Draguflies swarming around the sisters who were tending to the orange Lullamarie patch. *To each their own, but not for me. I have other plans for my talents.* Rediquin's thoughts trailed off as she entered the double doors.

Once inside, she caught the eyes of a group of sisters carrying lighted lamps and walking down the hallway. The prayer night watchmen. The four watches of the night, ever vigilant against the forces of spiritual darkness. *I guess I have retained more about the sisterhood than I care to admit.* Her silver band lit up as she passed through a narrow transparent nano wall. *I must be going the right way.* Rounding the final turn, she found the quarters. "Mother's home," she said. Just a few short steps inside, she paused. "It feels so…safe." She basked in the unfamiliar security in this unknown environment.

She continued down the wide hallway, to an open door. "This must be my room," she commented quietly and walked to the other side of the bed. "These are nice." She fingered the soft cloth of the garments neatly folded on the dresser. "Time for a bath, then to bed." She quickly undressed, eager for sleep and rest.

Some time later, unable to sleep, she fluffed up her pillow, then gazed through the top half of the window at the twinkling stars. Sudden images flashed through her mind—infant children crying, and blood dripping from an onyx blade. She sat up with a cry, clutching at her head. Blood ran down her nose and pooled atop her lip.

Then, the pounding headache left as quickly as it appeared. "What was that all about?" she said, perplexed. There was so much she didn't understand.

With a sigh, she slapped her palms on the mattress, and gave up waiting for her restlessness to leave her.

Jazrene walked slowly through a secret passageway to home. Her mind raced with thoughts about how Minna could fit into the new sisterhood. Minna's experience as a mercenary was a perfect fit to be a Semdressa and an instructor in the Criss Lumbra. Time felt extremely short and her heart squeezed with the conflict of how she should break the news that she was going home to Gannah El. *Meshua, how will I tell my daughter that you are calling me home?* She swallowed hard and picked up her pace.

A smile lit her face as her thoughts turned to what she imagined her grandchildren might look like. *I am so pleased our legacy will start anew.* The front door slid open and she quietly made her way down the hallway to the meditation room. There she found Minna bathed in the blue white glow of the moonlight, sitting on a mat near the window.

"Welcome home, Mother. I felt someone enter. I knew it was you. I hope all is well?" Minna's adult voice was something she had quickly gotten accustomed to.

"I apologize if I interrupted you." Jazrene entered the room. "I have something very important to tell you."

Minna sprang up and walked over to her with fluid, nearly soundless, steps. "What is it?" she asked.

"First of all, I'm very pleased to hear that you have been studying the new sisterhood governance and tenets." Jazrene's voice was subdued, almost hesitant. It was not like her to be uncertain.

Minna tilted her head to the side, seeming to know of the tumult in her heart. "Mother, it occurred to me that there are going to be five new Hadassahs ceremonially placed as the leaders of the sisterhood. Does that mean you will be stepping down?" Her daughter's brow furrowed in puzzlement.

Have I waited too long to tell her? "Yes, I am going to ordain the new Hadassah, which will complete the reformation of the Marium Kahnet." Jazrene stared into her daughter's eyes.

"Mother, I didn't read anywhere in the governance and tenets that those who hold the highest offices retire. They hold office until they die... Have I missed something?" Minna's voice held a note of bewilderment. Her expression looked deliberately blank to Jazrene, as if she was waiting for the other shoe to drop.

Jazrene exhaled a slow breath. "Minna, my dearest love. I have reached the end of my life's journey in this corporeal body. I am being called to Gannah El." The calm serenity of her tone was more convincing than the actual words themselves.

"You are going to paradise? What are you talking about?" Minna's voice was sharp with alarm. "If there is a plot against you, I can, and I *will* have them eliminated for you." Her whole body was tense and ready to fight.

Jazrene reached out and gently cupped Minna's shoulders and peered deep into her eyes. "That I don't doubt." She squeezed gently. "Abba El sent HIS messengers to inform me of my departure. It was only a short time ago that that I was told my transition to paradise would be after the ascension ceremony." She watched dismay wash over Minna's face.

Minna grabbed her wrists. "No!" she wailed. "It's my fault—you are being punished because of what I have been doing all this time. Please, I plead to Moshiach for my mother's life." She began to sob.

"No, my dearest love, do not blame yourself," Jazrene said gently, but Minna wouldn't look at her. It seemed that she was sinking into a pit of despair with the bronze gates of self-condemnation slamming behind her. She collapsed to her knees.

"I am cursed and now I am reaping what I have sown. I love you so much, Mother. I can't stand to lose you… I'll have nothing left," Minna said harshly between sobs.

Jazrene sank to her knees and held Minna by the elbows. "I have seen that not all is lost and that I will be a grandmother." She gently pulled her daughter to her feet. It seemed that statement had finally broken through the storm of emotion.

She saw that Minna was puzzled but was also listening intently.

"What? I am chaste…I don't know a man."

"You will continue our family's legacy, as ordained by Abba El." Jazrene was firm and matter of fact.

"Mom, is this a mistake? Maybe it won't happen for years to come." Minna's eyes pleaded sadly. Her stone-cold heart had obviously begun to thaw. Jazrene knew her unconditional love and embraces were making an impact.

"I once said that of all my children, you had a special journey." Jazrene smiled, beaming with such pride. Minna reached out and held her hand. Jazrene stroked her thick red hair and looked into the spirit for her future. "Here is what I see, Minna Lavine Vallo… You will have many children. Some you will give birth to, the others you will adopt. They all will have their own journeys. But now you will be given a chance for a new beginning and a clearer direction for your life, my beloved. So, here is a clue. There is a new threat emerging, even as we speak. The messiah of the Dragon's seed and the false light of the Saurcine Order. We must do all we can to mitigate their spheres of influence and stop the Dragon's seed from coming into existence." Minna looked sharply at her with tear-swollen eyes. But a spark of interest flared in them. "One day you will understand, my dearest Minna." Jazrene lifted her hand and caressed her daughter's beautiful face.

"Minna, repeat after me. *I break the bronze gates of condemnation and the iron bars of despair from my mind and heart in Meshua's name,*" Jazrene said loudly.

Minna breathed deep and repeated the pronouncement in the same tone as Jazrene. A moment passed. "Mom, I feel better.

Something has changed. I no longer feel the weight of oppression pressing against me. Now, it occurs to me I never realized it was there." Her eyes held a glimmer of hope.

"A repentant heart moves Moshiach. You did what you thought was right at the time, but now the eternal consequences of your actions have been removed. What was used for evil will now be used for good." Jazrene's heart swelled with joy as her daughter embraced the ways of the sisterhood. "Our words literally have the power of death and life. Remember that."

"I feel somewhat at a loss as to what do. Where should I live?" Her uncertainty was clear. But it was encouraging that she was talking about it.

"Don't worry about that. I have made arrangements for Sister Timnah to look after you," Jazrene said.

"Timnah? She is a senior Semdressa member. I know that for a fact, I have a talent for such things, Mother," Minna stated confidently.

"Yes, she is. She suggested that you join the Semdressa to teach the others your particular skill sets to combat the new rising threat." Jazrene paused for a moment. *Timnah will discuss Criss Lumbra with her later.* "I agreed, I believe it is an excellent idea. But that will be up to you to decide. In any case, whether you join or not, you will have a family."

Minna still looked bemused and shook her head a little. "Family?" She wiped her wet cheeks with her sleeve and sniffed. "Mother, you keep referencing my family. I don't have any idea what you are talking about." Her cheeks reddened.

"Tomorrow you will sit with Timnah and others in the balcony. You will stay there until Timnah says otherwise. Tell me you will do as I ask." Jazrene saw that Minna understood that she would not say more.

"Yes, I will stay in the balcony until Timnah says I can leave. Mother, I give you my word." Minna hugged her and kissed her cheek. "Oh, I have missed this. My heart has not felt the love of my family in decades."

"One day you will walk through the Ruak'Tabar and all vestiges of your past life will be washed away... On that day, you will start your new life. Moshiach has revealed it to me." Jazrene smiled widely.

"I look forward to that." Minna returned her smile.

Jazrene drew her by the hand. "So, tell me about Solek." She smiled widely with a sparkle in her eye. They made themselves comfortable. Soon, after a short conversation about Zeta Three, Minna sat quietly, listening to her mother's experiences of the last thirty years.

Chapter Fourteen

GEROBON

"All personnel, report to your stations. We are approaching Gerobon orbit." The ship-wide announcement repeated itself. Captain Tshera made her way over to her station.

"Incoming message, priority one, Captain," said the communications officer. Tshera acknowledged this with a nod.

"This is Gerobon orbital defense station… Identify yourself." The baritone voice was typical of Thrakonan males.

"This is Captain Tshera, of the Krauvanok battle cruiser *Aurgog*. I am sending the required code at this moment." Tshera placed her hand on the illuminated section of the armrest. "Captain Tshera, *Aurgog*," she said clearly.

"Welcome to Gerobon, Captain Tshera. I will inform the proper authorities of your arrival," the Thrakonan said.

"Our arrival is a class 1 mission. Security clearances level twenty-one," Tshera ordered as she prepared to inform the Kravjin and Saurcine Orders of Khanon's arrival.

"Mission is recorded and sealed according to your specifications, Captain Tshera." The communications link disengaged.

Tshera observed the flames increase along the ship's shields as the *Aurgog* descended into the Gerobon atmosphere.

Khanon took a bite of Cymbratar and placed the rest in his vestments. He informed Captain Tshera he would be on his way to the disembarkation bay. *I have never been to any other Kravjin temples outside the Zhanifra galaxy. I have only seen images of the others. I wonder if they are as impressive in person as they are in the recordings.*

He felt the minute vibrations of the ship touching the ground. The bay doors opened, and the crack elite troopers immediately marched down the ramp to secure the ship's perimeter.

"Lord Khanon, the perimeter is secured. There is a convoy of hovercraft identified as Kravjin personnel approaching," Captain Tshera said calmly.

Khanon touched his left wrist. "They are Kravjin masters. Secure ship, code six," he ordered sharply.

"Yes, Lord Khanon, code six is now in effect," she replied.

Khanon strode confidently down the ship's ramp with heavy steps. The heat of the midday sun was bearable enough. His smart fiber vestments automatically shifted to maximize a more moderate internal temperature. The caravan of three long hovercrafts stopped on the other side of a platoon of military soldiers with their weapons at the ready. Clouds of dust flew around each one as they landed on the dusty ground. The three-meter-wide doors slid open with a hiss. Twelve middle-aged men seemed to float out of their crafts. Their bald heads shined in the sun. He noted a crimson tribal design around the crown of their heads. *Must be their unique way, I suppose. I wonder how I would look with no hair…would Adramina like it?* Khanon bowed in respect to his hosts and fellow brothers of the Kravjin Order.

"Welcome to Gerobon, Lord Khanon. I am Volek," said the tall man.

"Greetings, Brother Volek," Khanon said and acknowledged the others.

"Master Abaddon informed us of your visit and the business you must attend to." Volek's yellowish eyes made him appear part reptilian.

"The Saurcine representatives will meet us at Dregesh." Volek seemed a bit distracted as he watched some of Khanon's military guards pointing their weapons upward. A shrill shrieking noise split the air. Khanon couldn't see what was up there yet, but Volek and the others were not reacting one way or another.

"What do you know about this necromonic order?" Khanon asked.

Volek's gaze returned to meet his. "Their weapons will only anger it. We will deal with it," he said sharply. "I will answer your question shortly."

Khanon quickly turned to his guards and barked, "Captain, do not fire your weapons. We will handle that beast." They lowered their weapons.

The twelve Kravjin sorcerers lifted their hands toward the large multi-winged beast that was descending on them. It was very large with a sharp yellow, beak-like face. Its dull black feathers beat in the wind as it came, squawking in threat at them.

"Kush~Dendresh~Nocra~Thakus." The twelve repeated the necromonic invocation. Spheres of multiphasic energy flew from their hands and shot directly at the beast. Its massive frame cast a shadow over half of the ship.

The spheres struck, then engulfed its head. It shrieked in pain. Hot plasma shot out of its mouth blindly into the skies, as it tried to remove the energized sphere with its clawed hands. Two of the guards had to move out of the way as the hot plasma struck where they were standing and sizzled the vegetation instantly. Khanon watched the mighty beast continue to be tormented by the spheres as it flew and disappeared into the far horizon.

"This way, Lord Khanon," Volek said and gestured with an outstretched hand toward the nearest hovercraft.

Khanon felt the heavier than normal gravity of the large planet. It made sense now how naturally the biology of the Thrakonan race was imbued with increased bone and muscle density. *It definitely adds to their fierceness in battle.* The trio of hovercrafts darted through a graveyard of bones bleached by the sun. Up ahead of them, past the sacrificial boneyard, Khanon peered admiringly at the field of massive fifty-meter-tall tanzanite obelisks. They sped upward toward the main temple grounds and stopped at the gated entrance. He followed the lead of Volek and stood on the flat bronze stone surface.

"This way, Lord Khanon." Volek turned and made his way over the bridge. Khanon looked from one side of the bridge to the other, fascinated. Facing the bridge were two large winged and horn-headed dragons, with most of their bodies protruding out of the temple walls. *They look so lifelike.* Their sharp teeth looked as if they could puncture class II ship armor plating. Khanon was impressed. He drank in all the new structures that were not in his own temple. This place was much larger in scale and looked more like a fortress then a temple of worship. The importance of the moment struck him all at once as they entered the Sanctus Oculus. He felt a swell of power flood over him. *Yes, this is more like it.* This was a new layout, much larger than the one back home on Tartarus. It was more like an auditorium. He looked at the large crimson stone atop the statue of Navmolek, god of religion. *He looks just like his statue.*

"Welcome, Lord Khanon," said an old bald man.

"Master Gwog, I am honored to meet you in person. I must say, this is a magnificent temple. I am very impressed with the new architecture," Khanon said sincerely. He caught glimpses of a group of Nossorads hovering above the chamber's upper level seating. Everyone's eyes followed the eternal beings swirling around the top of the Navmolek statue. The Nossorads gently touched the multi-faceted crimson stone and spoke in undistinguishable language. *Their speech sounds a lot like Toxrokk.* Dark speech.

The stone glowed brightly and the space between the statue's hands morphed into multiphasic folded space. Both Khanon and Master Gwog took several steps back. A beautiful woman, in regal blue garments, emerged from the vortex. Her luminescent blue eyes were in sharp contrast to the onyx background. Behind her were twenty-one more women, dressed in similar vestments. They stood in groups of three near the statue.

"I am Rishna Atharva, Queen Mother of the Order of Saurcine, daughter of Lord Saurcine." Her silver hair shimmered in the lights of the crystalline domed ceiling.

"Greetings, Queen Mother. I am Master Gwog, elder of the temple Dregesh." Gwog nodded, then bowed.

"I am here as commanded by Master Navmolek. I am to make a blood pact with Lord Khanon," she said and turned to gaze deeply into Khanon's eyes.

"I am Lord Khanon. It is a pleasure to meet you Queen Mother." His voice wavered with uncertainty. He had never met such a high-ranking woman in the necromonic disciplines before. Khanon felt another presence emerging from the dark vortex. *Navmolek.* He looked much different than when Khanon saw him in Creminmorta. Navmolek emerged from the vortex and floated just above the bronze floor. His appearance was that of a glimmering gem in the sunlight. His face glowed with the radiance of omnipotence. His long hair was made of gold, and his eyes were like blue sapphires. He was huge with a stature over four meters in height.

"I am here to honor you most highly with my presence and to bestow you, my loyal subjects, with the desires of your hearts. You deserve power, riches, glory, and immortality. And by the power of my arm I will bestow upon your inheritance." His booming voice shook the ground slightly. Khanon and the others bowed low to the ground.

"Rise, my children," Navmolek commanded. "Henceforth, your wives and daughters will become members of the Saurcine Order. As of today, you will return to your respective regions of space and begin to build Amphosars and new Kravjin temples. Each will have its own Dragon stone. I see all."

All eyes darted behind the shimmering being as muscular bipedal creatures emerged from the multiphasic portal, pushing large metal platforms filled with precious gems and metals. They ignored the corporeal beings in the chamber, intent on doing their master's will. *There is enough to buy whole planets. My master is rich indeed.* Khanon's eyes feasted on the spectacle of wealth.

"After you take the blood oath between your Orders, you, Khanon, will travel to Fiero Prime with some of these daughters and begin building my temples." Navmolek took a step toward Khanon, who trembled fearfully, wondering what would come next.

"You will send for your wife Adramina. She will conceive twins, but one will be given as an offering for a Krevomax bloodline. My stone is in place already. It needs to be activated by the life force in the blood. You know what must done." His cold, harsh tone bit into Khanon's soul. But before he could protest this horrific command, Navmolek outstretched his hands over them and sent red and blue energy streams of pure necromonic energy streaking over the assembly. Everyone was enraptured by the energy's power and did not notice that Navmolek had vanished along with the strange bipedal creatures.

The multiphasic portal shrunk down in size, but was still large enough for Rishna to leave. "Lord Khanon, Sisters Yatta, Hulan, Drenda, Wue, and Synar will travel with you to assist in the building of the Amphosar on Fiero Prime." Rishna's voice was soft yet firm. Khanon turned to her and saw the five women take a step toward him. They nodded their heads. He knew what he had to do instantly. He removed a blade from his waist and slit his right palm. He handed it to Rishna, who took it and quickly did the same. She handed the blade back to him.

"I pledge the Chomtheke oath between my bloodline and the Kravjin Order to bind with the Saurcine Order for all eternity," Khanon said loudly.

Rishna proclaimed the same, after which they both gripped each other's blood-soaked hands. As their palms met, an energy ball of red and purple engulfed their hands, then vanished.

"I am looking forward to meeting your wife, Adramina," Rishna said with a grin.

"Yes, she will be pleased to know she was chosen to begin the Krevomax bloodlines." Khanon's heart filled with pride at the thought of the power and riches he was gaining. He set aside the more brutal thought of the sacrifice of a child as greed of the coming power overtook him. *More importantly, it will give me some protection from the higher ranks of the Krauvanok Alliance and Kravjin Order.* His muse was interrupted by Rishna, who handed him a small crystalline ruby box.

"Take care of that box. It contains special discs to be used by your wife. My daughters will show her how to use them." Rishna's pinned-up silver hair shined as if it was made of fine silk. He took the box and held it tightly.

"Lords, these Saurcine will travel back with you to begin the building projects as instructed by Navmolek." Rishna turned to the five that stood near Khanon. "As soon as Lord Khanon activates the crimson stone, you will make contact and report to me immediately, as previously instructed." Rishna's youthful skin made her appear much younger than she truly was.

"Yes, Queen Mother," they said in unison and bowed low.

"Until the next time we meet, Lords," Rishna said, nodded her head, and entered the onyx vortex. A moment later it vanished.

Khanon moved closer to the statue and felt his stamina weaken as the necronos essence in his DNA and blood began to be absorbed into the crimson stone. He stared at the glowing stone, then moved farther away. He immediately felt the reverse take place; energy rushed through him. *Interesting, the closer I got to the crimson stone the weaker I became. But the farther I stood from it the more strength I gained. Strange, I don't understand how that works, but at least I know the basics.*

Now it was time to go back to Fiero Prime. *Adramina. Surprise, surprise, you will have another son, this one for the Krevomax bloodlines.* He grinned widely.

Back aboard his battle cruiser, the *Aurgog*, Khanon sat in his plush chair facing his desk. He was preparing to interview the Saurcine aboard his ship to learn more about them. But more importantly about Avisha and what he had seen in Creminmorta. He needed answers and had nothing to lose. Khanon placed the Ambatanok sacred tome, written by the hand of the Lady of Light, Rishna Atharva, on the top of his desk and opened to read the middle of the book. He knew that this tome, which was also called the *Wisdom of Light*, would give him the answers he sought.

The words popped off the page as if they were coming up to meet him. *The vision of things to come, the book of Emosheb.* The prophecies were of special interest to him now more than ever.

Emosheb 36 ω 4

The covenant between the noble houses will be bound by the daughters of the prince of the Barracura Abyss.

Emosheb 60 ω 6

The daughters of the Tisrad Dragon shall bring forth the Krevomax.

Emosheb 77 ω 6

From the sacred wombs of the sacrificed will the Tisrad Dragon's messiah arise.

Emosheb 85 ω 6

The daughters of Saurcine will cast their shadow across the Quintástraya.

He closed the tome with a thud. "They will establish a new holy order of prophetesses and spread the ways of Saurcine to all civilizations in the Quintástraya, and so the prophecy unfolds."

Khanon's solemn tone reflected the shocking realization that he would most likely have to move his family to Fiero Prime and call it home for the foreseeable future.

He swiveled his chair around and looked out at the outer perimeter of the Bisgabeth neutral zone. "Yes, we were like gods once." He smiled at the rich thought. Satisfaction bubbled up in his spirit. "And now, from my bloodline will come one like a god." He laughed aloud at the thought of having the Tisrad Dragon's messiah son. It would bring the Mantis Alliance, his sworn enemies, to ashes. *I will crush them without mercy.*

He stared out of the viewport and visualized his power growing to match the unimaginably vast power of the Bisgabeth. He stood up and headed to the meeting with the Saurcine.

Chapter Fifteen

LEGACY

Fay stood near the edge of the cave where she had first arrived. She adjusted the collar of her overcoat against the gusts of cold air that chilled her cheekbones. *It's a blessing to know that not all of my relatives perished thirty years ago. Well, I count distant relatives as family anyway. I wonder when they will take us to the next step of repatriation. We all failed to walk through the cleansing stream. That accursed Cymbratar! Why are sisters not able to remove it from us?* She was still nauseous from consuming a very large handful of Victus. The repulsive-looking bluish green leafy substance had failed to remove the Cymbratar from her body. Their other attempts failed, too. *I hope Orisa and Mirinda recover soon.* They were still bed ridden from the cure. But that other woman... Victoria, as soon as she ate the leafy substance, her nose had begun to bleed profusely. *She almost fainted it was so deadly to her, poor thing.* Fay sensed someone approaching.

"Are you feeling better?" asked Fay.

"Yes, much better, thank you. And yourself?" Victoria said in a concerned tone.

"I am okay." Fay's nose wrinkled delicately. "Nasty stuff, that Victus." Fay knew that if her experience was anything to go by, Victoria must be feeling quite ill as well.

"Yes, it was…well rather traumatic." Victoria frowned dismissively. "Guess what I found out?"

"I'm listening," Fay said quietly.

"Once we rid ourselves of the Cymbratar and walk through the cleansing stream, we will be given resources to start a new life. We can adopt children and be given new names and start new lineages, some of whom were lost during the attack."

"The way you say that it makes it sound as if it is a bad prospect, Victoria." Fay gazed into Victoria's deep blue eyes. She couldn't tell how the sister really felt. *Wow, this sister is good. No wonder she got in so deep with the Overseers.*

"Since the cures didn't work, we are to leave Ramah and not return under any circumstances," Victoria solemnly said. It was now clear that her heart wanted something else entirely.

"Are you sure about that? Who told you that?" Fay felt agitation rise and couldn't hide her skepticism.

"Timnah," Victoria said loudly, with some frustration.

"Oh, Mirinda and Orisa have woken up. They seem to be in good spirits. They asked for you," Victoria said.

"Excuse me, Victoria," Fay said, feeling a lightness lift her spirits. "I am going to go and see them!" She turned and left Victoria out in the waning daylight.

Victoria blinked as small droplets of rain splashed her warm cheeks. *Those three sisters must have gone through many trying times, and most likely sacrificed for one another. I don't care; I will never forget you my dear beloved friend, Balese. I promise you, I will name the first girl I give birth to your real name, Mila. You finished well, my friend. I will see you one day in Gahanna El.* She shoved her hands into the plush pockets of her cloak.

Splashed across the horizon were a vast number of Mantis Alliance military ships. "The Marium Kahnet are now members of the Grand Assembly." She shook her head in awe at the stunning importance of this. *How did this happen? When I left long ago, most of Ramah was laid waste. The buildings and other complexes were completely destroyed. Along with my family.* Her eyes filled with tears. *I will press on and be victorious, Abba El willing.*

Just then, a powerful vision opened up in front of her eyes. "Not again," Victoria said.

Suddenly, she found herself standing atop a large hill, surrounded by petrified trees. A stone altar rose up from a mound in the center of the dusty barren surface. It came to rest just several short meters in front of her. Twelve-winged serpent beings emanating sulfurous curls of smoke all around descended like striking predators on either side of the rubescent oblong stone altar. The ominous serpent apparitions reformed themselves into humanoid forms. These tall, powerful beings were cloaked in ceremonial robes and stood motionless. She suddenly recognized them as the Tisrak.

Her body was picked up and thrust to the side of the altar. She felt paralyzed and couldn't even struggle to leave. The hoods of the robes hid the others' identities from her, but she looked from one face to the other nonetheless. She heard a serpentine whisper and shivered. "You have the essence of necronos. It calls for sacrifice." She blocked the strong influence the best she could. She glanced down at her own garments and was not surprised that she too wore similar ceremonial robes. "What is going on? I don't want to be here." She could sense her mouth moving, but no sounds came out. A wave of cold descended upon her and she felt a strong presence above her. She looked straight up at the crimson stone. It transformed into the single eye of the Tisrad Dragon. She immediately recalled, from reading the necromonic tome, that it was one of the five spirits of the Tisrad Dragon, called Spirradeus. This one was Navmolek, god of religion.

"With the Ruaphesh blade, you will make a holy sacrifice to me," a powerful voice thundered from within the eye. The power of it shook her bones.

In that instant, a weighty object appeared in Victoria's right hand. She clutched it—it was a holy blade that had been forged in the lake of sacred blood, deep in the realm of Hemosongra. As she marveled at its dark beauty, it came alive and began to speak. *I don't know what it's saying, but I know it is dark speech.* The mysterious language was used in the five realms of Creminmorta. She sensed the blade's overwhelming thirst for blood.

Just then, a small human female child appeared on the altar. Her young flesh was olive, her tiny head thick with dark, silky hair. Her eyes were tightly shut, and tears were streaming down her rosy plump cheeks. *Strange, I can't hear her.* Seeming far from herself, she considered the soundless phenomena, then sharply looked at the holy blade of Ruaphesh that was writhing in her hand. "Sacrifice her to me and become my daughter, and you will live forever with power and influence," the slithering voice commanded.

"No!" Victoria screamed as loud as she could. She clawed at her right hand, prying the blade out of her white-knuckled grip. She reared back and, with all of her will, pulled herself out of the trance.

"Victoria…Victoria, it's all right, it's me, Timnah." The elder pulled Victoria away the high cliff's edge. Unresisting, she allowed Timnah to turn her and peer deeply into her blue eyes with compassion.

"Why is this happening to me?" Victoria said with shock and trauma wrestling in her spirit.

"Not only you, but the others as well, Fay, Mirinda, and Orisa," Timnah said with concern. "It will be all right, you will see. Abba El is in charge." She seemed a strong tower in that moment and Victoria knew that there would be powerful help with the sisterhood.

Jazrene and Karina made their way down the brightly lit hallway and entered a warmly decorated room. Fay, Mirinda, Orisa, and Victoria stood up from their lounge chairs and nodded their heads. "Mother Vallo," they said and waited, looking inquiringly at the other woman they did not yet know.

"I am glad to see you are doing much better my daughters. This is Hadassah Karina Calero," Jazrene said, beaming at all of them.

"Hadassah Calero, it is a pleasure meeting you," said Victoria for the group. The others nodded their agreement with smiles.

"Please be seated." Jazrene's genial and calm demeanor helped ease the sister's apprehensions. "Again, I want to apologize to each one of you for the pain and discomfort you endured after you consumed the altered Victus substance. I thought it would purge your bodies of the necronos essence. Don't lose hope. There is a way, Moshiach will at the right time reveal what must be done in order for you to have your new lives and start your families." Jazrene's strong faith was a welcome refuge for them all in this difficult engrafting into the sisterhood.

"So, it's true you want us to marry and bear children?" Victoria stated boldly.

"Not only that but take names of the families that were cut off during the Hoshkadish. All of your family's bloodlines are still with us today and are in no danger of dying out. So yes, you will marry, adopt, and bear children." Jazrene's firm tone was filled with authority.

"I don't know any men here. How will the groom accept a surname other than his own?" Fay asked the question they all needed an answer for.

"There are many honorable families whose sons have agreed to restore the family lineages that were cut off. You will meet them after you adopt your children," Jazrene said, then paused, waiting for the sisters to completely comprehend what she was saying. "They are associated with the Veth'Shars brotherhood." Jazrene began to pace, stopping in front of them one by one. She looked into their unnaturally blue eyes. "You will be given a substantial dowry to begin your new life after you are wed… And then you will leave Ramah. You, yourselves, will not return until one generation has passed. Do you understand?" Jazrene needed them to accept and partner with the plan that would help reset the history for them all. *Why do I have to leave now, Abba El? Look at these wonderful women that you are restoring.*

"Yes, I understand, Mother Vallo," Orisa said meekly.

"Yes." Mirinda nodded her head.

Victoria glanced over to Hadassah Calero, then back to Mother Vallo. "Of course, I will do what is required of me. But, how exactly am I going to accomplish this while I have this substance in my body? Isn't there danger to my family if it is not removed?" Victoria said calmly, with a hint of a frown on her face.

Jazrene nodded her acknowledgment of this but looked to Fay before answering. "Yes, I will do as you ask, but my question is the same as Victoria's." Her soft tone matched her demeanor, acceptance, and resignation.

"It's a valid question. If you decide to move on without going through the cleansing stream, the spiritual forces will haunt you for the rest of your natural lives. Not only that—it might endanger your families." Jazrene sensed an ugly hopelessness overtake them.

"Stop, it is not hopeless. I know a thing or two about bleakness and despair, my dear ones. Don't allow it to overtake you." She waited for them all to look at her before continuing. "Now then, there is a solution. I strongly believe the answer will come very soon. I can discern in the spirit that you will not live here too much longer."

Jazrene gazed at each of the sisters. "A more relevant question is: what will you do when the opportunity presents itself? Will you take the challenge, or will you leave with haunting dreams and visions? The choice will be yours." Her questions and statements were both a challenge and an encouragement to strive to enter rest. She reached out and touched Victoria's left hand. "Do not be afraid, we will give you all the support you need to accomplish what seems impossible. You, my dear ones, are not alone anymore. We are your family. We are sisters in the beloved." Jazrene then gazed deeply into each of their eyes with an endearing look of trust and hope she freely gave to them.

"Now, tell us about your dreams and visions as best as you can recall," Jazrene said seeing the shift to hope that she was waiting for.

Karina pulled a thin data disc from her vestments and held it in the palm of her right hand. She tapped the center with her left index finger. "Ready to record, Mother Vallo." Karina's silver eyes glistened like sparkling gems in the bright light.

The meeting would go on far into the night with a sense of community and courage that the four sisters had not experienced in a while.

Chapter Sixteen

LINEAGES

Through the window, the fading night sky announced another new day. Jazrene turned with a big welcoming smile on her face to greet her daughter. "Good morning, Minna. It is a blessed day indeed." She lightly embraced her.

"Good morning, Mom." Rediquin held on tight and took in the precious moments as if it would make up for a lifetime of not having them.

"I see you are an early riser like me." Jazrene grinned, then noticed something different about her daughter.

"What is it?" Minna asked, smiling.

"Your face has a glow. It's Solek… isn't it?" Jazrene waggled her eyebrows, teasing.

She blushed. "I don't know him very well. But I didn't expect this to happen to me. I have to admit I'm starting to have feelings for him." Jazrene could see the open doors of her heart ready for the promise of love to enter and bring complete restoration.

"He is a faithful man. He could not come from a more honorable lineage. I would be blessed to have him as my son in-law," Jazrene said.

"Solek said he met you and that he knows I'm your daughter… Wait, what…son in-law?" she blurted out in shock.

"The shadow of your past life will fade like the night sky as the dawn's light appears." Jazrene pointed out the window as the dawn's early light pierced the night sky. "Like the rays of a new day, so will your new life's journey begin. You will join the sisterhood and continue our family's heritage." Her words came straight from Moshiach. Minna didn't know it, but she was prophesying her future.

She did not rebuff her mother's statement. "You will be glad to hear that Solek agreed with you and that I would be a good fit for the Semdressa." Maybe I could be useful there?" Minna said with a thread of hope in her voice.

"Yes, that makes me so happy." A sense of peace that her daughter would walk the path Abba El had chosen washed over her. "I will speak with the Semdressa leader about your interest." Jazrene turned toward her and cupped her shoulders. "We will prepare a place for you to live." She could see the uncertainty on Minna's face. "I wish we had more time together this morning, but I have urgent matters to attend to. But first, let me take you to the dining hall so you can eat. I have arranged for Sister Wue to accompany you to the cleansing chambers to undergo Konia Kofesh. This will remove all chains that bind your mind and heart and the cloud of uncertainty from your life. But first things first, let's go." Jazrene took hold of Minna's hand and reveled in the satisfaction of having her daughter near. *Abba El restores what he did not take away. Thank you.* Her spirit was dancing with joy.

"Mother, I'm struggling with you leaving me, I'll be alone again. And, another thing… I am having strange visions of blood and sacrifices. I know it has to do with the Cymbratar I consumed. Actually, the voices I hear say so. Is there be a way to remove the Cymbratar from me?" Minna's heartbroken tone matched her tear-glistened eyes.

"I know about the dreams and visions and had hoped you would be spared. But like the other sisters who consumed that substance, you are also suffering. Minna, as the sun rises, so also will the solution to cleanse yourself of the necronos essence for good." Jazrene reached out and held her hand bracingly. "And you will not be alone. Timnah and the other elders have given me their word, you are a daughter to them." Jazrene kissed Minna's forehead, released her hand, and headed out to attend her duties.

Jazrene stood in the sanctuary hall. She looked through the large windows at the brilliant orange-hued rays of sunshine that washed over the snow-covered mountaintops. It was clearly a new time for them all, but especially for her. She quietly turned to the four newly appointed Abesses. Sisters Karina and Timnah were also in the room, making their prayers and supplications known.

One by one, they stood up. Jazrene led them across the copper stone floor and through the open bronze gates. Sisters Adah, Janan, Kalani, Wen, Karina, and Timnah maintained a close distance as they followed her across the skyway to the complexes built into the mountain. *The time of my departure is near.* She looked down at the fruitful grounds of the Monastarium. Her heart was filled with satisfaction. *Meshua, your love casts out any fear of death, for my victory is in you.* Her eyes followed a group of sisters at the edge of the fruit orchards. A moment later an eruption of hundreds of multicolored winged birds flew upwards. The wings beating the air were exactly how her heart felt, fluttering in joy.

My last season. I have come full circle; the fruit of my life is ripe for the harvesting. She stopped smiling as she imagined her daughter's face. *My sweet Minna, I love you to the ends of all eternity. I am sorry to have to leave you so soon. Take heart knowing you have many sisters, my beloved daughter.* Her steps slowed. She paused then pivoted around. It was time.

"The news you have heard is true. One of my daughters survived the day of Hoshkadish. She has returned. Her name is Minna." The sisters standing before her looked pleased. She could see no division amongst them at this revelation. "I ask that you make a place for her in honor of my service to Abba El and HIS Messiah." She noticed Timnah looked puzzled. It took a second or two for the others to understand her unusual statement. Jazrene waited, then continued in a tone they had rarely heard from her. "I have been informed by the Malakphos that I will shortly depart at the conclusion of the Barayalad tomorrow." The serenity in her voice made it clear she had accepted her fate with bravery and faith.

"Blessed is Abba El in the highest, for HE is faithful," the sisters said in unison.

She saw tears rise in the eyes of both Timnah and Karina. "It is well and in Abba El's timing, my dear friends. Now then, Timnah, Minna said that she is interested in joining the Semdressa. She is also a perfect candidate for the Criss Lumbra. In either case, once I depart she will be in your care." Her voice held a certainty that was reassuring, while at the same time compassionate at this passing of the torch.

Timnah stepped forward and kissed Jazrene's hand. "I am both honored and delighted without measure, Mother. I ask for your Ruahnaush blessing," she said.

Jazrene's face glowed with radiance. "Yes, in the name of Meshua, she will be a daughter and sister to you with the blessing of Patriarch Modroya. She is after all a daughter of Sarai." She reached out and squeezed Timnah's hand before embracing her.

"She will be as you have spoken to me, as my own daughter, Mother Vallo." Timnah crossed her hands over her chest and bowed.

"Mother Vallo, I see Minna's life's path. Although different from your own, she will be blessed nonetheless." Sister Karina's words resonated in Jazrene's spirit. The others nodded in agreement.

"Our spirits confirm this to be true," said Abess Adah.

You said that I was special. Jazrene recalled Minna's words through her broken sobs the other day. *Minna, my beloved daughter, you are special indeed.* She peered through the veil of prophecy.

"Sisters." She didn't wait for a response but turned and led the way once again. All the while she was mulling over how she'd broached the subject of her departure with Minna the other night. *I am sure she will not accept my leaving so soon no matter what I say. She is so strong-willed, and stubborn…Minna is definitely her mother's daughter.* She laughed to herself.

A familiar cool air filled the landing as they exited the skyway. Just ahead was a new MC56 multipurpose mechanoid that was polishing the stone floor. It ceased when it detected their presence.

"Good morning sisters, I am TR387." Its warm, monotone voice suited its golden-plated frame.

"Good morning, TR387. How many are you?" Vallo asked.

"We number five, Mother Vallo," it replied.

"You may carry on with your work, TR387." *Well that's new, I am so grateful for so much more help.* They stepped around the grounds maintenance droid and within a few short moments reached their destination. Just ahead was a large opening in the mountainside with blending technology that hid its presence.

"Tell no one of this access," Jazrene said firmly, looking at each of them. The sisters agreed with a nod. She placed her hand on the stone wall. "Mesh Thula." Her authoritative tone was clearly more than just a mortal position. It resonated in the spirit realm as well. A door immediately opened, and she led the way down a spiral sloping walkway of what seemed to be a large silo with a tall stone pillar in the center.

The ancient Reshmek and prophecies written in code on the

pillar had been carved into its surface. Soon they reached the base. "Gematah," she said and touched a sequence of Reshmek letters on a circular panel imbedded in the pillar. Momentarily, a weighty stone door slid into the wall of the cave. A cool rush of ionized air wafted over them. They breathed deeply, but a sense of anticipation filled the atmosphere.

"Come." Jazrene took a deep breath. *"I am here,"* said the well-loved voice of her beloved Lord. The sound of rushing water from the Ruak'Tabar multidimensional cleansing waterfall grew louder as they walked around the curvature of the cave. Just ahead on a stone platform were the lifeless bodies of the rogue sisters Nia and Taona Xongol.

Jazrene walked around the platform, then circled each of the corpses as if inspecting their vestments. She stopped between their heads. "Meshua Adda Mekka," she said with her hand over each of their faces. A powerful sense that she was rising off the floor moved her to step back. *Abba El, thank you.* She looked at each of the glowing faces of the sisters. "Abesses, now."

Indescribable peace straight from Bayit El flooded the platform. The four separated and moved to the head and foot of the prone bodies. The sound of rushing waters grew louder, then louder still. *That is a sign of the sister's rebirth. Only the Pheragim, the gatekeepers of the realm of Bayit El, control the flow of the Ruak'Tabar.* Jazrene began to worship, completely enraptured. The presence of Moshiach was so strong that Sisters Karina and Timnah were on their knees with their heads bowed.

The Abesses moved from Nia and Taona's heads to their sides.

Each took hold of their hands and with loud voices uttered a single command: "Lakum Zoe!" The roof of the cave seemed to roll back as Bayit El broke into the room. A light so bright with a spectrum of color not seen in the natural enveloped the Abesses and the prone sisters.

The breath of life hit Nia and Taona at the same time and they opened their eyes. Multi-dimensional harmonies of sound from the host of Bayit El broke into their midst, and they shouted with joy as Nia and Taona sat up.

"Jazrene, daughter of Abba El. Your departure is at hand." The sudden voice felt like a current of electricity on the top of Jazrene's head. "Tomorrow you shall leave your temporary vessel and walk in Gannah El, paradise, with me." The omniscient voice of the Most High God boomed loudly in the cave. Jazrene opened her eyes and looked around to see the others staring at her wide-eyed.

"Do as you have ordained for my life. For you hold my first breath and my last." She lifted her arms with palms out and shouted with joy. "I praise you in Meshua's name." She smiled widely.

"Behold the sign of my departure." Jazrene gestured to Nia and Taona, who were now standing looking bewildered and overwhelmed at the same time. She smiled, then immediately moved toward them and welcomed them home.

"Don't do be afraid. I am Mother Vallo. You are on Ramah." Her firm, warm voice seemed to calm their anxiety.

"How is this possible? I remember that we were dying of radiation…" Taona's voice trembled with uncertainty.

"You are correct… You died several days ago. You were then brought to us. These sisters were used by Meshua to bring you back to begin a new life." Both Nia and Taona wore a twin look of remorse. It moved Jazrene deeply to see this genuine repentance.

"Why us?" Nia said with a frown. "Do you know what happened on Letalis? Are you aware of what we did?"

"You have been brought back by the hand of Abba El to start a new life and family. If it was not to be, HE would have not allowed it. We do not question HIS motives. We are only to obey. For those who turn to HIS immeasurable grace will find peace." She smiled gently.

"Family?" Taona looked puzzled.

Jazrene's welcoming gaze embraced them. Her wholehearted acceptance of them seemed to be just the reassurance they needed. "Please follow me, sisters." She was pleased to see their nods of acceptance. They followed her to a stone bridge near the Ruak'Tabar. The supernatural waterfall had returned to its gently flowing state. "Daughters, you have been entrusted to continue bloodlines that were lost during the Kravjin attack, which is commemorated as the Hoshkadish. Just as you have been resurrected, so will a lost family lineage be restored. You will have new names as recorded in the appropriate databases, and in due time you will have newly adopted children. You will no longer be known as Loreen Lesedi or Nia Xongol. Nor will you, Taona Xongol, have the name Dilia Tarsus."

They stared at her with wide eyes, clearly shocked that she knew their true identities.

"Tell me, are you prepared to start your new lives and restore your family's lineages?" Jazrene asked, looking deeply into their eyes.

"Yes," they said in unison.

"I will do whatever you ask of me, Mother Vallo," said Nia, looking greatly humbled. Taona's eyes were filled with tears as she nodded wordlessly. It was enough.

"Come then." They crossed the bridge.

"Please stand on the other side of those two pillars and face me." Jazrene gestured to the two massive stone pillars where the purifying waterfall would appear. "This is now the age of HIS grace. For the Mantis Messiah has successfully fulfilled all that was required of him on Shalem, as it is written of HIM throughout the Kodashah and the book of Yaqal. Glory to Abba El in the highest and to HIS Messiah. Now there is a new covenant between Abba El and the fallen creation known as Konia Berit. One that we urge you to receive in your hearts and minds." She moved closer to them. "Search with your hearts. Do you believe that Meshua has come and has fulfilled all that is required for redemption of your souls?" She waited silently, feeling the heavy presence of Moshiach fall on the two.

"Yes, I believe that Meshua is Abba El's Messiah and that HE redeemed my soul." Taona yawned several times and then tears began to streak down her face. "I feel HIS great love for me," Taona choked out between sobs.

"Receive HIM, my dear daughter." Jazrene's voice was filled with the same love. She looked at Nia, who was visibly struggling. She reached out with her spiritual eyes, searching for the problem. In the spirit she saw Nia trying to break down a dark stone wall with her bare hands.

"I want to, but I don't feel worthy," stammered Nia. "I have caused so much harm and destruction. Abba El won't accept me. How could HE love me after what I have done?" She burst into tears. Her face twisted with grief and the torment of regret.

Jazrene immediately moved into action, extending her hand. "Nia, in the power of Moshiach and in the name of Meshua I break off the chains of shame, guilt, and regret. I release you from the torment of your past in the power of Meshua's name." Her voice rang with authority, and in the spirit, she saw the wall crumble to dust and blow away. Nia began to cough hard and her eyes watered. She bent over and braced her arms on her thighs, catching her breath. Within a few short moments, she quieted and rose from her bent position. "I receive Meshua as my savior and LORD," Nia shouted, wiping her tears on her sleeves.

"Now daughters, you must walk through the Ruak'Tabar to remove all DNA alterations by the necronos essence and as a step of your newfound faith. Don't be afraid, the dark essence was removed by the same radiation that killed you… Now." Jazrene clapped her hands three times and walked to the other side of the stone pillars. The iridescent stream of water with miniature bursts of glimmering gold began to fall between the two pillars. All eyes rose to the cavern's ceiling, from where the water had emerged. The Ruak'Tabar was beautiful to behold. The soothing sounds of the stream of water filled the cave like musical notes.

"Walk through the water and come to me," Jazrene said loudly, in awe at the work of restoration. The Ruak'Tabar glowed brightly as they stepped through the multidimensional cleansing stream. All vestiges of altered DNA were removed. Only their youthful appearance remained. The unrelenting driving force for retribution and violence had been forever washed away.

"Welcome home, daughters of Abba El." Jazrene warmly embraced them. "Now, take the Shabauh Oath. Do you remember it?"

They nodded yes.

"I pledge my life as a vessel of light as I step through the veil of divine purpose. I am cleansed in purity. My head is adorned with humility. The ways of the Marium Kahnet are my life, my heart and my soul belong to Abba El, and in HIS Messiah is my salvation." Taona's voice was filled with contentment and peace.

"As a member of the Marium Kahnet, I bestow upon you this symbol of your Shabauh oath." Jazrene extended her right hand with the palm open. In her hand was a Semsa ring with a glittering brilliant stone. Taona took the ring and slid it on her finger.

"From now on, your name is Cara Vedagesh," Jazrene said. Taona's lips silently repeated the name.

"Now your turn." Jazrene looked into Nia's clear-eyed gaze. The sister repeated the sacred Oath and accepted her ring.

"Your name is Shamara Ronen. These are you new names. Both they and your new DNA are recorded in the core systems of the Ramah government and our data lineages records, a copy of which will be sent to Hagar Pathar, the galactic library on Mantacletos. Sometime in the next few days, you each will adopt your new families. You will be given sufficient resources to start a new life on a planet of your choosing. We strongly encourage you not to contact the other sisters once you start your new lives away from Ramah. For the sake of your family and for their bright future, you must leave behind your past to ensure a worthy legacy for your family's lineage." She waited for Cara and Shamara to accept. They did with a nod.

"Yes, Mother, I will do as you have asked," Shamara said and looked at Cara. "I will miss you, my beloved friend Cara." Shamara embraced her for what they both knew would be the last time. They kissed each other's cheeks.

"Now then, Cara and Shamara, the old has been washed away. Do not mention this holy place to anyone. Please follow your elders. They will assist you in every step of acclimating to your new life. She dismissed them with a nod. The bowed low and left with their escorts. *It is a mystery how they all forget that this place exists. I don't know how that happens, maybe Moshiach removes that memory…who knows for sure?* Jazrene mused, watching them leave the cave.

She turned toward Sister Karina, who was smiling with deep satisfaction. "The Ruak'Tabar of restoration and new beginning is for those whom Moshiach leads." She removed her data pad from her vestment and softly recited the names on the list.

```
Alias Name:                    New Birth Name:

Nia Xongol                     Shamara Ronen
```

Taona Xongol	Cara Vedagesh
Orisa Sotasen	Allete Dubane
Fay Sinadendra	Rayna Bantu
Mirinda Kuffa	Xennette Tansu
Victoria Maja	Sabrina Cento

"Activate new user," Jazrene spoke into the device. "Karina, place your hand on the surface." The sister's hand was immediately engulfed in a blue light. "Take it…it's now yours to use for future needs," Jazrene said, graciously handing the device to her.

"Karina, as you know, the four sisters that returned are not able to proceed with this part of their new life. The Cymbratar they consumed can only be removed by exposure to the multiphasic Cremindraux radiation."

Karina frowned. "But it caused the deaths of those two. How can it be done without causing their deaths?"

"They would have to be exposed on a much smaller amount with it controlled somehow," Jazrene said then immediately turned to the only one who had all the answers. "Moshiach, I pray you show us the way to their freedom." She opened her spirit and listened to see if an answer would be forthcoming.

"I hear in the spirit, in the Rakia Expanse you will find the answer," Karina said softly.

"Yes, their journey is not finished. I hear the spirit saying they will join the Semdressa and be given an opportunity to remove the necronos essence from their bodies…. They all will decide shortly." Jazrene's measured prophetic utterance matched her faraway gaze. "The necronos essence within the eye stone of the Tisrad Dragon is the source from which the dreams and visions emanate. It is also the key to their freedom. They must take hold of it." Jazrene reached out with her hand as if grabbing it for them. She took in a large breath and released it after she made the pronouncement.

There was silence for a moment. Jazrene looked deeply into Karina's silver eyes "I could not see or hear what the outcome would be if they take this journey." Her eyes pleaded for the answer.

"I will make sure they will be given all the tools and assistance necessary to accomplish their goals. It will also be an opportunity to destroy that eye stone," Karina firmly said with authority and purpose.

"The crimson stone is in the Rakia Expanse. It is a very dangerous region of lawless space. Thankfully those selected as Criss Lumbra among the Semdressa are ready to be deployed." Jazrene pondered those ready to fight against this new threat.

"Isn't it interesting that their eyes and hair color changed after they consumed the altered Victus substance?" Karina's question was more of a statement of fact. "Fascinating."

"And how many of our daughters will lose their lives fighting against this threat?" Jazrene frowned, then took Karina's hand. "I am so sorry that I won't be here to confront this new threat and burden with you and my other daughters." She swallowed hard and her eyes moistened with tears.

A single tear ran down Karina's cheek. "I will miss you, Mother. You've been such an inspiration to me and the others. We owe you so much." She seemed like she was choking back tears. She lifted her hand to her quivering lips and took a deep, shaky breath, quelling the tide.

"It is time for my departure and Moshiach has informed me that all will continue to unfold as it is written… Ultimate victory is ours already, my beloved daughter," Jazrene said and gave Karina a warm embrace. "My daughter Minna, she will continue on her journey." She paused for a moment and smiled secretively.

"What is it?' Karina asked.

"I will be a grandmother. Minna will marry and have many children," Jazrene said with a wide grin at this revelation.

"Very well, Mother Vallo. Spend some time with Minna before you leave." Karina kissed Jazrene on her cheeks and wiped the tears from her eyes with the sleeves of her robe. In peace, the legend of the Marium Kahnet left the cave, although she never saw herself that way.

Chapter Seventeen

REBIRTH

The orange hue of dawn's early light covered the snowcapped mountains. *I truly enjoy sunrise. Will Bayit El look like this…? So beautiful.* Hearing a rustle, Jazrene turned to the plush overstuffed sofa across the room, where Minna was just waking.

"Good morning, Mother." Minna's voice was alert.

"Good morning, my dear." She turned and began her morning Kohyim routine; her heart was blessed as she watched her lithe daughter mirror her movements. "You haven't forgotten," she said between measured breaths.

"I see some differences in how I have been doing them." Minna's voice was filled with energy.

Outside the window, vast numbers of ships filled the sky around the Monastarium, announcing the conclusion of the Barayalad. Jazrene stood silent, watching her daughter finish the routine. She walked over to tightly embrace her and laughed joyfully and looked into her eyes. "Minna, be strong and be at peace." Her voice was imbued with the power of Moshiach. She saw it envelop Minna in bright white light.

Minna swallowed then opened her eyes and said solemnly, "Yes Mother."

"Come now, let us get dressed." Jazrene left to go to her room for the last time. Minna went to the guest room to change clothing.

A short time later Jazrene and Minna stood in the meditation room looking out the window. A knock on the door sounded throughout the residence. "That must be Timnah. She has come to accompany you to the ceremony." Jazrene looked at Minna with a warm grin.

"Sister Timnah, please come in," Jazrene said loudly.

The elder sister walked in. "Good morning, Mother Vallo… Minna." Timnah bowed low to the ground, then kneeled and kissed Jazrene's hand. Her sadness was clear, but Timnah's pure faith was also very evident. "I will miss you. You have blessed me and my family so much." Her voice was thick, but she quickly got her emotions under control once again. "I will watch over your daughter as if she were my own." She repeated the vow she had taken the other day.

"Thank you, Timnah. I love you. You are like a daughter to me." Jazrene opened her arms and Timnah hugged her tightly.

"Go with Timnah, she will look after you," she quietly said to Minna when she pulled away.

"Yes, Mother." Minna embraced her, seeming to not want to let go. She took one last loving gaze into her eyes, kissed her on the cheek, and then gathered her into another tight embrace.

"Minna, it is not forever; I will see you again with our Lord," Jazrene reassured her. She squeezed her one last time and leaned back. Minna smiled at her with tear-brimmed eyes. She nodded her agreement with that, then followed Timnah from the room.

Jazrene lifted her hands into the air and spoke in the spiritual language of Lingue, pronouncing blessings and safety for her daughter and for her future family. The rays of the morning sun accompanied by the chirping of Lumossi songbirds filled her bedroom. With a calm spirit, she walked around her home for the last time and left her quarters.

In contrast to the quietness of her living quarters, the Monastarium was filled with a bevy of activity. She was so happy that the halls echoed praises and songs of hope once more. She met and warmly greeted the elders who were to escort her to the auditorium. As they went along, she acknowledged and gave encouraging words to the sisters of all ages and various positions of office, who lined the hallways and gardens. She enjoyed the warmth of the sun and breathed deeply of the floral scents from the flower petals strewn on the path leading to the auditorium. The silhouettes of Reyna class super fighter carriers and battle cruisers dotted the sky, and the distinct sound of the wake of passing Mantis Alliance military ships streaking above the Monastarium added to the grandeur and importance of the sisterhood's ceremonial ascension as the spiritual leaders of the Marium Kahnet and the end of the Barayalad.

Inside, the auditorium was filled to capacity. Among the attendees were high-ranking officials and dignitaries from among the five galaxies of the Quintástraya. Seated in the center, closest to the platform, were the prophets of Mantis. On either side of the prophets were the Marium Kahnet elders of the Kilodromus, Malgavatta, Praxvarna, Vlberium, and Zhanifra galaxies. Jazrene felt the strong celebratory atmosphere as she walked down the center aisle.

"Congratulations, Mother Vallo," said a young lady dressed in royal robes.

"Princess, may you be blessed with a loving family." Jazrene discerned her heart's desire.

"Thank you." The young lady beamed with hope.

Jazrene's heart quickened with excitement as she met the gazes of the Mantis prophets and Marium Kahnet elders she was passing. Just as she reached the bottom step of the platform, the auditorium's transparent dome fully retracted. A rushing gust of wind billowed her white and silver ceremonial vestments and cooled her pink cheeks as she walked up the steps. She turned and faced the audience that was coming to attention.

"Welcome to our home. We are honored and blessed to have you here with us as we conclude the Barayalad." Her voice, aided by the auditorium's perfect acoustics, was clearly heard by everyone in attendance. She saw Minna seated with Timnah and some of the other elders of Chawah in the upper concourse. Minna nodded and smiled at her.

Jazrene lifted her hands. "We ask Abba El and Meshua to bless this ceremony and those in attendance." Her eyes were drawn to the five Hadassahs in the front row. *How beautiful they look wearing the Kallah veils. They truly are the brides of Meshua, for as many that receive the new covenant are one body.*

"Sisters, please come forward." She took a step back as a stark white, gleaming marble column rose from the platform floor. Atop it were five sparkling rings. Just as they had rehearsed, the five women stood to the left of the marble column. _

"Sister Azinnia, please step forward." Jazrene looked into her silver eyes that so beautifully matched the colors of her holy vestments. Azinnia bowed deeply. "Do you, Azinnia Mannasa, agree to accept the office of Hadassah and uphold the laws and tenets of the way of the prophets and the way of the sisterhood for the rest of your life?" Unlike herself, the new leaders would live well beyond a hundred years.

"Yes, Mother Vallo, I accept the vow. I will live out my life serving Abba El and HIS messiah," Azinnia responded firmly. Her face seemed to glow.

"Then, by the power vested in me, I bestow upon you the office of Hadassah." She picked up one of the rings and placed it on Azinnia's left ring finger. Jazrene stared intensely into her eyes. "Now it is for you to bestow the tiaras of the Office of Modroya for your galaxy. Our master jeweler has the first set completed for your Grand Assembly representatives." She said this for the benefit of the witnesses. "Please take your position, Mother Azinnia."

Azinnia moved to the side near the edge of the platform facing the assembly. It seemed to take such a short time for the sacred oath to be repeated with Sisters Mella, Nomi, Amadi, then finally Karina.

The marble column vanished into the floor of the platform. The five Hadassahs stood an arm's length from each. *Is it my imagination or has the day become much brighter than usual?* Jazrene noticed everything around her had a glow to it.

"Please welcome and honor these new leaders of the Holy Order of the Marium Kahnet." Her voice echoed throughout the auditorium. Her eyes swept toward Minna. *Be brave, my daughter, don't be afraid. Moshiach will guide you to your true destiny.* Minna lifted her hand to her mouth as if she could hear her.

The loud thunderous applause disrupted Jazrene's thoughts. *Am I moving or is it my imagination? No, I am moving.* She looked down and saw thin air between the platform and her feet. *No steps. Am I going?* The applause abruptly ceased, and the auditorium fell into complete silence. Instantly aware what was happening, the five Hadassahs turned to witness Jazrene rising slowly on a transparent gold object that was separating from the platform. Everyone froze and stood, staring.

Jazrene's heart began pounding. She looked up, unsure of what would happen next. Thick golden rings emitting pulses of light flashed around her feet. She couldn't see the bottom of her dress. Just then, a wave of supernatural power penetrated everyone in the large auditorium. Some fell to their knees under its strength. A white sphere appeared above her head and wrapped her completely in an intense blinding light. Everyone shielded their eyes, for it was too bright for them to look at.

The white sphere lifted and moved to her back, making Jazrene glow brightly. Her silver eyes caught and held Minna's. At her back the globe of light continued to expand over a large area. She vaguely noted the gasps of wonder filling the air, as yet another multidimensional force of energy washed over the crowd. Jazrene turned as she saw what everyone else saw. A glittering cityscape made of brilliant jewels in a dimension of light that no physical eye had ever seen appeared within the large white sphere. The perfect atmosphere of the supernatural city streamed into the auditorium—all were captivated by its beauty.

A white cloud formed in front of her. A moment later the cloud moved back, revealing two Watchers. Just behind them were her husband, children, and a multitude of others.

"Jazrene Vallo, come forth and enter Gahanna El," said a loud clarion voice. Without hesitation, Jazrene bowed low then gracefully walked between the Watchers and towards her family.

Then one who shined like a sun in its strength appeared above the Watchers. "Mothers of the Marium Kahnet, and those gathered here, do not fear; I give you my peace." The powerful voice caused the entire crowd to kneel and reverently bow before Meshua.

Then, suddenly, HE vanished and the portal to Gahenna El closed.

One at a time, the Hadassahs rose. There was a long silence as the magnitude of what they'd just witnessed settled in their hearts.

Yaqal 101

The radiance of HIS glory parts the dark clouds of despair; under HIS wings is safety. He redeems the humble with hope and to the faithful eternal life.

"Minna, you may go back where we first met, I have some things to discuss with you," Timnah said.

"Of course, Timnah, I will be there this evening." Minna stared at the place where her mother had stood just moments earlier, then left for her ship.

Minna stood staring at the lights below on the cliffs above the Monastarium. She had spent much time thinking and wrestling with the decision she knew she had to make by herself. To do that she had flown to the moon where it was reported that people like Nia and Taona had risen from the dead. During that time, she also had contacted other mercenaries to find out what they knew of the secret organization forming to mimic the sisterhood, and turned down death contracts she had received since she returned to Ramah.

Now she stared out of the mouth of the cave, replaying in her mind her mother's ascension. She vividly saw her mother's glowing face. *When the time is right you will know for certain if you are to join the Semdressa.* The words spoken in that well-loved voice echoed frequently in her mind. It had been three days since her mother had spoken them.

"Really, Mother, me marry and have a family… and give you grandchildren?" She laughed aloud. "Mom, I love you, but I doubt that will happen." Love for her mother and loss swelled in her heart. But the peace that had flooded her soul that day when she saw her mom walking and then breaking into a run to be united with her dad and her siblings made everything better. *To be honest with myself, I don't want to continue with my old life as a hired assassin.*

She sensed the approach of someone and looked over her shoulder.

"Welcome back home. I hope your business of your old life is concluded." Timnah's voice was welcoming. Minna trusted the wise words of this remarkable woman.

"Yes, I am finished with all of my old obligations. Now I am free to pursue other matters including ridding myself of Cymbratar." Minna's tone was somber.

"Have you come to a decision?" Timnah asked. A pause ensued, then Minna looked up at her.

"I have reports from very credible sources that the Saurcine are recruiting in large numbers. Their headquarters are in Gerobon… I also know that they are part of the Dragon seed bloodlines you spoke to me about." Minna's tone was firm and factual.

"That is exactly why Mother Karina needs to verify and if possible stop the bloodline from being established." Timnah cocked her head to the side, waiting. Timnah's casual glance at the *Furies Scepter* didn't fool Minna; she could feel the sharpness of her attention still on her.

"Cut off the bloodlines from being established. I assume that this mission would fall within the Semdressa scope of operations?" Minna's face got splashed with rain as a strong gust of wind swept into the cave.

"Yes, somewhat. Before I say more you will have to take the Semdressa Oath, which would supersede any other oaths you have taken." Timnah's words and voice held no manipulation, just bald truth.

"If I accept and join, where would I live?" Her face was slickly wet from the downpour now. She was staring intently at the sister. Inside, her mind was racing with the fire of a new challenge.

"Your new life would be here for now," Timnah said in the same vein.

"Aside from looking after my wellbeing, thank you for your loyalty to my mother. In her honor, I will join the Semdressa with all my mind, body and soul." Minna folded her arms and stepped into the light and out of the deluge. She could feel the water streaming off her body armor.

Tinman's face broke into a calm smile. "Welcome, Minna. Your mother prophesied that you would join us. Come with me."

Mother also said I would be married and raise children of my own. She watched Timnah walking away, then followed, beginning to feel a real anticipation and a sense of new purpose.

Minna stood in the center of a brightly lit, barren room. She welcomed its warmth. Twelve elders stood before her, with Timnah standing slightly in front of them. Everything about them was familiar to her. Even Timnah exuded a sort of hard expertise that she had not shown previously. It would sharpen and challenge her more than she could ever anticipate.

"We, the senior members of the keepers of secrets and that which is sacred, are in agreement. You would be a valuable member to the sisterhood. Minna Lavine Vallo, do you willingly take the Semdressa Oath, knowing that it is irrevocable and is for life?" Timnah said with a sharp, piercing look. She seemed to be probing for any double-mindedness with her eyes. But Timnah seemed to like what she saw and dipped her head slightly.

"Yes, I, Minna Lavine Vallo, do vow to pledge my life in the service to the sisterhood as a Semdressa member." Minna's strong tone resonated from her chest. She knew that she sounded a bit like her mother just then. She extended both hands toward the elders. Timnah stepped forward and wrapped a thin ribbon of silver around her wrists once, then poured anointing oil on her hands.

"We accept your pledge. You are now bound to us," the elders said in unison.

Minna felt a strange tingle on her head. Goosebumps rose on her forearms and the silver ribbon melted into her skin, becoming forever a part of her.

"Now we must see if you are one of the chosen to carry one of the sacred items to cut off the Dragons seed bloodlines," Timnah said, then moved back to her previous position.

"Yes, we will see. We are in agreement," Sister Rahma said, then carried a wooden box on a tray and stood in front of her. "There are many gemstones in this box. Put your hand through the hole on top and pull one out."

Selection by divine providence. Let's see if Mother's words bear witness that

I will have a special life's journey. Minna boldly reached into the opening on top of the box and plunged her hand inside. She swirled her hand strongly around, hearing the scraping of the stones against the bottom of the box. She clutched a handful of stones. In her mind's eye a vision of a red stone appeared then vanished. She paused with narrowed eyes at this unfamiliar experience. Then she pulled her hand just above the stones but not all the way out of the box. They could all hear the drop of the stones one by one. She looked up and caught the gaze of Timnah.

"I have picked one," Minna said pensively. She pulled her hand out of the box with her fist tightly surrounding the rather good-sized gem. Minna extended her arm and opened her hand, exposing a red Mevaseret gemstone. *I wonder if I have to give it back.* She smiled at the thought, but her smile faded when she saw the shock in the eyes of the elders. They were looking at each other in surprise.

"You have been chosen to carry the Vavresh blade," said the raspy voice of Sister Valora. This sister was short and looked rather harmless but had the reputation of being a shrewd master of Krav Naga. "Your quest to remove the necronos substance will be reached when you achieve your objective." She looked at the others.

"You may keep the stone as a reminder that you have been chosen by divine providence to cut off the bloodline of the Krevomax," said another sister.

"Sister Timnah will give you specific instruction as to what to do. Be blessed, highly favored daughter of Mother Vallo," said a stately ebony woman who reminded Minna of Tamar Ogesh, an old and trusted Choshek agent.

"Minna, please follow me." Timnah turned to address the Semdressa elders. "I will continue to give you updates on our progress." With that, Timnah beckoned, and Minna followed.

Minna smelled minute traces of stone dust. Six highly polished workstations stood along the stone wall. *Those must be new. This must be the Semdressa headquarters.* She noticed she was garnering curious stares from the sisters who were making system checks on various workstations. She nodded to one or two along the way, then rounded the curvature of the artificial cave, arriving at a set of closed doors. Timnah placed her hand on the white door. Her hand glowed and the door slid open. Minna followed her into the room.

The complex was quite a bit more expansive than she had anticipated. She had wrongfully deemed it an amateur spy network. *Considering the time it takes to cut through Thermathite granite, they must have been building it for a while.* They entered a multilevel room bustling with Semdressa going about their duties. Near the center was a holographic galaxy map of Kilodromus. The 3D map highlighted sector 523 located in the Cji Expanse. It was a sector of space sparsely populated with sentient beings and celestial bodies similar to that of the Rakia Expanse.

"Sister Timnah, I have relayed all pertinent information of sector 523," a young Semdressa agent said as she reached them. Her large green eyes had streaks of silver.

"Sister Minna, this is Marta Bellasova. She is the Semdressa operations advisor for this mission," Timnah said.

"Your experience and that of your partner in the Rakia Expanse will be valuable. I'm sure that you will benefit from our knowledge and contacts already established in your assigned region. I look forward to learning more about your unique skill sets, Sister Vallo." Marta's tone was admiring and accepting at the same time.

"I am pleased to meet you," Minna said, nodding.

"Down to business, then." Marta turned then scaled the map for a more detailed look at the solar system. She tapped a planet that changed from green to red. "This is the planet Gerobon, the home of Princess Rishna Atharva. You and your partner will leave immediately. Once you arrive on Gerobon you will make contact with the individuals listed on this disc." Her voice held a fine thread of urgency. She handed Minna the disc.

"You mean right now, this very moment?" Minna asked, somewhat alarmed.

"Yes, you will report to us when you arrive… Your Semdressa code name is Satavar. Use it for all future contact." Marta quietly waited for her reply.

Minna turned to Timnah, who wore an agreeable expression. "The name chosen is that of your grandmother. I knew her personally and the name will suit you well."

Minna nodded. "I accept with gratitude my Semdressa code name…Satavar." Her voice was firm and unwavering.

"Honor your forefathers and never waiver from your oath," Marta said.

"I will," Minna said and crossed her arms over her chest.

"Have success, Satavar, and be blessed by Moshiach." Marta nodded and left.

They were not alone. In the dim light above them were five women dressed in distinct vestments. As Minna looked more closely, she could see body armor under their thin fabric overcoats.

"Who are they?" Minna looked at them with narrowed eyes and burgeoning curiosity.

"Criss Lumbra," Timnah said flatly.

They looked like an elite squad of some sort. "I want to know more about them," she said in earnest They felt familiar somehow. She reached out, trying to discern why she felt instant kinship with these mysterious women.

"In due time, but for now, we have to go somewhere else, so you can be properly outfitted and given a detailed briefing for your mission in that region of space." Timnah waited for her nod of acceptance, then headed to the back section of the complex at a brisk pace. Minna trailed behind, her mind spinning with the rapid changes in her life.

Chapter Eighteen

CRISS LUMBRA

Inside the Semdressa headquarters, Fay, Mirinda, Orisa, and Victoria had just completed their initiation into the sisterhood's spy network. They were now undergoing various tests to evaluate the probability of success for this off-world mission they'd volunteered for.

"Are you ready, Orisa?" Agent Spalda barked in a hard tone. She was a tall, stately, somewhat humorless woman. Standing outside of the combat training room, the well-seasoned agent took her job very seriously. She had been tasked with getting the recruits ready for the mission to destroy the crimson stone of the Tisrad Dragon's eye on Fiero Prime.

"Yes, I am ready!" Orisa shouted and gripped her staff tightly.

A green light flashed in the training room. Just entering it was an athletic woman dressed in sparring apparel, brandishing the same staff. Without a word, she kept her forward momentum going and thrust her staff into Orisa's mid-section, knocking her backwards. Orisa quickly regained her balance, then darted to the side, feeling the air whoosh by her cheek as the staff narrowly missed her face. Using the opportunity of Orisa's defensive posture, the woman was able to kick Orisa in the back. She fell flat on her face.

"Yield," the woman shouted.

That hurt, thought Orisa, wincing. *So, you want to test my combat skills, do you? Very well.* She bounced up off the ground, undaunted to continue the contest. *That woman moves fast, but I'm much quicker.* She focused all of her energy and unleased it with a blinding strike to her opponent's midsection with the staff. Then in a blur of speed she struck the women's lower jaw with her foot.

"Yield," Orisa said loudly, standing over her unconscious opponent.

Long moments passed, then a medical technician came to attend to the woman. Orisa stayed nearby, nervous that she had severely hurt the woman. *I wonder how my friends faired in this test.* She was not surprised at the outcome. Although she was the smallest of the four, she was an expert in Krav Naga. She definitely could defend herself. She was relieved to see the woman brush the hands of the medic away and get to her feet without help.

A look of respect shone in her opponent's eyes. "I was told you had enhanced strength. No one mentioned your speed. Aside from that, you have excellent fighting technique, sister," she said. "Well done."

Agent Spalda broke in. "Sister Orisa, please exit the training room. After changing your attire, report to the medical center."

"Come with me," said the medical technician.

Orisa nodded once at her opponent and followed the technician to the prep room.

Inside the medical center, Victoria sat on an opal crystalline chair inside a semi-transparent cube. *I guess this is what those modified soldiers felt like when we experimented on them.* A soft tone alerted her to a visitor. She turned her head expectantly. As the doors slid open, a woman holding a data pad entered. Her thin overcoat swayed in her wake as she briskly strode straight towards her.

"Sister Victoria, I am Doctor Dura. The strength test results are amazing. You scored slightly higher than Fay and Mirinda. Still, even their strength levels are higher than the strongest Mantis Alliance Commandos. The blood samples we have taken from you three—so far, I might add—confirm that the necronos essence has fused with your DNA. As you may already know, one of the side effects of consuming this essence is that your bone density is much higher than normal." She pushed her black-framed glasses up more firmly on the bridge of her nose. The doctor gazed into the Victoria's eyes, looking a bit baffled.

"If I am correct in my analysis, your semi-luminescent blue eyes are a result of consuming the Cymbratar?" She let the data pad come to rest on her knees as she waited for a response.

"Yes." Victoria felt no need to elaborate. She leaned forward slightly. "And what is this next test?" She looked around the cube that was beginning to feel confining.

"This next test will record your cellular repair responses." She nodded reassuringly and smiled. "Don't worry, it won't hurt exactly, but you might feel some discomfort." Dr. Dura's soothing tone was meant to make her feel more comfortable. Victoria fought an urge to squirm.

"Can you find a way to remove the necronos essence from me?" Victoria waited with a sense of hope.

"Fay and Mirinda asked the same question. Unfortunately, although we have the most advanced bio-science technology here, we are not able to remove the necronos essence." Her lips pursed as she seemed to mull over the matter. "I will remain here for your safety and observe the molecular activity in your body. Are you ready?" She waited with raised brows. Victoria relented and gave her a sharp nod. "Okay, test will commence now," Dr. Dura said and entered a series of commands on her data pad. The interior surface of the cube erupted with multitudes of tiny dots of various colors. A few short moments passed in silence.

"How do you feel?" The doctor's tone was compassionate.

"I sense tingling on my skin, but it's tolerable," Victoria said. She plucked at the top of the thin two-piece medical exam clothing and felt vulnerable at being so scantily clad.

"Your cellular repair response is higher than both Fay and Mirinda's. What do you attribute that to?" It was clear she was keenly interested.

"Its most likely due to the fact that I consumed a whole portion of Cymbratar just before I returned." Victoria remembered she had taken her last allotment right before she destroyed the Mecropex. "There is no more, just in case you did not know. The creators of the substance have been destroyed." Victoria leaned back and breathed a sigh of relief as she felt her cells stop repairing themselves.

Dr. Dura entered another series of commands into the data pad. "There, all finished, Victoria. You may get dressed. There is a person outside the door who will escort you back to the prep room. From there you will be escorted to the debriefing room." She pushed her glasses back up on her nose and stuck out her hand. "It's been an honor to meet you." Victoria shook her hand and watched her leave with the same fast walk she came in with.

Relieved, Victoria immediately exited the cube, going directly to her neatly folded clothes on a nearby table. *I just have to hope this is worth a new beginning for me. Why else would Abba El have saved me all that time ago?* Just then, she recalled the mighty white hand that had scooped her up out of the way of the explosion. She felt the awe of the miracle all over again…*Oh, yes, now it makes sense. The Matriarch.* Humbled, a swell of the love of Abba El overcame her. "Thank you, Moshiach, for reminding me. Now I know," she whispered, tugging the last of her uniform into place. She headed out of the room with new hope welling up in her spirit.

"Victoria, this way please," said an elderly sister who was rising out of a seat in the hallway.

Victoria smiled at her and waited. *I wonder how the others faired with all these tests?* She couldn't help but notice the stares of other Semdressa agents in the hallways as they passed.

Fay and Mirinda stood up to greet Victoria with open arms and smiles as she entered the briefing room. She felt the welcome relief of being around trusted friends. Her spirits lifted as she hugged them.

"What have we gotten ourselves into this time? It sure is more involved then I first imagined." Mirinda's tone was filled with stress.

"I know, they said a solution to remove the Cymbratar from me had been found. I assumed it was going to be in the medical center." Victoria voiced her disappointment. They settled next to each other in a row of cushioned seats.

"I believe that our problem will be solved with something on the mission we volunteered for. They said they will do everything in their power to help us," Orisa speculated with some optimism.

"Dr. Dura said they don't have the technology here to do it." Fay's brows were pleated, concentrating on the matter. "So, yes, I believe it's safe to assume, the mission is to rid ourselves of this necronos essence."

The door opened and Orisa entered with Agent Spalda and two others who held folded clothing. They wore the sisterhood silver bands.

"Sister Orisa, please take a seat," said Agent Spalda. She held four data pads in her capable hands.

The two other women placed the folded clothing on an oval table at the end of the room. The elder agent maintained their attention. "When I leave, you are to put on those suits. They are for your mission, designed specifically for where you are going. They will defend against most necronomic energy blasts. The headbands will dampen any connection to the crimson stone." Her confidence was reassuring. Done with their task, the other two women left. The sisters remained silent, waiting. Agent Spalda stood in the center of the row of seats and held the thin data pads against her vestments.

"Your mission is to get as close as possible to the Crimson stone. It emits small amounts of multi-phasic Cremindraux radiation. We have calculated that if you get close enough it will actually remove the necronos essence from you." Her eyes narrowed but she continued in the same strong tone. "But here is the warning—if you stay too long near it, you could lose your life." Her words and warning were clear. They had gotten used to her plain, direct manner.

"You mention Crimson stone, but I have never heard of it," Orisa said, twisting her mouth.

"It goes by many names, but it's the stone in your dreams and visions. The others you are going with are responsible for destroying it." Agent Spalda looked piercingly at them, as if she would say more. She pressed her lips together, then she took the top data pad, activated it, and handed it to Orisa. She moved to each of the others, giving them their data pads.

"These data pads are for you to study the information about the Fiero System and its ruling governments, demographics, and other pertinent data." She moved to stand in front of them, folding her hands behind her back. "You will stay here until you leave on your mission. May Moshiach guide your path to success, Sisters." The agent nodded approvingly at them, then left.

Orisa darted out of her seat and rushed to the table. "They each have a single letter attached to collar," she said excitedly.

"Let me guess, an F, O, M and V, right?" Victoria said dryly as she made her way to the table.

"I love it, makes me feel like royalty." Orisa gushed as she placed the silver headband on. "Introducing Princess Orisa." She smiled widely with outstretched arms, as if a large audience was adoring her.

"All hail Princess Orisa." Mirinda played along, clapping, and waving at her.

"I'll just be happy to get rid of this accursed Cymbratar and start my new life in peace," Fay mumbled.

They set about getting dressed and began to pour all their attention into studying this planet they would be traveling to. To Orisa it all felt very familiar.

Fay, Mirinda, Orisa, and Victoria remained in the debriefing room as they continued to study and immerse themselves in the information. They were deep in discussion of the governmental hierarchy when they sensed someone at the entrance of the room.

"The mission is a go. It is time for you to depart. Please leave those devices here," Timnah said. They immediately followed her to the flight bay, where they would begin this final death-defying mission.

Multiple levels flashed by platform as they continued their ascent until it stopped in the transportation bay. They caught the occasional glances of the technicians working on transport ships as they made their way to the other side. Rounding a second ship, they reached the imposing military ship they would soon board.

"A military ship. I suppose this mission is more dangerous than I thought," Mirinda said quietly. There were five women standing at parade rest at the bottom of the ship's ramp.

"At least we'll be safe traveling in that Class IV Mantis Alliance recon ship," said Fay under her breath.

"Are you guessing, or do you know that as a fact?" Victoria said with a sharp edge in her tone.

"As a Semdressa, I asked Timnah for the Mantis Alliance general databases on ships." Fay grinned reassuringly at Victoria. "I really enjoy ship propulsion and communications. It's in my blood."

Timnah halted near the five soldiers and introduced them to the four sisters. "This is Major Lystra, and Commanders Omari, Emiko, and Captain Berene and Lieutenant Sonja," Timnah said proudly. The sisters noted their luminescent violet eyes, and their pinned-back platinum hair.

"Major Lystra, they have been briefed as to their mission. They are proficient with Krav Naga and have Class II strength and Class III cellular repair ability." The slightly amazed looks of the Criss Lumbra unit skimmed over the sisters at Timnah's back.

"I leave them to your charge Major, may Moshiach guide you to a successful mission… Commanders." Timnah nodded at the other four.

"Thank you, Sister Timnah." The Major placed her clenched right hand over her protective breast plating. The other four followed suit.

Timnah turned to the four sisters. "I strongly believe, as did Mother Vallo, that you can accomplish anything if you trust the path the Moshiach has placed before you. I will be waiting for your return. You will not fail." Timnah's confident tone was reassuring on so many levels. It meant acceptance and forgiveness was truly theirs. With that, Timnah excused herself and left their presence.

"You will each be paired with one of my team members." Major Lystra had everyone's attention. She eyed them with a sharp gaze that didn't miss anything. "We are the unit assigned to this mission alongside of you. You will follow their instructions as if they came from me. Any deviation from your orders could cost your life. My unit is aware of what you must do. But as we infiltrate the enemy stronghold, circumstances might change. Mother Calero made it clear that we give you a chance to remove necronos essence from your bodies. And so, we will give you that opportunity. One thing above all else that must be accomplished, however, is the destruction of the crimson stone. That is my unit's primary goal. "Do you understand?" Major Lystra's strong voice and hard expression were typical of a battle-hardened soldier. Without waiting for a response, she inspected the sisters' light combat vestments made of the same material as their own. "Interesting," she commented, looking at the silver metallic headband they wore to block the crimson stone visions.

"We have Class 21 security clearance and have been debriefed on the particulars of your travels and subsequent return. I'm impressed you survived. Let's hope this mission will be just as successful…" The Major stepped to the side of them. "Fay, you are assigned to Commander Omari; Orisa with Commander Emiko; Mirinda with Captain Berene; and Victoria with Lieutenant Sonja… Now, let's board. We have no time to waste. The quicker we get there the less likely their defenses will be fully deployed." With that said, Major Lystra turned and headed up the ship's ramp.

The sisters followed her up the ramp with their Criss Lumbra counterparts at their side. The ramp retracted as the cargo door sealed them in. Just scant moments later, the sleek military ship exited the bay rose swiftly into orbit. The main power core was engaged and vanished in folded space as they sped to their destiny in the Fiero Prime System.

Adrenaline flooded their bodies as they watched the multi-colored drift of space travel out of the view ports. It would be a long while before they would be able to settle during the journey.

On the other side of the planet Ramah, in the tropical Tumaline jungle, Minna continued practicing with her newly acquired energy pistols. "Perfect shots, I really like these weapons," she said with a grin and holstered them, watching the smoldering pieces of drones fall to the floor. They were light but deadly. The whine of the cleaning bots coming from the bottom of the wall to remove the debris filled the shooting practice range.

This gear was meant to protect her against most necromonic energy blasts. "It fits really well…very flexible and light." She held out her gloved hands and inspected them. "Nice, I almost like this more than my signature red and black bodysuit." She donned her helmet and said, "Satavar." As soon as she spoke her name, the visor lit up and scanned her face. A green dot at the top of the visor indicated authorization to use the suit.

```
Incoming message:

Sender: Abasca

Message: On my way to station 4.

End transmission.
```

"Jaya is on her way back to Kilodromus. It's time to get going," Minna said, then motioned to the attendants to open the sealed range. She strode confidently down the sloping hallway to the bottom level of the secret complex. She came to the stone door exit. "This is Satavar, I'm a go." A few moments passed as the thick slab of stone slid back.

As was her nature, she stepped into her new mission without fear or doubt. She felt the heavy door shut behind her. Her body hummed with anticipation and purpose. Thick, impenetrable jungle surrounded her immediately on the other side. It was raining and looked like it had been deluging, as the water streamed from the vegetation. A path that was less than a meter wide led to her ship. Minna forged ahead down the path leading with her right shoulder. She slid along until she reached the platform. "There you are, my friend. How did they treat you?" She inspected the *Furies Scepter* with appreciation. "Where is my partner in this mission?" she said with some irritation. She did not like waiting. Her visor indicated that a stronger metal alloy now covered the entire hull. She entered a series of codes to connect her new bodysuit to the ship. She was more than happy to board as the cargo bay door opened.

Inside, Minna removed the helmet and continued her inspection. "Great, upgraded energy canons. New high output auxiliary power cores. They gave me the latest in cloaking technology. This is like a whole new ship," she marveled aloud. She strode to the bridge and stashed the Omni currency disc, which contained a vast amount of wealth, into a secret compartment under her seat. "I'm sure I'll need this to complete the mission and for whatever comes my way in the meantime." She double-checked her ship's computer systems and engine cores, then sat down. Still waiting for the other agent to arrive, she unsheathed the Vavresh blade from her utility belt. She lightly balanced the weight of it on her open palmed hands. The edge was so sharp it cut at the slightest of touches. She had found that out right away.

"So, my partner and I are to go to some lair where conventional weapons are ineffective to destroy blood eggs of the Prince of Grythinmor. Wherever that is. What are you made of, my beauty? You will surely secure my success and maybe I will get to learn more about that that Criss Lumbra squad. They sound like my kind of people." Minna re-sheathed it, then powered up the ship. "You are better than new, my dear friend." She smiled patting the console. "Now, where is this Veth'Shar agent?"

She peered into the jungle, hoping to see him. *We have no time to waste.* She'd sent him a message some time ago. He should have been here already. "Maybe I'll just leave. That will teach whoever it is not to be late," she muttered mockingly, starting to get a little angry.

The round device on the control panel lit up. It was the Semdressa communications device. "Let's see here..." She attached the device to her communications screen. "Satavar, receive message," she said aloud.

```
Incoming Message:

Sender: Agent Marrex

Message: I am here, open your cargo bay door. End
of Message.
```

"Terminate communications," she said, pressing her lips together in annoyance. *Finally.*

Minna activated the rear ship viewer. A man wearing an overcoat and holding two large travel bags stood in the downpour. *I hope those are weapons. Maybe I should let him stand out in the rain for a bit longer.* She laughed, then opened the cargo bay door. The thud of the bags hitting the metal floor resounded all the way up to the bridge. *I want to see this sacred vial he was chosen to carry.*

Not waiting for him to appear, she pushed the controls forward. The ship lifted off the pad and shot out of the cave, throwing the Veth'Shar heavily in the co-pilot's seat. She glanced over to glare at him. "You're late, I was going to leave you," she snapped.

He remained silent, just calmly lifted his hand and slid his cowl off. "Admit it, you missed me," said Zeta Three with a cocky smirk, in that familiar provoking tone of his.

MARIUM KAHNET OATH

Every member of the Marium Kahnet sisterhood must take the sacred oath and those who wish to live their lives accordingly are also encouraged to take the oath.

THE SHABAUH

I pledge my life as a vessel of light as I step through the veil of divine purpose. I am cleansed in purity. My head is adorned with humility. The ways of the Marium Kahnet are my life, my heart, and my soul belongs to Abba El and in HIS messiah is my salvation.

Marium Kahnet Book Trilogy

RETRIBUTION Available

DECIMATION Available

REBIRTH Available

I sincerely hope you enjoyed reading this book as much as I enjoyed writing it. If you did, I would greatly appreciate a short review on Amazon or your favorite book website. Reviews are crucial for any author, and even just a line or two can make a huge difference.